THE MYTH MAKER

THE MYTH MAKER

A NOVEL

Alie Dumas-Heidt

CROOKED LANE

NEW YORK

This is a work of fiction. All of the names, characters, organizations, places and events portrayed in this novel are either products of the author's imagination or are used fictitiously. Any resemblance to real or actual events, locales, or persons, living or dead, is entirely coincidental.

Copyright © 2025 by Alie Dumas-Heidt

All rights reserved.

Published in the United States by Crooked Lane Books, an imprint of The Quick Brown Fox & Company LLC.

Crooked Lane Books and its logo are trademarks of The Quick Brown Fox & Company LLC.

Library of Congress Catalog-in-Publication data available upon request.

ISBN (hardcover): 979-8-89242-126-3
ISBN (paperback): 979-8-89242-249-9
ISBN (ebook): 979-8-89242-127-0

Cover design by Meghan Deist

Printed in the United States.

www.crookedlanebooks.com

Crooked Lane Books
34 West 27th St., 10th Floor
New York, NY 10001

First Edition: July 2025

10 9 8 7 6 5 4 3 2 1

In memory of my Grandma Janice, who loved a good detective
story and always put her name on these first pages
of the books she gave.

1

April 7, 2009

Forty-five minutes late. Jenna checked her watch again, the pink plastic band nearly identical to the purple Swatch her best friend wore. The normally punctual best friend who was now forty-six minutes late. They had been best friends since they were eight years old. Thick as thieves, as her mom always said, even though that never made sense to her. Her parents would be home any minute, and if she was still sitting here, she'd be trapped. They'd insist on having dinner together, or worse, renting a movie and having a night in with their youngest daughter.

Lately, her parents had been holding on extra tight. It was the worst part about being the youngest, and why she desperately needed her ride to get here. She was fighting so hard to grow up. Her oldest sister was living in an out-of-state dorm for her first year of college. Her middle sister came and went as she pleased, using work as an excuse to be away from home, even if she didn't have a shift at the burger joint. Stood up or not, if Jenna didn't get away from the house one way or another, she would find herself the only sixteen-year-old starting spring break playing Scrabble with her parents at the kitchen table.

Hurt and angry, she grabbed her carefully overstuffed backpack and locked the door behind her. She wished she still had her cell phone, but her dad had confiscated the hand-me-down device for going over on her text message limit again. If she had it, she could text her best friend and find out why she was standing her up tonight of all nights. She needed to pass her damn driving test next time so she could get a job. If she could do that, she could pay her own phone bill, and she would be able to reach out to her friends instead of being left behind.

She trudged down the sidewalk, away from her street of cramped row houses. Her boring white siding stood out among the houses of blues and greens. She knew them all. They'd lived on this street since she was four years old. The Masons in the sea-blue house at the top of the hill where she'd met her first friend at the kindergarten bus stop. The elderly neighbors next door who'd made sure she and her sisters got in safe after school as young latchkey kids. At the end of their steep street was an attempt at a park. She couldn't check her bestie's house two streets over without giving their plan away, but the park had been designated long ago as their emergency meet-up spot, so that's where she was heading.

"Hey, Jenna! Do you need a ride?" An aged white car stopped haphazardly along the sidewalk, not quite out of the narrow lane.

Jenna leaned into the open window of the passenger side. "Are you going to the party at Alex Lavine's house?"

The laughter from the driver's seat was bitter. "No. I don't get invited to the cool-kid parties. Is that where you're going?"

Jenna shrugged. "I was supposed to, but my ride hasn't shown up and I don't know where he lives. I was hoping you did."

"Sorry, I'm out of the loop. Get in if you want. I mean, you don't have to, but we could hang out. I stole some weed from my brother and I'm going up to Dash."

"By yourself?" Jenna asked.

"Me and the weed, the water, and the moon."

The idea that someone her age would plan to spend a Friday night alone made Jenna shudder. The popularity game in high school really could be a bitch. "All I've got on me is half a bottle of my parents' cheap vodka and fourteen dollars."

"Good enough. Get in."

Jenna giggled, feeling rebellious as she pulled the passenger door open. She shrugged out of her backpack and tossed the green bag on the cracked brown vinyl of the back seat. The bass line from a guitar-heavy punk song she didn't recognize vibrated through her chest as she closed herself in. On a Friday night, when your best friend blew you off, spending time with any friend was better than spending it with no friends. Or your parents.

2

It takes a flattening of all senses and instincts to walk into a room and stand over a dead body. It's a learned skill. A skill I'm still learning after four months as *Detective* Cassidy Cantwell. Everyone talks about the acrid smells, the nausea, the nightmarish scenes. They equip you with menthol rub for your nose, ginger gum for the rolling stomach, and there's red wine to help clear the images you take home with you.

What no one talks about is how hard it is to tamp down your own sense of survival. The reality of your own mortality is right there, front and center. The trick is to dull those feelings, not turn them off. A detective who goes numb will miss things. A detective who can quiet the emotions and still take in what's around them solves cases.

I reminded myself of this lesson as my partner, Bryan Ramirez, parked our unmarked black Dodge Charger in front of our next crime scene. I was new to this team but not new to Bryan. When I first started with the Tacoma Police Department as a wide-eyed, twenty-two-year-old female rookie, Bryan Ramirez was my training officer. We rode together as partners for seven years before he made the jump to detective. When I pushed for a spot on the same violent crime unit, Bryan was my greatest supporter, and when I got the promotion, we paired up again as partners. Working together worked well for us.

I climbed out of the car and moved with the long strides necessary to keep up with my partner's quick steps. A gaggle of nosy neighbors were gawking from the other side of the street behind a police barrier as we made our way across the lawn. We were greeted at the door by a baby-faced patrol officer named Derek North. Derek took a lot of ribbing for the multiple times his patrol car had been reported as a stolen vehicle since he'd started with our department. Each call came from a concerned citizen sure they'd seen a wayward teen taking a joyride in a patrol car.

"Get turned in for stealing your cruiser lately?" I asked.

Derek flipped me the finger before checking that Bryan and I were wearing our required blue paper shoe covers and adding us to the list of personnel on scene. "Did you hear the last guy actually followed me to the station?"

"I think everyone with a radio heard that one," I teased. "Were you the initial here?"

"Cory and I arrived with medical. He's still inside." Derek waved us inside the redbrick bungalow with a sweep of his clipboard. "This one is all yours now, Detectives."

"Hey, guys. Sorry for the end-of-the-day call," Cory Stevens, a dark-haired patrol sergeant, said as we made our way through the front door. "The crime scene guys have already started, so be careful around the doorjambs."

The entry opened to a tight living room where it was clear a fight had taken place. A potted philodendron was toppled, leaving a knotted pile of roots on the floor and a choreography of footprints in dirt on the beige carpet. A large abstract watercolor was on the ground, and a spiderweb crack splintered its way through the glass of the frame. A glass coffee table was centered by a dark-blue sofa, and in front of the table was the body of our victim. You could almost mistake her for sleeping if you ignored the deep-purple stain that circled her throat. She was a petite woman with a loose blonde topknot and delicate features highlighted with smoky eyeshadow and red lips. She was on her back, hands resting in the center of her chest, her filmy red dress smoothed straight at the hem above her knees. Her bare feet were crossed at the ankles, and the stem of a white rose was trapped under her bare heels.

The floor crunched under my feet as I stepped into the living room for a closer look at the body. Soil and shards from crushed seashells were visible in the carpet along with blooms from what had been an impressive bouquet of red roses and anemones. The remains of the bundle of flowers lay on the table next to a blue glass bowl containing a glossy pink conch and a collection of smaller shells. It seemed someone had righted the bowl without cleaning the mess, putting it back with the flowers after the fight. Like the shells, some of the flowers had been pulled from the original bouquet, but even with the petals ground into the floor, the fragrance from the roses spiked the air.

"What do we know so far?" I asked as a camera flash from one of the crime scene technicians lit up behind us in the kitchen.

"Delivery guy called it in," Cory said. "He was bringing flowers that were ordered for this address. He said he could see the body through the front window, tried the door and it was unlocked, so he came in to see if he could help. He came in far enough to decide he couldn't help her, then called us."

"He came all the way into our crime scene?" Bryan shook his head and pulled at the open collar of his blue dress shirt.

"He only came in as far as Cas is now, and I don't think he'll ever do it again, if that makes you guys feel any better."

"Nope, not feeling any better." I started for the next room as my back pocket vibrated for the fourth time since leaving the station. I ignored the buzzing, knowing who was calling and why. "So he was bringing another bouquet? The one in there is pretty fresh. Is someone making up for something?"

"Possible," Cory said. "Neighbor across the street says our vic came home with her husband last night about eight PM and they were arguing in the driveway when they got out of the car. Husband left, alone, about an hour later."

"Looks like the fight might have escalated once they got inside," I said as my phone buzzed again.

"You might as well answer him, Cas," Bryan said, stepping around me into the kitchen. "He's not going to stop until you do."

My phone had been buzzing like a force of angry bees for the past hour, and I knew Nicky, my boyfriend of almost two years, was holding out hope I'd make it for the dinner date he'd planned. I also knew I wouldn't make it to dinner. *Again.* The growing list of canceled plans was responsible for more than one argument between us over the past few months. His own hectic schedule as chef and owner of a popular restaurant was enough of a struggle. My new schedule with unpredictable long days and random callouts made our time together even more sporadic. All of that combined had me ignoring calls more often when I knew I couldn't give him good news.

I moved around the tiny kitchen peninsula, which was topped with a white stone flecked with vibrant green, as I decided to take my partner's advice. I watched one of our crime scene technicians push clear strips into smudges of black powder on the back door and waited for Nicky to answer.

Nicky had already braced himself for disappointment. "Reservations are in less than two hours. What are my chances you're going to be there?"

"We just arrived at a crime scene, and we're going to be on this one for a while."

"I knew this was going to happen." His irritation came through loud and clear. "I guess I'll see if your brother wants to do dinner."

"I can come to your place when I get off if it's not too late," I offered.

"Brandon is off for the next seven days, so I have to be back here first thing to accept deliveries," he said, dismissing my compromise.

His growing unwillingness to give me a pass on my long days while he ignored his own overwhelming schedule had my teeth on edge. "I didn't do this on purpose. I don't have just a regular end-of-shift time anymore."

"This is the third time I've made these reservations."

"I know." My eyes stopped on a large painting over the kitchen table. The mass of shapes in their vibrant colors appeared abstract at first glance, but with a closer look, details unfolded. The forms in pink, red, and black came together as ballet dancers. If you didn't know to look for them, you would miss them. My heart jumped for a second time since we'd left the station. "I gotta go." I didn't wait for Nicky to reply before ending the call.

I made my way quickly back to the living room. "Do we know what her name is?"

"Dana Mayhew. Neighbor says she moved in four months ago with her husband—"

"Ethan Mayhew," I interrupted.

"Yeah. Do you know him?" Cory asked.

"Worse," I said, sucking in a deep breath. "I dated him."

Bryan smirked. "That's a plot twist. Did you know this was his house?"

I stared down my partner. "I would have mentioned that bit. Ethan is an artist. These paintings are all his. Last I heard he was teaching art at the community college, but I haven't seen him in years."

"When exactly were you two involved?"

"For a few months during the first year of college. We didn't last long, though. Like I said, it's been years since I've seen him, but out of all the guys I've dated, I'd vote Ethan *least* likely to choke his wife to death. We'd argue and he'd take off, he couldn't do confrontation, and he was definitely not violent."

"According to the card and the receipt, he's the one who sent the flowers that were being delivered. The neighbors don't seem to know either of them very well. So far, we've heard a lot of *nice but kept to themselves* descriptions," Cory said.

"Sounds about right. I don't see him attending many block parties with the neighborhood. He was difficult to date and even worse at general socializing back in the day because he was introverted and awkward; he wasn't like this. I can't see him being responsible for this."

"Are you telling me Nicky isn't the worst decision you've made in your dating life after all?" Bryan laughed as he circled back toward the front door. "You do have to admit, Cas, this scene is feeling textbook."

At first glance, it was easy to agree with my partner. Parts of the scene I was looking at did feel textbook. A married couple. A fight witnessed by neighbors. An obvious physical altercation inside with the grim inclusion of a dead body. A missing spouse. It would be easy to agree with Bryan and put a target of suspicion on the husband. But this time, I knew the guy. As complicated as our young relationship had been, I couldn't ignore the memories of a shy, passive man who'd never had a penchant for confrontation.

"The old guy kitty-corner saw a man walking away from the house about an hour after the other neighbor said he saw the husband leave," Cory said. "Problem is, he has no idea who the guy was, what he looked like, or if he stopped here. He was just letting his cat inside, noticed the guy on the sidewalk walking away from the general direction of this house, and then went to bed."

"There's a flower petal near the back door in the kitchen from the mess in here. If she didn't answer the door, maybe he came in the back door."

"Or went out that way." Bryan anxiously cracked his knuckles. "Did you see the broken glass? It looks like someone threw a wineglass at the wall, but no one cleaned it up."

I hadn't noticed a broken glass, but I had noticed her bare feet. "She's barefoot in there; she wasn't walking through glass."

"We've got people trying to make contact with the husband at work to bring him down to the station, and dispatch called the ME the same time they called you, so Shannon should be here soon," Cory said. "I'm going to have my guys clear, since the scene techs have the house now. We'll have reports on your desk before we clock out tonight, Detectives. Good luck."

As I stepped back outside, I twisted a few strands of my dark hair and tucked them behind my ear, wishing I'd pulled it all up today. It had been years since I'd given much thought to the part of my past Ethan Mayhew occupied. We'd met as freshmen at a party neither of us wanted to be at and spent the next nine months together. Our relationship went through ups and downs because of his temperamental moods and my inexperience with relationships in general, before imploding on itself, as teen romances do. Still, I couldn't accept the idea that he'd gone on to murder his wife.

It wasn't simply that I didn't think Ethan could have committed this murder. Standing in the chaos of the crime scene, I wasn't as convinced as my partner that it felt *textbook*. I was mulling over the images when the black ME van backed into the narrow driveway. Shannon O'Mara was in the driver's seat. He was the lead for the county medical examiner's office and, by far, my favorite creepy guy. He showed up at crime scenes looking like Alice Cooper cast as a balding professor, with nerves of steel. Even at the cruelest scenes, I'd never seen him react with anything other than calm. He pulled his equipment and stretcher from the back of his van, delivering orders to his assistant.

"Let's see what you all have today," Shannon said, skipping the pleasantries and charging into the house. I followed the pair inside, leaving Bryan on the porch on a phone call.

Once inside, Shannon made a circle around the body, getting to his knees to examine the bruises on her throat. "She was strangled, manually," he started. "She's in rigor, so she's been dead at least twelve hours, possibly a bit longer. I'll get you guys my report as soon as I can."

I knew that was his way of excusing me from what was now his crime scene. I stepped over his kit and rejoined my partner outside.

"Patrol is bringing your friend to the station," Bryan said. "Are you ready for a reunion?"

* * *

I opened the door to the nausea-green interrogation room and found Ethan Mayhew staring blankly at an unopened Coke can. The harshly bare room, with its small metal table and four straight-backed chairs, did little to ease his discomfort.

"Cassidy? Hi?" His eyes locked on to my familiar face, looking for answers. "No one will tell me what's going on." With his shaggy hair hanging in his eyes and a shark-tooth necklace hanging out of the collar of his black Henley, I was startled by how little he had changed since college.

I took a seat across from him and introduced my partner. "There's no easy way to tell you this. We found your wife at your house this afternoon. Ethan, she's been murdered."

"Murdered?" The word swirled heavily in the air between us, and I watched him struggle for a full breath before dropping his head to his hands. "How did you . . . where is she?"

"A flower delivery guy found her," I said.

Ethan sat up, panicked. "I sent those. I sent her flowers today. Did he . . . how?"

"He could see through your front window and was worried she needed help, but it was already too late."

"How can you be sure it's Dana? How do you know she was murdered?"

I slowly opened the thin folder I'd brought with us and slid it across the table to Ethan. Inside was a photo from the crime scene. I'd been careful to crop out the bruising from her neck, but there was no hiding the lifelessness in her face.

Ethan sucked in a sharp breath, reached across the table, and pulled the folder closer, studying the image through tears. "What happened to her?"

"We're trying to put that all together. Right now, we need your help so we know where to start."

"She wasn't like that the last time I saw her. Why is she wearing all this makeup? That's not my wife, that's not Dana."

I glanced at my partner, who responded with a subtle shrug. "Ethan, this woman was found in your home. Are you saying this isn't your wife?"

His teary eyes were lost. He ran his hands across his cheeks, swiping at the tears he couldn't control anymore. "The makeup. That isn't how Dana does her makeup. Ever. She doesn't like the heavy-makeup look, never has. When I left the house last night, she did not look like that. She looked like she always looks."

"Why did you leave the house last night?"

"I have an apartment near campus. I use it as my studio, and I stay there sometimes if I'm working on bigger projects."

"Is that normal, staying the night somewhere else and not talking to each other during the day, or were there issues last night?" Bryan asked.

"I don't do it a lot, but it happens. I had a full schedule today, so I figured I'd talk to her when I got home." Ethan sat back in his chair, took another swipe at his eyes, and wrapped his arms across his chest. "We went to dinner last night, then I dropped her off at home and went . . . and then I went to my studio."

Bryan reached for the folder and closed it before sliding it back in his direction. "What time did you leave your house last night?"

"I'm not sure. Sometime around nine or nine fifteen. Dana had opened a bottle of wine and was going to catch up on one of those *Housewife* shows." His shoulders rose with a sad chuckle. "She calls it her hobby. I paint, she watches bad reality TV."

"So she didn't have any other plans you were aware of? Why would she have done her makeup after you left if her plan was to just be home?" I asked.

Ethan retreated into the back of the chair, his head back, eyes fixed on the speckled acoustic tiles of the ceiling. "I'm telling you, Dana didn't do her makeup like that. And no, she didn't have plans."

"Would she have been having company over? Does she have friends who would just stop by?"

"At nine PM on a workday?" Ethan shook his head. "She's been at the same office for five years, and most of her friends are work friends. They're not the type that just show up late at night in the middle of the week. She was just going to watch some TV."

Bryan let the quiet settle for a few moments, then rolled up the sleeves of his shirt before changing direction. "You sent your wife flowers today. Was there a special occasion?"

"She loves sunflowers. Other women want roses, but Dana wants sunflowers. We, uh, we argued last night at dinner, and I didn't want to have it still sitting over me when I got home, ya know?" He rested his elbows on the table and put his head in his hands. "I was just trying to say sorry for being an ass."

"What was the fight about?"

Sorrow turned to defense. "It wasn't really a fight. I wouldn't call it a fight. She made some last-minute plans... plans for next weekend with some girls from work, and I didn't know until last night at dinner. I just got the last girls' trip off our credit card, and I said some things about her spending."

"Are there financial issues?" I asked.

There was one quick laugh from across the table. "We just bought a house, and we have two college degrees between us and all the debt that goes along with that, but we aren't drowning. I was just being a jerk last night about it. I don't know why. She grew up traveling, but I can't always get away during the school year, and sometimes it gets to me—her girls' trips. I sent the flowers to say sorry."

I waited for Bryan to catch up with the notes he'd been taking and to give Ethan time to catch his breath. "Can you think of anyone who would want to hurt Dana?"

"I need to see my wife. How do I get to see her?"

"I can have someone take you to make the ID when we finish here, if we can get through a few more questions. Is there someone who would have wanted to hurt her?"

"How is this real?" Ethan stood and pushed his hair out of his eyes again. "Why would anyone want to hurt her? We're your basic, everyday, boring married couple, Cassidy. I teach art history and painting classes. Dana works at a real estate office. She got her license last year. We work, we go to movies, we hang out with friends on weekends and do the family thing on holidays. She doesn't have enemies. Especially not enemies like this, not ones that would want to kill her. I need to see her."

"We can allow that," Bryan started. "But your house is still a crime scene, so we need you to not go home until we've let you know it's clear to go back in, all right? Not at all, not for anything."

"Is there someone we can call for you? We can have them meet you before you do the ID," I offered.

"My sister. I need to get ahold of my sister." A heavy realization hit as Ethan left the room that almost took him to his knees. Bryan reached out and grabbed his elbow to steady him. "I'm going to have to tell her mom."

The pain in Ethan's words struck me. That was the familiar Ethan, the guy who'd walked out when I wanted to fight. The guy who broke up with me by trying to hide on campus rather than confront me. Before my eyes, his new grief was deepened by the difficult news he was going to have to find a way to share. He wasn't going to be able to run away from the heartbreak this time.

* * *

When I finally dragged my tired body into my kitchen after eleven PM, I expected Freddy, my yellow-eyed guard cat, to greet me. The sound of the TV coming from my living room pitched me into instant irritation. I knew it wouldn't be Nicky, and an uninvited visitor was not what I was in the mood for. I rounded the corner and found my little sister sprawled on my purple sofa with Freddy on her chest, watching Dorothy, Rose, and Blanche bond over cheesecake.

Meghan's usually light-brown hair had been bleached to a lemon meringue and clashed severely with the fuchsia and peacock-green eye shadows she was wearing. The hair color was jarring, but it was what I knew was coming next that had me counting off calming breaths in my head. The last time she'd shown up like this, it took me three months to get her out of my guest room.

"How did you get in here, and why are you on my couch?"

"Sorry, Jamie gave me his key."

I groaned, making a mental note to confiscate any other spare keys my twin brother had, since we clearly disagreed on what they should be used for. "So that's the how; now, *why* are you on my couch?"

"I fought with Mom today, and she said I should stay here until I get into my own place, on account of the dead woman on the news and you sleeping with a gun. True quote." Meghan sat up on the couch, cradling Freddy like a baby, which oddly enough the demon cat didn't fight. He was best known for his sneak attacks, having left multiple guests bloody, but he'd always had a soft spot for my younger sister.

"This is not a good time for me, Megs." I slouched into the recliner in the corner and tucked my feet under the crocheted blanket gifted to me from my grandma when I bought my town house. "I just started a new case at work, and I'm running on negative hours of sleep. I haven't even had dinner. I'm not up for having company."

"If you would put a TV in your guest room, you wouldn't even know I was here."

"If I put a TV in my guest room, you never would have left in March."

"Probably," my little sister admitted with a laugh. "Jamie told me you and Nicky are going out of town soon, so we can call it preemptive house-sitting and I'll feed the cat monster while you're gone."

Exhausted, I pulled my grandma's blanket over my head with a groan. "Jamie only told you I was going away because he doesn't want you to stay with him."

"Nah, he told me that too. His exact words were 'The last time was the last time.' He also said that if I stayed with you, he wouldn't have to feed the cat monster when you go away and he wouldn't have to worry about me being on his couch if he brought his date home."

"His idea would make sense if I was actually going out of town, but like I said, work is hectic and I'm probably not . . . wait, Jamie said he had a date? It's not Adam again, is it?"

Meghan shrugged her bony shoulders. "I didn't ask for details after he said I couldn't stay."

I didn't want her to stay. I didn't want to deal with the chaos that followed my little sister like a storm cloud. There were six of us Cantwell kids. My twin brother, Jamie, and I had come along less than two years after our older brother, who himself had been born less than two years after our older sister. A younger brother followed and was the baby of the family for eight years before we found out Meghan was coming. I was ten when she was born and thrilled to help take care of a new baby, but twenty years later my family was still relying on me to keep her from spinning out. "You can stay, but it's two weeks, Megs. You need to work things out with Mom or work on getting into your own place this time. And I'm not getting involved in any drama. Right now, I'm going to eat some cereal and go to bed."

"I won't make a sound, promise."

"Two weeks. And no weed in my house."

Meghan held up her right hand and promised with a smile. "Oh! I almost forgot, there's some mail from Mom's house on the counter she wanted to make sure I gave to you."

I covered both eyes with my hands and pressed my fingers into my forehead, today's stress nearing the critical point. "I haven't lived at Mom's house for ten years; why would someone leave mail there? What is it?"

Meghan shrugged bony shoulders and lifted Freddy into the air to adjust him on her lap. "I didn't open it. There's no stamp, so Mom said someone must have put it in the mailbox today."

My body was getting heavier with the weight of the day as I pushed myself out of the chair and shuffled to the kitchen. As much as I wanted to sleep, I needed to eat, and figuring out strange mail sent to the address I hadn't lived at for over ten years sounded like an easy win I could use. I picked up the manila envelope with my name and my parents' address across the middle and studied it while I made a bowl of cereal. Along with no postage, there was no return address, but there was something vaguely familiar about the block print in thick black marker.

I grabbed a pair of scissors from my junk drawer, sliced open the top of the envelope, and shook the contents onto the counter—a single photograph. It was a four-by-six glossy picture that I didn't recognize, but I knew both of the people in frame. It was me during my sophomore year of high school with my best friend, Jenna Sutton. We were wearing our matching blue-and-white swimsuits for the swim team, arms around each other poolside. We were both smiling, not quite looking at the camera, and I had no idea who was on the other side of the lens.

A rush of emotions had my hands trembling, and I abandoned my unfinished dinner in the sink, grabbed the photo, a sleeve of crackers, a coffee cup, and a bottle of wine, and retreated to my bedroom. My entire day had been questions, and right now, why someone would leave an old photo of me and Jenna in my parents' mailbox instantly moved to the top of the list.

I locked myself in my bedroom and pulled a small clear tote from under my bed. The more I looked at the photo, the more I was convinced I had actually seen it before. I ran my finger across the face of my best friend, wide, happy smile, one arm around my shoulder, the other flashing a peace sign at the camera. The orange date printed in the bottom corner showed *11/17/08*. Five months before she was ripped out of my life forever.

I pulled the blue hardback yearbook from the tote and held my breath for a few beats, trying to get my heart to settle. It had been a long time since I'd opened the yearbook. This one, sophomore year, contained only one message written in the pages—a long message of grief from my twin brother that I'd only made it through once—and at the end of the book was a memorial page for Jenna. I'd looked at that page often.

In the pages dedicated to the swim team, I found what I was looking for. Almost. It was black and white in the yearbook—the cost of color photos being reserved for the senior class pages—in the middle of a collage of five other photos. We were there, poolside, with our arms around each other and Jenna's famous peace sign, but it wasn't the same photo. More specifically, it wasn't the same photographer. The images were identical, right down to the exact position of the other swimmer climbing out of the pool behind us, but the one I was holding was from a slightly different angle. A picture taken by a photographer we were not paying attention to.

I stared at both photos until my eyes blurred with new tears. Why? Why would anyone leave this for me, at my childhood home, without saying who it was from? Who would think I needed this photo in my own collection of life before Jenna was murdered? No one who knew me would think I needed additional reminders, and something about it felt cruel. It didn't feel like someone trying to share a moment—the public setting of the photo, the mystery photographer—it felt like someone trying to force me back into fear. The fear that enveloped sixteen-year-old me after the murder of my best friend.

I sipped on my coffee mug of merlot and closed the book on my lap. I knew I couldn't lose myself in this one right now. I had to shuffle it back into place and focus on the case in front of me. I didn't let myself pull things out of the large totes on the floor of my walk-in closet that contained everything I knew about Jenna's unsolved murder. I popped the lid on the newest one and placed the photo and the envelope inside. I would make time to circle back to the question the photo presented, but not tonight. *In this business, you have to be able to compartmentalize.* My partner's early training advice played in my head.

My mind wandered back to work, a gruesome slideshow from the crime scene flashing behind my eyes. I knew where Bryan stood, but I wasn't yet convinced Ethan was guilty. The easy answer would be that Ethan Mayhew killed his wife. Easier as far as declaring the case solved, anyway. I still couldn't make that idea fit with the Ethan I had known or the man we'd sat down with today. I also couldn't clear the unsettled feelings that stuck with me from the crime scene. There was something else there I couldn't put my finger on yet. Something intentional. Something sinister. The person who left Dana Mayhew on her living room floor had gone there for that reason. I was sure of it. As sure as I was of the cruel intentions of the person leaving me photos in mailboxes.

3

I slammed through the doors of the station the next morning at 7:57 AM with an extra-large espresso in hand and three minutes to spare. The images from the Mayhew crime scene mingled gruesomely with my vintage collection of nightmares from a restless night of little sleep. My long, dark hair was pulled up in a tight twist, and I'd pushed the dress code a smidge with a pair of dark jeans, a black V-neck sweater, and my favorite pair of emerald-green ballet flats. I'd gone the full-makeup route in an attempt to cover the puffy, dark circles under my eyes. Bryan was already at his desk when I rounded the corner, his *World's Greatest Lover* coffee mug and the local paper in front of him.

Bryan Ramirez was five years older and had started with the department four years before me. He was hot-tempered and high-strung at times and a perfectionist always. With his short-cropped dark hair, nearly black, deep-set eyes, and charismatic personality, I'd told myself early on it was inappropriate to crush on the guy showing me the ropes in my new career. Even without my reminders, our attempt at being anything other than friends had never left the ground, and he eventually took on the role of another older brother, overbearingly protective at times and never letting me drive.

"How'd we come out?" I asked, sliding into my seat and flipping on my laptop.

"The usual. 'Woman found dead in her home. No arrests made. Police have no answers,' that kind of babble." Bryan sipped his coffee without taking his eyes off the paper. "How was your night?"

I took a swallow of my own morning coffee. "Besides the normal nightmares, I gained a roommate." There was no rush to share anything about the taunting photo someone had decided to send me. Bryan was aware of my side investigations, but we'd agreed early on that I'd keep it out of the office.

My partner let out a snort. "Meghan came back to the nest, huh?"

"Mom thinks it's safer for her to stay at my place because I, according to my mother, sleep with a gun."

"Please tell me you don't keep it under your pillow." Bryan laughed. "I'm going to drive up to Ethan's apartment and poke around. Wanna come?"

"No. Shannon said he'd have more for us later this morning, so I figured I'd go down there and talk to him, then build up our copies of the photos from the crime scene guys."

"Come around to the idea of Ethan being our guy?" Bryan asked.

"Not yet. I know you're set on it being a domestic, but there is just something off about it. Something felt almost staged. And what about her makeup? I believed Ethan truly was surprised to see her made up like that when we showed him the pictures. He wasn't faking that."

"So you're thinking someone confronted Dana Mayhew, strangled her to death, trashed the house, then stuck around to play beauty salon?" Bryan tented his fingers together on his desk, and I suddenly felt like I'd stepped into the middle of my own interrogation.

"What if Dana was expecting company and did her makeup and changed her clothes after Ethan left? Let's say when she found out he was leaving for the night, she decided she didn't want to watch her TV shows alone."

My partner flashed an arrogant smile. "It wouldn't be the first time a happy couple fell to the dark side, but you could be right, maybe there is someone else in Dana's orbit besides her husband. You know that also gives Ethan a motive, right?"

"I think we need to find out who else was sending Dana flowers."

"I'm going to check out the apartment. You see where you can get on finding the guy who didn't know to send sunflowers." He pulled his dark neoprene jacket over his athletic shoulders. "We'll see where we stand at the end of the day."

Once alone with our files, I worked on color-coding the statements that had made their way to my desk the night before. Some colleagues preferred to work with the digital files, but despite being one of the younger detectives at thirty-two, I was old school. I preferred my paper files and my highlighters. As I went through the written records, I looked for any quirk. Any scrap of information relayed by one of the neighbors that would signal there was someone else to look at. Once I'd hit the end of my stack and the end of my coffee, I hit the break room for a refill and then headed to Shannon's office. The space had the clinical feel of a medical office, with a light-gray metal desk and multiple standing filing cabinets lined up under his framed degrees and certifications. There were no personal photos or decorative touches to give anything away about the occupant of the office.

"Did I miss the memo about a new dress code?" Shannon eyed my jeans.

"You must have. It's in place of hiring me a personal assistant to pick up my dry cleaning."

Shannon chuckled. "Let me know when your top brass approves this personal assistant idea. I could use one or three."

I took a seat in one of the green vinyl chairs at his desk. "You have more pull around here than I do. If you pushed for it, you could save us both."

"I'm guessing you're here for yesterday's homicide?" Shannon flipped open one of the few folders on his desk and turned it in my direction.

"What do you have for us?"

"No pressure at all in declaring this a homicide. We won't have the tox screen or the details from the nail scrapings for a few more weeks, but I can tell you she died no earlier than ten PM and no later than two AM. Cause of death was manual strangulation. It didn't contribute to her death, but I did find this." Shannon passed me a small plastic baggie with a gold ring inside.

I turned the trinket over in the palm of my hand. It was a small size, probably a pinkie ring, with a small gold apple in the center of a thin band. I squinted at the faint engraving on the inside of the band. *"Beautiful?"*

Shannon nodded. "It was at the back of her throat, and I'd say whoever killed her put it in her mouth after she was already dead on the floor."

* * *

Bryan sauntered back to my desk after noon and tossed a new statement on my ever-growing pile of papers. "File these along with Ethan's statement."

I scanned over the chicken scratch on the statement from Ethan's neighbor at the apartment complex he claimed to have gone to after leaving Dana at home. A woman named Joanne, who lived down the hall from him, confirmed he was at the apartment complex before 10:00 PM. He'd held the elevator for her in the parking garage so she wouldn't have to wait alone for the next one.

"So that puts him at the apartment before the time of death."

"Yeah. I'm going to agree with you and say Ethan probably isn't our guy." Bryan slouched out of his jacket and hung it on the back of his chair before sitting down.

"We got something else from Shannon too." I tossed the baggie with the ring across his desk.

"What's the significance of the ring?" Bryan twisted the ring around in his fingers.

"Shannon found it in her mouth. He said it was put there after she was dead. He cataloged two other rings and a link bracelet, so I reached out to Ethan. I didn't give him details, just asked if he could describe what clothes and jewelry Dana had been wearing when he left. He doesn't remember anything other than her wedding ring and her grandma's ring that she always wears, and maybe a bracelet. Also, he says she was wearing leggings and a purple sweatshirt when he left. I've checked the evidence logged, and we didn't collect any clothes, but there's photos from a hamper in their room and it was empty other than a towel."

"If she changed her clothes, where did they go?"

I shook my head, a nonanswer to a question I couldn't make sense of. Like the ring my partner was still examining, the missing change of clothes could only offer more questions. "There's an inscription on the band, *Beautiful*. I would guess that was something personal, but when I asked Ethan if he remembered her wearing an apple ring, he said he doesn't remember her having a ring like that, period. It wasn't anything he gave her, so who did the inscription?"

"Why'd the guy put it in her mouth? Did she turn him down? Was she ending things?"

"Why an apple?" I added to Bryan's list. "The apple, the engraving, it feels too specific to be insignificant." The apple was worth questioning, I was sure of it. It was the type of symbol that was adopted and gifted, like hearts or butterflies. The type of personal attachment that meant I had both a frog pendant and frog key chain from Nicky. A simple mention of frogs and a favorite T-shirt I wore until it was holey had cemented a connection to me with the amphibians, even if I'd outgrown them. The apple felt like that. It wasn't an accidental charm. It meant something.

"So where does this leave us?" Bryan asked, tossing the ring back to my desk and opening a canned soda he'd pulled out of his jacket pocket. "We're supposed to be answering questions, not creating more of them."

I shook my head with a pensive sigh. Not even eliminating Ethan from our suspect list—something I was comfortable with—gave us a real win. Until our request for the digital part of Dana's life came through and we could build a map with bank transactions and phone records, our best chances were going to come from those in Dana's circle. Someone was going to know if apples meant anything to her, and with any luck, someone was going to know who would have sent her roses.

* * *

I sat in my car on the tree-lined street I grew up on with my radio up, hitting redial. The number was my twin's, and for the third time Jamie wasn't answering. My annoyance grew as another minute ticked by on the dash clock of my ice-blue-and-white Mini Cooper. I hit his number again, then jumped when he drummed his fingers on the passenger-side window of my car.

"You're late. Why aren't you answering your phone?" I asked, meeting him on the sidewalk with a hug.

"Because I was on this street when you started calling me, and I was going to be parked in less time than it was going to take me to fish my cell out of my pocket." Jamie returned my hug, then stepped back to straighten the black button-down he was wearing with dark denim that we'd unintentionally matched. "You knew I was coming. Why so edgy?"

"I thought you were going to make me go in on my own."

"It's just Mom, Cassidy."

"Easy for you to say; you're not the one with a new murder investigation on the news and a new roommate Mom is fighting with. I'm tired, I need backup."

"I offered to talk to Mom for her, but Meghan said she wanted to stay with you. I figured you'd tell her no if you didn't want her there. As for tonight, it's Isaac's birthday, the grandkids are here, she'll be distracted. You're safe."

"You also didn't tell me about your date." I wasn't ready yet to give up on playing hurt. "You tell Meghan, but you don't tell me?"

"Don't worry, it wasn't Adam." Jamie laughed and took my hand, leading me up the walkway.

Being fraternal twins, Jamie and I are easy to peg as related. We share the same straight tawny-brown hair, Cupid's bow lips, and hazel eyes. Actually, all of us Cantwell kids look alike. We all look like our mom, but only the three boys got her height and metabolism. I was average at five foot five and proud I could still wear my jeans from college, but this did not compare to my twin's effortlessly trim, six-foot frame. Jamie was the older twin by a full thirteen minutes, and he'd been using his position as the oldest as an excuse to boss me around since we were small. He was also the only one who always knew when I wasn't okay, even when I tried to hide it.

Jamie opened the front door, and we stepped into the common state of bedlam that erupted whenever we were all together. Hannah had followed in our mother's footsteps, deciding to leave college and stay home to raise children. Her four kids were now joined by Isaac's two boys, and all six were swirling around the living room in a sugar-fueled frenzy. Dodging sticky fingers and an unnecessary Nerf gun, Jamie and I made it to the kitchen miraculously unscathed.

"You made it!" Hannah wrapped herself first around me and then Jamie. "Mom said she wasn't sure if you were going to make it, what with having to work that case on the news. I saw you and Bryan on TV this morning." Hannah threw me an evil wink and waited for Mom to react. I mouthed a few choice words to my older sister, who loved playing Mom's favorite child.

"I watched that on television last night, and it's just awful," my mom started right on cue. "Peggy Mason even called to tell me she saw you on the news. I told her I wished you did something else, and you know what she said? At least my kids weren't on the news with mug shots. Poor woman, her kids have put her through a lot, but I still wish you didn't want to see those kinds of things when you go to work, Kissy."

I bristled at the childhood nickname Jamie had stuck me with. "It's not that I want to see dead people when I go to work, Mom, and I can't help it if the neighbors think they need to call you because they saw me doing my job." The conversation wasn't a new one. My parents—mostly my mother—had been uneasy about my career choice since I'd made the announcement in college. I'd been defending myself ever since, and the conversations were exhausting. "I want to catch bad guys. If I just wanted to see dead people, I would have been a mortician."

That idea was enough to make my mom shudder. "You could have taken a job at the terminals like Isaac did. Dad could have helped you too, probably could have helped you get into the port office. Or you could have followed Jamie. You two could have your own firm as twin architects."

"Do you not remember her in art class, Mom? Cassidy designing office buildings would make as much sense as her trying to cook with Nicky in his restaurant. Straight lines and hot surfaces are not in her wheelhouse." My sister cut in to save me from what she'd started, still grinning. "They did get a pretty good shot of you on the news, though. Kelsey Sutton messaged me to make sure I saw it."

The mention of the Sutton family stuck my breath in my chest. I thought about the two older sisters of Jenna Sutton and her parents regularly. From the age of eight until I was sixteen, the Suttons were a second family to me, and mine to Jenna. Our older sisters were friends first, but our bond developed into a stronger friendship than theirs. By the time our sisters were in high school, they were merely acquaintances. By the time Jenna and I made it to high school, we were inseparable. Holding on to her family after she was gone was a harder ask than I could master at sixteen, and I'd never made my way back in.

Guilt had kept me away when they gathered to memorialize the fifth anniversary of her murder. And again for the tenth anniversary. Earlier this year I'd watched from a distance as her mom released thousands of ladybugs into a local park to commemorate fifteen years without her. Ladybugs, like my frogs, had always been a symbol of Jenna. That day this past April hit me harder than the previous years. Fifteen years since my best friend had disappeared. Fifteen years with no answers as to who killed her. Almost as many years gone as she'd had of life.

"You still with us?" Jamie tossed a chunk of his bread at me but missed, sending crumbs in an arc across the floor.

"I'm here," I said, feigning a smile that I knew might fool my mom but would never fool my twin. "It was a late night last night with the new case and somehow getting a roommate again." I was hopeful a mention of the problem child in the family could get me out of going further.

"I hope she gave you the mail I sent with her," my mom said, then started handing out plates of spaghetti and red sauce for us to put on the kids' table in the corner.

"I got it; it was just someone dropping off an old swim team photo." I moved out of the way as Hannah directed her kids to their seats for dinner. I needed to change the conversation before everyone sat down. My mom would want to reminisce, reminiscing would lead to talking about Jenna, and talking about Jenna would push me past my threshold. "I'd appreciate everyone giving me a heads-up, though, next time you decide to send Meghan to live with me. Last night was a rough night to come home to a roommate."

Jamie laughed and slung an arm around my shoulders. "I didn't send her to you; that was Mom's doing. She just asked me for a key." Then he leaned in closer and whispered, "I'm onto you, so we'll talk later." I never could hide anything from him and what he called our twin senses.

"Do you talk to Kelsey a lot?" I asked Hannah as she took a seat between me and her husband. Her mention of the Suttons had caught me off guard.

"We chat now and then," Hannah said. "Not as much as we used to. She always asks about you."

While we sat for dinner, I leaned into an old practice of moving food around on my plate and laughing in time with the others to stories I wasn't listening to. My dad and my older brother told work stories about a new ship at the terminal, and my sister celebrated sending her four kids back to school for the year. When my mom tried to turn the conversation my way with questions about Nicky, Jamie helped me out of it by talking about his most recent date at Nicky's restaurant.

I was struggling to keep up with the dinner conversation and keep hold of everything else wanting my attention. First on the list, of course, was the investigation into the murder of Dana Mayhew. By the end of the day, even Bryan had completely moved off Ethan being a suspect. The discovery of the ring, the change of clothes, the mystery bouquet of flowers—all of that made us certain we were looking for someone else in Dana's circle. With any luck, the sit-down we'd scheduled for morning would give us at least some of the answers we were looking for.

The invading memories I couldn't push away were more deeply rooted. Hearing that Hannah had spoken to Jenna's sister had me thinking about the photo left in the mailbox. I'd instantly attached a sinister motive to the memories being forced on me, but what if I had it wrong? Could one of Jenna's sisters or another of our friends from school have left it for me, innocently thinking I'd want it? I mulled around the idea that I might have jumped to the wrong conclusion, but I couldn't quite convince myself of it. The anonymity kept me suspicious.

* * *

After dinner and cake were done and dishes were cleared, Jamie gave the signal to make our exit and followed me outside. When we reached the curb, he stopped at the front of my car, and I knew he wasn't going to let me drive away without letting him in on what I was dealing with.

"Are you doing all right? You were somewhere else tonight, and I know it's not just because you've got a case, and it's not because you've got a roommate."

"If you're making a list, don't forget pissing off Nicky," I added sarcastically.

Jamie shook his head with a laugh. "I know where things are with Nicky; I got treated to dinner last night. What else is going on?"

"The dead woman from yesterday was Ethan Mayhew's wife," I blurted.

"Your Ethan Mayhew? The art guy from college?"

"He was never *my* Ethan, but yes, that Ethan. It was strange seeing him yesterday. The case just has me in a weird place."

"Cas, are you telling me your ex-boyfriend killed his wife?"

I paused, trying to choose my words carefully so I didn't open any more doors for my brother to walk through. "He says he didn't do it, and I think I believe him, but I have to prove it one way or another. Finding out what happened to her is on me."

Anticipating

Satisfaction. That was what he was feeling watching the back of his brother's head as he made his way out of the crowded bar. He'd orchestrated the meeting in this spot because it was close to him and on the opposite side of town from his brother. It was small and trendy, with brick walls and dark wood. One of the dozens of establishments meant to look like a 1920s speakeasy, where the drinks were small in size, big in price. It wasn't the type of place his brother would frequent on his own. At least he didn't think it was. They hadn't lived like brothers for years, but he had another reason for picking the trendy night spot—he was sure *she* would be there. He was right.

He'd been watching her for weeks now, ever since the Fates brought her into his path. She had finished her morning ritual and stopped for a coffee when he first spotted her. Her gold-streaked brown hair gathered in a long ponytail, dewy skin, flirty smile. The signs were strong, but he kept his distance and called in with another sick-mom emergency to observe her for the day. It was amazing how much you could learn about another person from a safe distance. What she drove, where she lived, where she worked, where she went to unwind after a long day on her feet.

His plan was simple. He picked a smaller table next to her and her friends and waited for his brother to arrive. When he finally arrived, his annoyance creased across his forehead, he ordered himself his favorite top-shelf whiskey, gave his brother the paperwork from his lawyers, and waited for him to run his mouth. To tell him no. To start one more argument about the situation they'd been fighting over for months. It had to be draining his brother by now, trying to pay the legal fees. The money his lawyers told him he could get just by settling was almost worth giving in to, but he wasn't sure the increase in his bank account would be as satisfying as screwing with his brother.

He stole discreet glances at her table while his brother read through the latest incendiary demand his attorneys had drawn up for him. The reaction was as expected, and the fight in the spotlight he'd created was loud and unavoidable. He'd pushed until the vein along the side of his brother's neck bulged, and then he threw back his final swig of whiskey and laughed at him. His brother spit a long string of threats and then stormed out, just as he'd known he would. With mock embarrassment, he looked around the small bar and, when he caught her looking at him, raised his hands and shrugged in an innocent *don't know what just happened* way. Her smile widened.

When she skuttled past the others in her group to take her turn filling the pitcher, he went to pay for his drink. He stood next to her at the bar and waited for the busy bartender to return to their side. He interrupted when she started her request and asked the bartender to add her next pitcher to his tab, he said to apologize for his brother. He offered a smile dripping with humility, and she accepted the beer.

"I know this is going to sound like a pickup line, but do I know you?" he asked.

She tilted her head and studied him curiously. "Do you hang out here? Because I'm here a lot."

"No, my brother named the spot; it's my first time. Unfortunately, I spend most of my time working. I barely even find time to run anymore."

"That must be it!" She beamed. "I'm a runner too, never miss a day. I usually run on Ruston."

Excitement. That's what he was feeling when she made him an offer to join her table, but he still had too much to finish to risk it. He turned her down politely and regretfully, stumbling over the excuse of an early morning at a busy office. The Fates had guided him correctly tonight, and he would thank them soon enough, but he had to be patient. He considered waiting for her to leave, but there was no need. She was making a valiant effort to live life in secret, but he knew who she was, and he knew how to catch up to her again when it was time. There was more to do first, and he had to stay focused. Anticipation surged through him as he drove away.

4

The sound of my fingers drumming against the tabletop in the interrogation room was starting to annoy even me, so I placed both hands flat with a huff. The first real break in the murder of Dana Mayhew had come out this morning after the first quick sit-down with her best friend from work. Before we'd even asked the hard questions, she'd clued us in to the fact that not only was Dana having an affair, she was having an affair with someone from her office. It wasn't the first time either, although her friend described the last encounter as merely a fling. Dana had never said anything that made the friend think Ethan was aware of what his wife was doing when she worked late. Or the real reason for the girls' trip he'd only recently paid off on their credit cards. She gave us a name, and two hours later I had him in the office struggling to tell the truth.

"Look, Randy, we know you've been spending time with Dana. We have witnesses." I pushed a blank witness statement form across the table with a pen but avoided the folder of photos. I was saving that in case of denial. "I need the details of where you were the night Dana was murdered."

The teary man sniffed and pulled another tissue from the box on the table. Physically, he couldn't have been more different from Ethan Mayhew. He was in his forties, ten years older than Dana, with dark hair and a gym rat build he was proud of. The yellow dress shirt he was wearing was too tight on his biceps and across his chest. When he sat down, he had been full of confidence, but after he'd spent nearly thirty minutes brushing off his relationship with Dana, insisting they were simply work friends, his resolve was crumbling. "Fine, yes, you're right. Dana and I were messing around, but I don't know why you think I know what happened to her. I never would have hurt her."

"If you loved her, why did we have to come find you?" I was dug in, not trying to be the good cop in today's questioning. "Your coworker and girlfriend was murdered, and we had to come find *you*. Why didn't you contact us, tell us what you know?"

"I didn't have anything to tell you." His panic intensified with each new question, and the fear coming off him was visible—shaking hands, sweaty forehead, red cheeks. "She's really careful. I know that sounds bad, I know we shouldn't have been messing around, but what's done is done, ya know? I don't know anything, so I didn't want to make Dana look bad."

My partner laughed next to me. He'd been in terrier mode since we'd been able to confirm Dana had a lover, more convinced than I was that we'd be sitting down with the killer. "Were you trying to protect Dana, or were you trying to protect yourself?"

"Okay, sure, I didn't see any point in blowing up my life when I knew I didn't have anything to help you with her case. But it wasn't just about me. Dana was beautiful, inside and out. People will judge her for something like an affair, and that's not the kind of person she was."

"The woman you were having an affair with wasn't the kind of person who would have an affair? You need to let us decide whether or not we believe you had anything to tell us about what happened to Ms. Mayhew."

Randy Lloyd sniffed again into his tissue. "Dana had some strict rules for what we were doing. I'm not proud of it. As of right now, my wife has no idea anything was going on, and I'm trying to keep it that way. We talked at work. We made plans in person. She didn't allow me to text her after hours unless she texted me first, and she never texted from home. I have never stepped foot in her house; I don't even know where it is."

"You've never been to her house?" The news, if it was true, blew another hole in my running theory.

"Never. We saw each other at work, we've met up for dinner after work a few times, and we went away for a weekend. We weren't alone—there were other people from the office for this real estate seminar thing—but we spent a lot of our time together. We were planning on going away again next weekend. It was wrong, I know that. Sometimes you can't help where your heart goes, ya know? I just didn't want to come forward with all of this and risk ruining my marriage for nothing."

"You'd rather risk being a suspect in a murder than admit having an affair?"

His defensiveness shot up, and he crossed his arms tightly around his body. "I never thought I'd be a suspect because I didn't kill her. I didn't talk to Dana that night. I picked my kid up from her basketball practice right after work, grabbed pizza for dinner, and monitored homework time. I don't know who hurt Dana. I wish I did, I wish it never happened, but all I know is that I did not do this. I wouldn't do this."

"Can anyone confirm where you were?" I asked.

"Yeah." Randy laughed through new tears. "I mean, if I really have to tell her, my wife could tell you I was home taking care of our daughter while she was at work. She manages a nursing home and is covering an overnight shift right now, so I have the night shift with our kid all week. She talked to our daughter before bed. She didn't see me until the morning, but she knows I was home; she can tell you that."

"Right, but she can only tell us you were home when she talked to your daughter," Bryan argued. "Who can verify you were home all night and didn't sneak out after bedtime?"

"And leave my kid? She's seven!"

Bryan shrugged. "Wouldn't be the first time I've seen selfish parents leave kids unattended to do what they want."

"No, no, no. I did not leave the house all night. I had an affair, Detective, and I feel like shit about it now, but I'm a good dad. My kid is seven; I would never leave her alone at night. Besides, I've never been to Dana's house—she didn't allow that. I'm not your guy."

I sat up straight in my seat, elbows on the table. "What about gifts? Did you ever give Dana any special presents? Buy her jewelry, send her flowers?"

My question brought more frazzled laughter from Randy Lloyd. "We've been sneaking around for six months, and the most I've done is pay for lunch. I told you, she was careful."

Before I could ask my next question, there was a rushed knock on the door and Gabe Hutchins, Bryan's first partner as a detective, stuck his bald head in. "Hey, can I chat with you two real quick?"

I stepped out in front of Bryan, and he closed the door behind us, leaving Randy Lloyd alone. My hopes of Randy being a viable suspect had already significantly dimmed. "What's going on?"

"The husband of the dead woman from the other night is on the phone and insisting he talk to you. I guess he was notified he could go home and he's freaking out, I think about the state of the house. I tried to talk to him, but he's being vague, and he wants to talk to you. He's just sitting on hold."

"We've had this guy over an hour, Cas; I don't think we're getting anything else out of him," Bryan said. "I'll finish up with him, you go take the call, and we'll meet up in a bit and compare notes."

I blew out my cheeks, tightened my ponytail, and headed to my desk, uncertain of what I was walking into. "Ethan?" I said after hitting the blinking button on my office phone.

"You guys need to come back here and finish the job, Cassidy. There's stuff here . . . it's everywhere." Ethan was breathless, and his emotions bled through in his voice.

"Ethan, I'm sorry. I wasn't aware you'd been told you could go back to the house, but they should have given you the numbers for some agencies that can help with the cleanup. It's not something the department—"

Ethan shouted over me. "I'm not talking about a cleanup, I'm talking about evidence. Literal evidence that you guys left at my house."

I'd studied the crime scene photos of the Mayhew scene enough to have the images burned into my eyes. I couldn't pinpoint anything I remembered feeling out of place beyond the dead body. "All right, I am on my way there. I want you to step outside of the house, wait in your car if you need to."

* * *

There was a wave of déjà vu as Bryan parked our black Dodge Charger at the curb outside Ethan Mayhew's red-brick home. Instead of neighbors and other officers, Ethan was in the driveway with a woman I recognized as his sister and another man I had never met.

Ethan greeted us in the yard and introduced us to his sister and brother-in-law. All three had entered the home to gather some belongings. "I can't stay here. I don't know if I'll ever be able to stay here, but when I saw the stuff on the table . . . it took a minute, but those things on the table are not ours. I don't know where they came from, I don't know how they got here, but they do not belong here."

"Specifically, what items are you talking about?" I asked. "I can say we gathered everything we considered relevant to the crime scene."

Ethan had his fingers laced together at the back of his neck, and I was concerned he wasn't stable on his feet. His brother-in-law reached for him as his knees buckled, and for a quick second we all thought he was going to pass out. We helped him take a seat on the porch, and his sister spoke for him.

"He doesn't know where the bouquet came from because he sent sunflowers, that's the first thing. But also, there's some seashells in a bowl and some sort of bird statue on the coffee table. None of that has ever been here. They don't even really go with Dana's style. All that's ever been on the coffee table in all the times I've been here has been photography books."

"Could this be something new that Dana bought this week?"

Ethan shook his head, which was now in his hands, his elbows pressed into his knees. "Dana doesn't do knick-knacks. Look at the rest of the house."

* * *

Bryan and I entered the house, and minus the body of Dana Mayhew, the living room looked eerily the same. Petals from the red roses and anemones were still scattered, now with browning, wilted edges. The single white rose that had come to rest under Dana's feet was still there on the floor; the remaining bits of the bouquet sat at the corner of the coffee table. My partner held up a copy of a photo taken from the same vantage point we had now. The blue glass bowl, with a pink conch visible inside, as well as the marble statue that clearly resembled a dove were in the same place on the table. I could find reasons for Dana to do her makeup or change her clothes, but what reason would she have to redecorate? And if the decor didn't belong to the Mayhews, what reason would a killer have to bring knickknacks to a murder?

"It's all exactly the same," Bryan said, the confusion furrowing deeper lines across his forehead.

"This doesn't line up with an affair, Bry. I was willing to consider it. I was willing to consider she changed her clothes and did her makeup different than she does it for her husband because she was waiting for another man. I was willing to buy all of that even after talking to Randy. I was even willing to buy the idea that the ring was a gift from a rejected lover. That isn't what this is. We need to figure out what we're really dealing with."

After taking more photos, I snapped on my rubber gloves, opened our collection of evidence bags, and got to work. This time, I took every petal, shell, and flower from the room. Together we walked the house first, looking for anything that seemed out of place. We also made another pass through the bedroom and only bathroom, looking for the leggings and purple sweatshirt that Ethan swore his wife had been wearing when he left home. After coming up empty for the clothes, we had to bring Ethan back into the house. He'd admitted he only went as far as the living room, so we had to make sure nothing else had been left behind. We cleared each room with the new widower and went back to our office, the box of new clues and confusion on the back seat.

* * *

Fat, pelting raindrops smacked my kitchen window in the murky light of the early morning. I'd spent most of my night tossing and turning over the details of the Dana Mayhew murder. I'd given up on sleep and set myself up in the kitchen with some of the records I'd brought home, determined to put something together. I was standing over the kitchen table with a bowl of Special K, the array of crime scene photos spread out in a gruesome collage, when Meghan came in unexpectedly. The new hair shade of neon yellow had been streaked overnight with what I could only guess had started life as grape Kool-Aid.

"Step away from the table," I said, going for another mouthful of cereal. "This is an official investigation space right now."

"OMG, is that a real dead girl?"

"Don't look! This table is now official police business," I repeated, ineffectively pushing my cereal bowl over the screen of my laptop, leaving the scattering of photos on the table exposed.

"Is this the case you've been working on, the one they keep showing on the news?"

"Megs..."

"It's not a secret, it's on the news. I won't tell anyone." She plopped herself down next to me, willfully ignoring my request to be left alone. "Whoa, those are different dead girls."

"Like I said, official police business."

"But they were only talking about one dead girl on TV. Why are you looking at two dead girls?"

It was a hunch. A feeling I couldn't shake after we'd finished collecting the second round of evidence from the murder scene of Dana Mayhew. I'd pulled the case file, not even big enough for a paper box, of a murder from the end of last year. It was the murder of an elementary school teacher that Bryan and Gabe had worked together. Sarah Goodall had been strangled with a garrote hastily crafted out of the shuttle of her weaving loom, but her case went cold quickly.

I hadn't yet been promoted to the detective unit when she was killed, but after reexamining the crime scene of the murder of Dana Mayhew, I couldn't stop going back to images we'd all seen during briefings in the office and details I'd discussed at the time with Bryan. Everyone familiar with the crime scene agreed that Sarah Goodall was most likely strangled in her living room, meaning her killer had taken the time to move her body to the second room in her duplex that she used as a craft room. No one had ever doubted the scene in the craft room was staged, and I couldn't help but compare it to the staging we now knew existed at the Mayhew scene.

The craft room held a large loom that displayed a work in progress depicting an owl on a bare tree branch. The shuttle from the loom had been used to strangle her with a gold cord from the project, and feathers, later determined to be owl feathers, were thrown around the room. The thick, gold cord was unraveled from its spool across the floor, and the body of Sarah Goodall was placed in the middle of the mess. A third item cataloged was found clutched in the palm of her hand: a black-and-red spider made out of wire and glass beads.

No one was sure if she'd been holding on to the spider trinket when she was caught by her killer or if it had been placed there after he'd strangled her and moved her body. And if it had been put there after the fact, no one had a guess as to why. After a night of mulling over the images, I couldn't help but think there was a connection between the two scenes. The feathers and the gold string, the flower petals and the seashells—all mess created by the killer as if to simulate a fight. And if that was true, was there a link between the glass spider and the golden apple?

After half a pot of coffee, something I hadn't noticed in the first few passes of the grim photos jumped out at me. The more I looked at the arrangement of the threads, the more I was sure the body of Sarah Goodall, a weaver, had been placed in a web. We knew that the apple ring did not belong to Dana Mayhew; it had been brought by the killer as some sort of message or icon. I didn't know why he'd picked an apple, but I was sure it was going to be specific to Dana, like Sarah the weaver being left a spider.

"I'm trying to figure out a connection between spiders and apples."

"Ooh. Is that a clue?" Meghan asked casually with a yawn.

"I think so. I'm just not sure how to tie it together or what it means to our suspect."

"You should talk to someone like Professor Gentry. He taught my humanities class, and he did a whole class on symbols like apples. I mean, a golden apple is what started that war with the fake horse, remember?"

"War with the fake horse?"

"Yeah, in the Greek stuff," Megan said. "Professor Gentry said it was started because Paris traded a gold apple for the woman he wanted to marry, but she was already married, and it started a war. It might have been a real war too, not just a myth."

"Anything in Professor Gentry's classes about bird feathers?" I tried to keep the desperation out of my voice.

"Um . . ." Meghan thought physically, an index finger tapping her bottom lip. "I don't remember feathers. Maybe I'll remember later, but I can give you his email; maybe he can tell you what they mean?"

"At this point it's the only break I've got."

"And Mom thought I was wasting time taking humanities in college." Meghan beamed at me.

"I think she thought you were wasting time in general," I said sarcastically. "You have been handier than the Google gods this morning, and I will take the email of your professor. But first, you need to swear on your life that you won't repeat any of this conversation. This whole thing never happened. I only allowed it to happen because I'm too exhausted to know better right now, but I will deny this conversation to my death if you make me."

"I swear this conversation that never happened between me and my awesome sister will never be repeated." Meghan cheerfully spilled out her impromptu oath before giving me a hug. "Can we count this tremendous bit of help I'll never get to take credit for as rent for a month?"

"A month? I thought we agreed this was for two weeks and you were going to figure out your situation."

"I was going to move in with Paige, but her other roommates are weird."

My eyes rolled to the back of my head as my proudly weird sister emphasized the word. "I'm sorry? You can't live there because her roommates are *weird*?"

"They are! It's not my kind of weird, it's like a decaf kind of weird. We got together last night, and none of us thought it was a good fit."

"Were you going to tell me that you weren't going to be moving out?"

"I just did."

I could fight it. I could tell her no, but there was no point. I had more pressing issues to worry about without dealing with calls from my mom about being a terrible sister. She never used those words, but she'd perfected the guilt move, and I didn't need to hear it. What I needed was to talk with my partner about the first possible break in our case. "As long as this conversation never happened, we'll call it even for rent, but only for a month."

I gathered up my files and headed back to my room to get ready for an early morning. I pulled a blush-pink sweater and black blazer from my closet, then sent a text to Bryan explaining my new theory. The cryptic items had definitely been left with Dana Mayhew by our killer, and I was increasingly certain that the same killer had left the strange items at the other crime scene too. Within a few minutes my cell was ringing, and I outlined my new idea about the connected cases while Bryan listened in silence.

"I'm trying to figure out why you didn't bring this up last night," he said when I finished by telling him I'd be speaking with a classics professor about possible symbology.

"I wasn't sure what I was linking in my head until Meghan mentioned talking to her professor. There could be a whole world of symbolism that we've missed here, and if these two are linked from last December to now, we might have missed others. I'm heading into the office now."

"You really think you've linked the two cases?"

"I do. I also think what he's leaving behind is related to them, and that might mean he's not picking these victims at random. We might be looking for a guy who is getting away with stalking victims, completely undetected."

* * *

"I'm not sure if I'm impressed or concerned," Bryan said, looking over the redecorating I'd done during my pre-shift takeover of our corner of the office.

The two corner walls were covered from eye level to knee height with printouts. Phone records, bank records, known acquaintances lists, and crime scene photos from both scenes. I'd started digging into each woman's financial footprints and found no major intersections. Besides the occasional takeout choices and a few Target shopping sprees, the only thing they seemed to have in common was that they were murdered.

I affixed the final printout to an empty space on the wall. It was a copy of Sarah Goodall's phone records, and I'd highlighted three calls that matched a number on Dana Mayhew's call logs, which we'd finally received. I'd spotted the repeating number straightaway, but it wasn't the breakthrough I was hoping for. "I can tell you that Dana and Sarah ordered pizza from the same Tony's."

"So, all this work and all we've found out is they both liked pizza and Target? What about your other mystery clues?"

I grabbed photos of the beaded spider and the apple ring and put them in front of my partner. "There's no doubt that the killer brought the ring, the seashells, and the flowers with him when he murdered Dana Mayhew. He's using them to say something about his victim, but I don't know what yet. You guys had the string, the feathers, and the little spider in her hand, at the scene of Sarah Goodall, and it was all assumed that they were there all along, but what if he brought those too?"

Bryan made himself comfortable at his desk and stirred a fat bunch of sugar packets into the sludgy coffee from the break room. "We figured the owl feathers were probably related to the weaving project she was working on. She taught at the elementary school and made tapestries that she sold online for extra income. Running theory was that she bought them from a craft supplier. The thread that was all over the floor we know was from the loom too."

"What about the spider? Why was she holding that? If she had it in her hand as he was strangling her, how would she keep hold of it? Especially while being moved from one room to another? I think it means the same thing to him as the ring, Bry, I just don't know what they mean together."

My partner leaned back and rubbed his jaw with a groan. "I don't like where this is going. I've never had a case go cold faster than the Goodall case."

"The file is short on suspects. Was there ever anyone who stood out?"

"No. She was originally from Oregon and had been here for about a year. She'd made a few friends from the school she taught at and was single. It was the school that called her in as missing. She was one of those never-miss-a-day-of-work kind of people, so it immediately stood out when she wasn't there for her volunteer breakfast shift. Without a lot of people in her circle, there weren't a lot of people to look at. She was one half of a duplex, but the bedrooms were each on the outside walls, so neighbors heard nothing."

"I emailed Meghan's professor already. He was a little too excited to have police asking for help, but he's referred us to an expert at the University of Washington. Professor Darcy is willing to meet with us at eleven thirty on campus at the university."

Bryan pulled a few more photos of Sarah's murder scene into the center of his desk, including the close-up of two loose feathers on her chest. "Are we brewing a serial killer?"

"I did not use the words *serial killer*," I quickly corrected. "But yes, I think it's the same guy. I said all along that Dana Mayhew was staged." I tapped a finger on the most detailed photo of Sarah Goodall's craft room. "You guys could tell Sarah was strangled in her living room, after he came in the kitchen window, and she was moved to the craft room. The killer put the gold string down first, then threw the feathers around after he moved the body. He did the same thing with Dana Mayhew. That living room was staged; there was never a fight there. He set a scene with each murder, Bry, and he brought his own props."

"We'll sit down with your expert, and then we'll need to put something together for Lieutenant Miller. I texted her after we talked to let her know we're working on a theory that links these two murders together."

My brain snapped to attention at the mention of sitting down with the lieutenant on what was still an early-morning theory, even if I did believe I was right. I knew there was more research to do, but I was certain I was going in the right direction with the tokens. We were looking for one killer who already had two victims in our city. Two that we knew of.

* * *

The late-morning traffic was slow and wet as a morning storm blanketed the west sound. We parked in a visitors' lot on the west side of the sprawling campus and located the office of Professor Amelia Darcy. The office itself was exactly as I'd imagined the office of a humanities professor with a specialty in ancient mythology and folklore would be. Dark-wood bookcases stuffed full of books, boxes, and statues lined two walls. Opposite a wall of two windows and low filing cabinets was a dark-wood executive desk as overflowing as the bookcases, with stacks of papers and more books. The only clear space was a round table in the corner with four wood chairs around it.

"Ah, Detectives, have a seat," she greeted us as we entered her office. She wound long, graying blonde hair around a yellow pencil and stabbed it into place at the top of her head.

"Good morning, Professor Darcy. Thanks again for meeting with us at such short notice." I took a seat at the table and put the folders we'd brought with us in front of me. Bryan shrugged out of his jacket and sat down with me.

"I have to say, I've been doing this long enough to get tenured, write seven books, and consult on a bad TV movie that didn't take enough of my advice, but this is the first time I've been contacted by law enforcement." The professor sat down across from me with a cup of tea in one hand, the string from the tea bag still hanging off the side.

"I didn't want to give you a lot of information beforehand, because I want to make sure that I'm not adding any influence. Ancient mythology is definitely not my specialty," I said. "But if you could look at some images—not graphic ones—just images that we think might have some deeper meaning than what we've assigned to them, it could really help our investigation."

I'd arranged the photographs in the files strategically and pulled out the first three from the scene of Dana Mayhew's murder. The floor of flower petals and anemone heads that had been pulled from the mystery bouquet were visible, along with the single white rose in the bunch. The second photo was the coffee table with the bowl of shells and the marble dove. The third photo had been provided by the ME's office and showed a close-up of the golden apple on the gold band.

One by one, the professor pulled the photos in front of her and studied silently, occasionally sipping from her purple *Home of the Huskies* mug. She picked up the photo of the flower petals for a better look, but her expression was pro poker level. "I know you're trying not to give anything away, but can I ask what type of crime this was?"

"It was a murder," I said.

"On Monday the fourth?" she asked.

I nodded. Easy guess, I thought. The case had made the news.

"Each of these items you've flagged, on their own, could actually be applied to various deities and myths. I mean, we have the apple at the heart of the story of Eve. The old Norse goddess Idunn had golden apples that kept the gods in

Asgard young, and a war was waged with the giants to protect them." She finished the tale and took another sip of tea. "Inanna was an early Sumerian goddess, and two of her icons are roses and doves. The image of the Roman goddess Venus emerging from a seashell is one most people are familiar with, and her mythology is influenced by Aphrodite in the same way Aphrodite was influenced by Ishtar and Inanna. So, as far as whether these items independently hold significance in mythology, the answer is yes, they show up in multiple places. But I can go one step further for you: I can tell you the specific myths relevant here."

Professor Darcy went to one of her many shelves and brought back a thick reference book with a row of headless statues across the cover. Bryan raised his eyebrows at me in anticipation while we watched her flip through pages. Finally where she wanted to be in the tome, she turned it around for the two of us to study. The first page depicted a full-size statue of a nude woman, her hair in a bun, holding a long cloth in one hand. At the bottom, beneath the image, was *Aphrodite of Knidos*.

"The goddess Aphrodite from Greek mythology is who I believe all of these items are meant to represent." She spoke with confidence. "The image of the Roman goddess Venus in a clamshell actually began with Aphrodite. Both goddesses were said to have been born as adults and emerged from the sea, so there's the seashells. The one white rose combined with the red ones is connected to Aphrodite, who was said to have cut herself on a white rosebush racing to save her lover, and her blood turned the roses red. The anemones are part of the same story. Her lover, Adonis, was killed, and when her tears mixed with his blood, Aphrodite caused anemones to grow. Some variants of the flower are called tears of Aphrodite."

I adjusted myself in my stiff seat and scanned ahead on the reference page. "She was the goddess of love, right?"

"That was part of her story, yes. The Greek goddess of beauty, love, lust, fertility, and even war. She was the goddess responsible for the Trojan War; that's where the apple comes into her story. In a fight with other goddesses over who was the fairest of the goddesses, it was decided that Paris of Troy would decide. Three goddesses each attempted to bribe him, but he picked Aphrodite, who offered him the love of any woman he desired. Paris fancied Helen of Sparta, who was already married to the king, but Aphrodite kept her promise and made Helen fall in love with Paris. The story of Adonis, the Trojan War, and so many other major stories in Greek mythology include Aphrodite. The item used to declare which goddess was most beautiful was a golden apple inscribed with the Greek word for fairest. That's your golden apple." She tapped a neutral polished nail on the photo.

I pressed fingers against my mouth, contemplating telling the professor about the inscription on our golden apple, but held back, and knew I'd made the right call when Bryan also didn't offer the detail.

"Couldn't the apple be associated to any of those other goddesses as well?" Bryan asked.

"Sure, but not with the flowers and seashells as well. Like I said, each of these items individually can be associated with other figures in and around the Greek myths. This type of iconology is quite common through all folklore. The most significant thing that you've brought me is the date. All of these added together with the fact that the crime they're related to happened on the fourth of September marks this as Aphrodite. The fourth of every month was celebrated as her festival day."

My shoulders slumped with an exhale as I tried to take in the information Professor Darcy had dropped on us. It was real. The details the killer had left behind were more than simply creepy; they were part of a game. It also meant that the images from the second folder I'd brought with me were going to tell us another story that had been missed nearly a year before. "Can I show you a few more photos to see if there is anything that stands out to you?"

"Of course."

I flipped through the photos in the second folder for the one I was looking for. The one I thought was most indicative of the iconology the professor had been able to explain from the Mayhew scene. Professor Darcy scooped it up as soon as I set it down.

She traced a finger along the image of the beaded spider in Sarah's hand. "The goddess Athena was a weaver. When a mortal named Arachne claimed to be more talented than the goddess, Athena turned her into the first spider."

* * *

"So, was the drive worth it?" I jumped with a squeak when Lieutenant Miller spoke up from the doorway of the conference room Bryan and I had moved our case files into. Her pale-blonde hair was pulled back in a neat ponytail at the nape of her neck, and she was buttoned into a black button-down shirt with a pair of pin-striped slacks. "Bryan said you've possibly connected this new case with one from the end of last year thanks to the help of someone at U Dub. What do we have that's linking two of them?"

"Cas made the connection, and after talking to the professor, I can't say it's definite, but there could be something to the theory," Bryan said.

Lieutenant Miller fixed her gaze on me. "Tell me what you got."

As I explained everything we'd learned from the professor about Aphrodite and the fact that there were objects left at the Mayhew scene that didn't belong to the homeowners, Miller's face became increasingly drawn.

"You're going to have to help me out here. How did you connect seashells and jewelry to craft supplies at a different scene?"

"It sounds like a stretch, I know," I said, losing some of my early-morning confidence on the exhale. "There's similarities in both cases—murdered in their own homes, both strangled, and the crime scenes were both staged. Both scenes were arranged to look chaotic, but looking closer, it had to be orchestrated, and it all means something. Professor Darcy thinks the items are meant to represent Greek goddesses."

"Keep going."

I explained the Athena connection, feeling like I was masquerading as a classics expert myself. "It's light, but I think we're on the right track that these cases are related."

Lieutenant Miller raised an eyebrow at my conclusion. "Let's not lose sight of the fact that the person we have saying the Mayhew items don't belong at the scene of a murder is one of the people we should be looking at for the murder."

"The husband, Ethan Mayhew, he's one I'm comfortable clearing," Bryan offered in my defense. "We know he was at his apartment at the time of death, and the electronic gate for the parking garage does not show he left again until morning for his class at the community college."

"Who knows about this myth angle?" Miller asked.

"The three of us and the professor, so far," I said, relying on a healthy dose of hero worship from my little sister to guarantee her silence and keep her out of the running total. "I've scheduled to sit down with a friend of Sarah's and her neighbor again. Now that we're looking at it from a different angle, I want to see if they remember any weird occurrences that might have been missed the first time around."

Lieutenant Miller nodded. "Keep it at only us at this point. None of this needs to be shared right now, especially no confirmation to the press that we might have connected two murders until we have more than a strong theory. Having the press run that we have another serial killer in the area is the last thing I need."

The message from our lieutenant was loud and clear: She wasn't convinced. As much as I'd sold myself on the idea that the murders of Sarah Goodall and Dana Mayhew were connected, and as much as I believed Professor Darcy was correct in the symbology she'd discovered in our evidence, I still had a ways to go to prove it was more than a theory.

* * *

I once promised Jamie that I'd never build a suspect wall covered in red yarn at the back of my closet. I was a rookie officer at the time and pestered Lieutenant Miller long enough that she allowed me access to Jenna's cold case file to look at on my off time. Instead of a wall, I had my binders—bins of them—and tonight I'd pulled the one with the chronologically newest binders into the living room as soon as I got home. My reasons for unpacking the grim collection of murders in and around the Pacific Northwest were twofold: I still didn't know who had sent me the photo of me and Jenna, so I hadn't let myself abandon the idea that it wasn't sent with innocent intentions. I also needed to add the details of the two murders I was working on to convince myself there was nothing similar to Jenna's case.

I made myself a plate of eggs and settled in on the couch with my earbuds and a throwback playlist. Meghan rattled through a story about her day and why it meant she wouldn't be home for the evening, but I wasn't paying attention, waving goodbye over my head as she ran out the front door. I started by putting the photo and envelope I'd received into an evidence bag and added it to a folder that fit the purple three-ring binder. I pulled out the pages of news clippings I'd taken from the end of last year on the Sarah Goodall murder. Reporting had ended once our department had nothing new to update the press with, so she didn't occupy many pages.

I'd developed a checklist years ago when I first started my clandestine investigation into Jenna's murder to compare it to others. Sarah Goodall hadn't checked any of the relevant boxes. She'd been murdered in her own home; Jenna's murder scene was never found. Sarah had been strangled; Jenna had been stabbed—a detail the adults in my life initially tried to hide from me until the specifics of her death certificate were published by the local media. That detail erased any possibility of Jenna's death being related to the water or of it being an accident. I was forced to accept the fact that because I wasn't there, Jenna ended up with someone who took her life away, but in the past decade I hadn't found any other victims that I could definitively connect to her murder. Including Sarah Goodall or Dana Mayhew, whose pages I was going to add tonight. Even if I didn't see an immediate link, I cataloged them all the same, my collection of voiceless victims.

Scissors in hand, I started snipping pages from the newspapers I'd brought home. Sometimes I had to buy them, but most of the time I took them from the office before Bryan could throw them out. Dana Mayhew had started on the front page, then her story was moved to the front of the local pages. Today, no article had run regarding her murder, but I doubted they'd printed the last of her story. My classic rock playlist shuffled from Led Zeppelin to Stevie Nicks, and I tossed the first paper to the floor, then jumped with a scream when it landed in front of a pair of feet in black Adidas. Nicky was standing with his hands in the front pocket of his loose-fit jeans, a look of irritation on his face. I pulled my earbuds out and stammered through an apology.

Nicky Danishevsky was tall, built, and Hollywood handsome. He had commanding gray eyes fringed in dark lashes, with a Marlon Brando jawline and chiseled abs to match. He had looks, success, and determination, but I'd still said no to him for weeks when he first asked me out two years ago. We met when we were eighteen, after Nicky was randomly paired as my twin brother's roommate our first year of college. Dating my twin's best friend seemed like a terrible idea back then, and he went on to marry someone else from their friend group before we all graduated.

When he asked me to dinner a few months after his divorce, I turned him down, but with Jamie's encouragement to keep trying, Nicky refused to give up. After weeks of flirty phone messages, he sent a giant bouquet of wildflowers to the station, along with a reservation card for dinner, and I gave in. In part because of the flowers and in part because Bryan insisted I put the poor guy out of his misery and show him exactly why he didn't want to date me. Nicky couldn't be convinced back then, and two years later we were still working on things, but the look he was giving me said he might be questioning his decisions.

"I tried knocking, but you obviously didn't hear me," Nicky said. He dropped himself into the recliner in the corner with a gruff sigh and grimaced at my half-eaten plate of eggs. "I take it you forgot we were going to dinner?"

Even without the proof that I'd made myself food, my oversized black sweatpants and fuzzy socks gave away how much I'd settled in for the night. "I am so sorry. I can get changed if you want to give me a few minutes. I completely forgot."

"It's been four hours since I texted you about doing dinner."

I pushed myself into the back of the couch and crossed my legs under me. "I've had so much going on this week, I completely lost track of my day."

Nicky sat quietly in the chair, his head back, fingers laced together over his head. "So, what connection do you think you found this time?"

"Nicky..."

"No, for real, it's not like I don't know why you pull all of this out. If Jenna's case is canceling my dinner plans again, we can at least talk it out, right?" Nicky's attitude was hovering somewhere between annoyed and sarcastic. "Lay it on me."

I tossed the blue-handled scissors into the tote and shuffled the rest of the newspapers on the coffee table. I was at fault for forgetting the text exchange making dinner plans and agreeing he'd sleep over at my place, but I wasn't in the mood for a guilt trip. "I always add the new cases to my files, you know that. Even if it doesn't pertain to Jenna's case, I might be able to compare other cases later on. That's all I was doing." Opening up about the anonymous mail I'd received and the nagging feeling that it was related to Jenna's murder was something to keep to myself.

"But why did you decide in the last four hours that you needed to do this right now?"

"I don't want to fight about this. I can get dressed and we can go get food." I gathered my binders and started putting them back in the plastic tote, but Nicky stood up and grabbed my hand. His unexpected switch to gentle mode caught me off guard, and I let him pull me to him.

"I don't want to fight either." He squeezed a little tighter and nuzzled his chin on the top of my head. "If you'll put this away, I'll order delivery, because I know it's questionable you even have eggs left."

I pressed my face into the soft blue cotton of his shirt and wrapped my arms around him. His shoulders relaxed, and I knew he was going to let my missed dinner date go. When I broke the other bit of news to him that I'd forgotten about, he'd be upset again, but for now this was as close to an apology either of us was going to give.

"You do realize it's been eight days since we've been in the same room, right?"

"I know," I said into his chest. The scent of his musky body wash and Downy was familiar and comforting.

"After eight days of not being with you, I just wanted a night together, that's all. Preferably with a tasting menu and a bit of you naked. Well, a lot of you naked, actually, but we'll order in, and I'll take what I can get." We held on to each other in silence for a full minute, letting our tensions release, before Nicky let go. He kicked his sneakers off at the front door and stretched out on the couch, patting the cushion for me to join him after I'd moved the blue bin back to its space in my closet.

I flipped through the channels on the TV, looking for anything to do with food, hopeful it would create the distraction needed to get Nicky over my mess-up of the evening. "What are my chances that you're still going to spend the night tonight?"

"I'm staying the night," Nicky said. He took the remote from me and adjusted the volume as the intro for a cake competition started. "What are my chances you aren't going to cancel the weekend plans I made for next week? Me, you, a cabin in the rainforest. I'll make you the new stuff I'm planning for my winter menu, and we can hide for a bit. Brandon promised he can handle the restaurant on his own for a few days, and I said I don't want to hear from him unless the whole thing is on fire. I don't even want to turn on my phone."

I rubbed my tired eyes with both hands and took in a deep breath. Even before I'd forgotten about our dinner plans, I knew I was going to have to do this part, and I still wasn't prepared to deliver more bad news. "Let's just play that conversation by ear."

Nicky laughed, but it was disappointment. "I have reservations, Cas, I can't just play it by ear. If I need to cancel them, I need to know."

"With this new case, I don't know if right now is the best time."

"Unless there's something specific going on, why can't you say yes? Is it because it's your ex-boyfriend? Because I know you're not on call next weekend. That's the whole reason we picked those days."

I stiffened at his quick shift back to angry and the mention of Ethan. I hadn't discussed much of the case with Nicky to this point, and I made a quick leap to how he'd found out. "Did Jamie tell you that?

"No, Jamie didn't tell me, but glad to know you told one of us. They named him on the news today, and I recognized him. I went to school with him too." His arms were folded tight across his chest now.

"I might have connected our murder to another murder from last year. I think we got confirmation today that they're linked. That's why I don't know if I can get away next weekend, because I'm not sure what we're dealing with anymore. Now you know something Jamie doesn't know." I sank into the arm of the couch and, to avoid Nicky's stare, turned my attention to a cheesy host talk contestants through recipe requirements. Neither one of us was willing to chance pushing the conversation past its breaking point. I wrapped up in my favorite crocheted blanket, and Nicky ordered himself Thai food for delivery, then we both became overinvested in watching how to make the perfect devil's food cake. When we finally made it to bed, the discord from the evening climbed in with us.

* * *

Pain punched through my chest, and I struggled to open my eyes in the darkness. I was bleeding, but I wasn't sure where the blood was coming from. My mouth was filled with the coppery taste of old pennies, and my face was warm and wet. A heavy weight kept me tethered in place. I pulled against the weight, fighting to get myself free.

Jamie was next to me, blood dripping from the side of his head. I shouted at him, but he didn't respond. I twisted in place, pulling wildly on my seat belt when a hand came through my window. Jenna crouched at the mangled car door, tugging at me until I was free, then walked away, never saying a word. Her ash-brown hair was a mess of tangled knots, and her wet clothes left puddles on the ground behind her. My heart pounded in my ears. Panic set in. I couldn't move, I couldn't breathe. My fear erupted into hysterical screams.

"Cassidy. Cassidy." I heard my name, and an alarm sounded in the distance. The man called for me again, and I pushed harder against what was holding me down to break free. A strong hand came down on my shoulder and shook me.

"Cassidy, answer your phone," Nicky said, still half asleep.

I opened my eyes, bringing myself back to the safety of my bedroom and out of the old trauma of my nightmare. Grabbing for the noise, I shifted out from under the weight of Nicky's arm and sat up in the dark, checking the blue glowing numbers on my alarm clock—1:39 AM.

"Hello?"

"Hey, it's me." Bryan's voice was thick with sleep. "I'm on my way to you. We have another murder."

5

Bryan was more irritated than his new normal as he drove his supersized black Ford through the gates of the victim's neighborhood. He was required to show both of our badges and IDs to the security officer before we could enter. The guard—a man in his late forties with a graying mustache and a hard-ass attitude—did not trust us without the reds and blues of the other squad cars on scene. Bryan grumbled about not switching vehicles as he was finally allowed through the gate into the Cherry Creek community. Cherry Creek was one of the city's newer, affluent communities, opposite of where Dana Mayhew lived.

A mixed fleet of private security and patrol and medical units were scattered in disarray in front of the victim's house. The tall wrought iron gate was open, and two larger-than-life stone lions stood guard on either side. The statues seemed ominous, if not a little over-the-top, even for this crowd. As ominous as the giant stone beasts was the black ME van backed up the brick driveway.

Looking past our rushing crew, I was caught off guard by a second cluster of vehicles stopped farther down the street. Every major news studio had caught wind of the latest suspicious death. The news trucks were filtering in at the opposite end of the street, smartly keeping their distance for now. I shook my head and sighed, thinking of what it had cost them to get past the front gate attendant.

I followed Bryan along the brightly lit walkway to the front door of the two-story colonial. We walked through the open double doors into a massive white marble foyer. A crystal-and-brass chandelier, which looked like it may have been stolen from Buckingham Palace, overwhelmed the space above an extravagant dark-wood spiral staircase. At the bottom of the stairway was a notably worn-out Cory Stevens.

"I tell ya, I will never willingly take an overtime night shift again," he said, leading us back through the long hallway past a formal sitting room. Three girls, all around nineteen, were huddled together on a sofa, the shock of their grim discovery still evident in their posture. The girl in the middle was sobbing while two friends offered comfort from either side.

"Our victim is Olivia Bower. Her younger sister found her out back. She's been strangled like your other girl."

"Are we sure this isn't someone she knew? I had to show five forms of ID to get by the asshat at the front gate." Bryan was still grumbly.

"That's because you went through the front gate. Notice the TV vans made it through just fine? Only parts of this neighborhood are actually walled up, and even then, it's not impenetrable. Parts that open onto city trails have unguarded access gates for people on foot. It's not a fortress. Besides, this doesn't feel like someone who knew her," Cory answered. "You'll see what I mean."

"Do they have a security system?" I asked. These days, even the neighborhoods without the Cherry Creek price tag had a spattering of home security cameras and video doorbells.

"They have a system, but the younger sister didn't set it because her sister was going to be home."

We followed Cory through a back door in a gourmet kitchen and out to a perfectly manicured backyard with a white-painted gazebo, a brick pizza oven, and a hot tub. In the hot tub was the body of our latest victim. Olivia Bower was not the debutante I'd expected to see. She was in her early twenties with a face full of piercings. Her head and shoulders were out of the water and her arms were draped over each side. Her wrists were covered in plastic bracelets, and small tattoos went up each arm. The woman's dark hair with random bursts of red was fanned out on the tiled edge of the hot tub in sets of meticulous braids of varying sizes.

With the help of portable work lights that had been set up to assist, Shannon O'Mara knelt next to the hot tub, painstakingly wrapping our victim's right hand. I stepped carefully to his side and could see that two of her long, daggerlike fingernails were broken. The water was dark, with pink foam in the corners where the bubbles from the jets had settled when they were turned off, and a strong metallic smell was mixed with the standard chlorine.

"Is that blood?" I asked, startled to connect the wet-penny smell with the darkness of the water.

"Quick test says yes, this is blood, but it's not hers, from what I can tell. I can't tell you what kind of blood either, considering *that*." He pointed to the right side of the hot tub, where the form of a suckling pig rested just past our victim's outstretched hand. "I think it might be animal blood but too much to be from that pig. Also, he's been frozen for a while. There's more blood and some flowers in there."

I stepped to the left of the hot tub and studied the next item Shannon had pointed out, just out of the ray of illumination from the work light focused on the body. A large silver bowl with an engraving of vines adorning the outside was on the ground and filled to the brim with blood. Resting on top of the blood was a posy of white blooms. "They're snowdrops," I said to the crowd around me. "My grandma always planted them to have something in her yard the deer wouldn't eat. I'm pretty sure they're poisonous." I didn't know what any of it meant yet, but I was also sure that when I reached out to Professor Darcy again, she'd be able to tell me of a Greek goddess who used snowdrops in her mythology. From the other clues left behind—the suckling pig and the blood—our killer no longer cared if the symbolism in his crimes was noticeable anymore.

It was easy to confuse the significance of feathers and flower petals in scenes of chaos. For both Sarah Goodall and Dana Mayhew, the items left to signify their importance had almost gone unrecognized. He was making sure we wouldn't miss his message again.

"I don't know what all of this is or how it connects to your last murder, but I can tell you at least the cause of death is the same: There's bruising on her throat, and I'd guess he strangled her right here. I've already checked her mouth, and what you see around her is it."

"The hair is odd." I crouched closer to the body of our latest victim to examine the braids.

"I'm also going to throw out there that besides the braids, there's salt in her hair."

"Salt?" I repeated.

"Yeah. I'm only guessing here, but it seems he dumped salt water on her hair before he braided it. You can see the bits of the chunky salt particles, and the whitish edge to where the water dried on this dark finish on the hot tub." Shannon pulled a wide strip of tape over the paper bag on the left hand of our victim and stood, wet marks showing on the knees of his pants from the soaked tiles. "We need to get her out of this water and try to preserve what we can. I'm going to look at her now, since I'm up. I'll get you my report as soon as I'm done."

I took in what I could of the disturbing array around our latest victim while Shannon prepared to move the body. "It doesn't look like she had much of a chance to fight."

"Headphones," Cory answered. "There's a pair of wireless headphones on the patio table. We're guessing she was wearing them when he attacked. He is probably the one who left them on the table on his way out of the backyard. Evidence-wise, we've found nothing else so far, other than an unusable shoe print in the flower bed along the driveway. I don't think he came through the house at all."

"Evidence at the last scene was also sparse. We came up with a partial print, not much else."

"I'm going to follow Shannon down to his office, see what he comes up with on the initial exam tonight. You want to ride with me or catch a ride to the station with one of the patrol guys?" Bryan asked me, already fidgeting on his feet.

"I've got to talk to the sister, then I'll ride back with you," I answered, even though that wasn't what I wanted to do. What I wanted to do was stop this snowball we were running behind and keep it from getting any bigger. I wanted to put the night on ice and climb back in bed. What I didn't want to do was make a teenager walk me through the nightmare she'd unwittingly walked into. I headed back down the hallway alone to the room Olivia Bower's younger sister was still sitting in with her two friends.

I introduced myself to the three girls huddled together on the tufted red sofa. There was a coordinating floral print across the rug and walls and draperies. I couldn't be sure if the roses I suddenly smelled were real or created by an overstimulated decorator.

"I'm Sophie. Olivia is my sister," the petite blonde in the middle answered. Her eyes were puffy and red from crying, but there were no new tears. Her blush-pink Hollister logo T-shirt and white denim were more in line with what I'd expected to see her sister wearing when we arrived.

"We're very sorry about everything that happened tonight," I said. "Where are your parents? Is there anyone else who lives here? Other siblings?"

"Our parents are in Chicago for a business conference. It's just me and Liv here. I tried calling my mom's cell and the hotel, but I haven't heard back yet."

"We'll get the contact information so we can get ahold of them for you, but if you do hear back before we get ahold of them, please have them call us, all right? We'll need to talk to you more, but for now, is there anyone you can think of who would hurt your sister? Anyone at all?"

Sophie shook her head. "I don't know anyone who would have done that. I don't even know what all of that was back there. Liv wasn't always nice to people, but I don't know who would do this. There was so much blood."

She set her eyes past my shoulder, and a new wave of sobs rolled in. I knew the young woman had reached her end for the night, and decided it was best to wrap things up with her and let her be comforted by her friends. But letting her go would have to carry a warning. "You're not going to be able to stay here tonight, possibly for a few days. We also have to warn you not to talk to anyone about what you saw here tonight, and I can't stress the importance of that enough. What you saw back there, no one should have to see that, but we have to keep these details to ourselves. You might hear from a journalist or want to get it out of your head by talking to friends, but it is important not to so we can solve this case, all right? I'll leave you my card for when your parents return. Is there somewhere you can stay for tonight?"

"She can stay with me," the blondest of the three answered.

"Officers will be here for most of tonight, probably into tomorrow. If there is anything else you think of in the meantime, no matter what time, call the cell on my card."

* * *

I rocked anxiously in the stiff-backed chair outside the city morgue, waiting for Bryan to finish talking with Shannon. I'd made the mistake of attending one autopsy early in my career, and it was something I'd worked hard ever since not to repeat. A body at a crime scene rarely got to me. Things changed once the investigation became clinical. The sound of small power tools, the snippers and scalpels, were bad enough. When you added in the strangely sweet acidic smell that had stayed with me for days after, it was too much to do again.

Queasy or not, our night was not over. Bryan was amped up and we needed to sit down and review our cases together, so I waited. I flicked on my cell—4:03 AM. My body was jittery from the mix of adrenaline and exhaustion weighing on me. I was fighting to keep my thoughts on track, but the new clues left at the Bower scene were competing for brain space in the early-morning hour. I needed to find the connection between what I'd just seen in the backyard of the Bower home and the myths. I opened my phone and pulled up the email address Professor Darcy had given me. I outlined in simple bullet points the new items we had collected: pig, scrying bowl, snowdrops, and hair braids in salt. I didn't include the blood, figuring that had been for our sake more than for myth accuracy. Bryan crashed through the black double doors into the main lobby as I hit send on my email.

"We need more guys. We need more guys right now to go over what we've got. Call Sam, see if you can get him and Gabe to come in with us. We've got to figure something out about this bastard, because you and I know he's killed three now, and he seems to be picking up speed."

"I'll call Sam." I had come to recognize this level of Worked Up in my partner. He didn't reach it often, but when he did, it was hard to bring him out of it. We were all in for a long morning.

"Tennyson," Sam answered on the first ring. Sam Tennyson and Gabe Hutchins were two detectives we worked with often from our unit. I hoped they could help me pull a ramped-up Bryan and our pile of so-called evidence into some sort of direction.

"It's Cassidy. We caught another murder tonight, and Bryan is itchy to get more eyes on what we have. We're leaving the body locker now. Is there any way I can convince you to call your partner and meet us at the station?"

"I knew this call was coming after I got the alert about the homicide on my phone. I'll get ahold of Gabe, and we'll meet you down there."

"Thanks for coming out."

"Anything for you, Cas. I'd hate for you to have to calm Bryan down on your own."

* * *

The sky outside our windows glowed with the purple hue of early sunrise, replacing the stark darkness we'd started in. I sat at one end of the banged-up table in the conference room we had been working out of with Bryan, Sam, and Gabe, stale coffees and scattered papers in front of each of us. We took turns for what felt like days shuffling the papers back and forth across the fake-wood tabletop, giving alternating theories on the crime scene photos and the dog-eared copies of witness statements Bryan and I had been dragging around.

"The last thing I expected when I went to bed last night was to wake up and be connecting multiple murders before sunrise," Gabe said, shuffling a stack of photos back into one pile. He rubbed his copper-skinned shaved head and gave in to a wide yawn. "Did we get anything traceable on the ring?"

"Nothing. There's no maker stamp, no way to trace it. I've contemplated putting it on the news, but I'm not sure if that's the right call yet," Bryan said.

"I'd say no on going to the press," Sam said. He scratched at graying stubble that was growing in where a full beard had been until a few weeks ago, shaved at the request of his granddaughter. "I think the last thing we want is to have them running with their own theories for the public on what we're dealing with. Especially because I'm still not sure how we're connecting what we first thought was a domestic to something that feels . . . well, a little Satan-y?"

"I don't know exactly what tonight means, but I'm confident it's Greek," I said. "Not Satanic."

"What about the Goodall case?" Sam asked. "Are we sure that's connected? The manner of strangulation was different for her. He wrapped something around her throat at that one. The strangulation at these last two doesn't involve a weapon. Even the timing isn't matching for me. Sarah Goodall was killed almost a year ago. These recent two were in a span of five days. Why?"

"Could have been because the cord was available in the craft room? I also think the timing supports the mythology. Professor Darcy connected all of the items left with Dana to Aphrodite over anyone else because she was killed on the fourth of the month; that's Aphrodite's day. Sarah Goodall was killed on the seventh of December, and she said neither of those are symbolic of Athena, but maybe he hadn't decided to incorporate dates into his symbology yet. Or maybe it just took him this long to find the next one."

"Why are the scenes getting so much more elaborate, then?" Sam asked. I knew he was only trying to make sure we weren't missing anything, but I couldn't help but feel slightly undermined by the series of questions.

"I don't think the killer wanted any of the scenes to be subtle. He knew when he went in to kill Olivia Bower last night that he was going to do that. It wasn't done on a whim. I don't think he wanted us to miss it. He wants us to know it's him, and he wants us to notice the tokens. I think he's trying to be more obvious."

"Dude, I don't want to say this, but do we think there are others that we've missed?" Gabe asked the grim question I hadn't given life to. "There was a big span of time between the Goodall case and the Mayhew case, and then barely a week between the Mayhew case and tonight."

Bryan stretched in his chair. "I've been looking at other cases that came in after the Goodall murder, and I'm not seeing anything else similar, but if there *was* anything else, it went entirely unnoticed. If we assume we missed tokens at any other crime scenes, we'd be looking for women attacked while home alone at night and strangled in one manner or another. These are the only three that match those similarities around here in the past year."

"I liked your case a whole lot better when we thought it was the husband," Sam said. "I see where you're going with the connection and I can even see it in the first two, but looking at these photos from tonight? This feels like something else. Feathers are one thing; these things were set up like she was trying to cast some sort of spell. This one is throwing your theory off for me."

"I want to see what the professor comes back with, because I'm betting that there was some spell-casting goddess out there, and this is going to fit." I flinched on a cold gulp of coffee and let my head drop against the back of the chair, exhaustion winning the fight. "I'm done for tonight. Or morning? Whatever time it is, I'm done. I need to get some sleep and come back to this."

Gabe glanced at his watch and double-checked it against the clock hanging on the wall. The ticking minute hand declared it six thirty AM. "I'm in, if Cassidy comes back with breakfast."

"Breakfast would be good. Maybe we'll get lucky after some sleep, and maybe I'll still be married," Bryan said as he slow-paced it out the door with the rest of us. I climbed into his truck, fighting my body's urge to sleep as soon as he pulled into the early-morning traffic. I allowed a few minutes to pass in silence before I decided it was time to poke the bear.

"What's with the divorce talk? What's going on with you and Ana?" I asked as we pulled out of the station parking lot to head home for a few hours' sleep.

Bryan took a deep breath and gripped both hands on the wheel. "Well . . . we found out Ana is pregnant again. I guess she's put off taking a test because she was trying to stay in denial, but her doctor confirmed she's about three months along. She wants to kill me because, of course, it's my fault, and she kicked me out of the bedroom. I've been sleeping on the damn couch for two weeks."

"Wait, I thought you guys were done having kids?"

"We were."

"No, I mean like snipped done. I thought you took care of that last year."

Bryan and Ana had had three boys in the seven years they'd been together, now ages six, four, and three. All the boys were hyperactive replicas of their father and had proved to be quite the handful.

"I chickened out," Bryan said quietly.

"Back up. What do you mean you chickened out? You took three days off!"

"I know! I got there, and they stuck me in that little room alone, and the idea of that guy coming at my junk with a scalpel was not working for me, so I left."

"And you still took three days off? I brought you lunch."

"I didn't want to tell people I wimped out. I spent the three days helping Ana with the boys and I promised her I'd reschedule, but I haven't. She's already scheduled me for another appointment, and if this one isn't a girl, one of us might be next in line for your guest room. Me and four boys might be too much testosterone for Ana to deal with." Bryan angled his truck into my empty driveway. Nicky was most likely on the way to the gym, not waiting for me to get back home to say goodbye if it meant messing up his morning routine.

"Many more weeks like this and I'll end up single too. Nicky already wasn't loving the new schedule, but last night I canceled on some weekend plans he's been trying to set up." I ran stressed fingers across the top of my jeans before opening the door of the truck. "You and I should've married each other when we first met, then none of this work stuff would matter. Why didn't we do that again?"

"Uh, there was the whole interdepartment-dating-rules problem, and your brother hated me."

"Jamie didn't hate you."

"He still hates me. His exact words the first time I showed up for a Cantwell dinner was 'Don't think I'm going to let you date her.' Also, you snore like a bear. It was never going to work."

I gave my partner a playful shove. "I don't snore."

"You do. You absolutely do. Now, get out of my truck so I can go sleep, or I'm sleeping on your couch."

"Keep telling Ana you're sorry. I'll see you back at the station in a few hours."

"Don't forget the coffee. Add some pastries, good ones. I mean, you were the one who threw a cold murder into our mix."

6

The heavy rain from the morning before came back for an encore as I dashed across the blacktop at the station with coffees in one hand and a bag of local pastries in the other. Gabe rushed to the door to help with the offerings I'd brought with me while Bryan paced in the corner on his cell.

"You are my favorite person in the world at this moment." Gabe flashed one of the smiles he was famous for. "I already downed some of the junk they make here, but I'm desperate for some real stuff." He took the lid off one of the paper cups and added a healthy dose of powdered creamer to the mix.

"Who's Bryan talking to?" I asked.

"MacAllan. They've been talking nice for a few minutes now."

Cole MacAllan was a unit leader in our local FBI office. The first assignment with Cole and Bryan together had started as a giant pissing contest, but they put their egos away when it counted and got the bad guy in the end. An offer from Cole or one of his crew was not something we turned down anymore.

Bryan finished his call with an unceremonious grunt and joined me at the table. He started the process of pulling the top off a lemon muffin, easily looking worse than he had yesterday. His wrinkled appearance and the dark circles under his eyes made it easy to guess any sleep he'd had was on the couch. "Cole offered his help if we decide we need it," he said around muffin bites. "Guess it's been slow for his team these last few weeks, lucky son of a bitch."

I reached for my own cheesy Danish and settled into my spot at the table. No one in the room was feeling chatty, so I concentrated on the gooey pastry and waited for my laptop to warm up.

"To recap from last night, we are all still in agreement that this guy is making these Greek connections, and that also has to mean he's stalking them first, right?" Gabe finally got the conversation started.

"He has to be, at least to some extent. There's no way the myth theory works if he isn't watching them to a degree," I said.

"Going back to all of that, we have the goddess of wisdom assigned to a teacher, the goddess of beauty and love assigned to a pretty woman having an affair, and the goddess of what, blood sacrifice to Olivia Bower?" Sam quipped, obviously not convinced of the working goddess theory.

I kept myself straight in my seat, trying to eke out as much confidence as I could for my early-morning mythology lesson. "It's not just the items he's leaving behind; the goddesses he's selecting match the women to some degree, and that's why I think he's watching them first. Once you know which goddess he's referencing, you can see the connections he's made to each victim in real life."

"But going over the first two—Sarah and Dana—there's nothing reported about either of them noticing any type of stalker or odd interactions they told others about," Bryan added.

I opened my emails, and the one at the top of the list was from Professor Darcy. I scanned the bullet points she'd listed and was again impressed by how closely the details she'd provided matched the scene. The professor had included a collection of pdf files from her classes that we might find useful. The three files were named "Athena," "Aphrodite," and "Circe." "Professor Darcy came through for us. I know who our third goddess is."

"What did the good professor say?" Bryan asked.

"Olivia Bower most likely represents Circe, the goddess of magic," I answered. "According to Professor Darcy, Circe was vengeful and a sorceress, known for using dark magic to turn men into pigs, which she then fed to the men's friends. It's believed she used snowdrop flowers in her potions. We need to learn more about Olivia to fully understand her connection, but it might be related to what her little sister told me—she wasn't always nice to people. Regardless, I don't think there's any mistaking the connection to the Circe mythology."

"It's almost obscenely exact," Gabe said, rubbing his eyes.

Bryan downed the last bit of his coffee and tossed the empty cup away. "Well, we have a few hours to come up with something worth sharing on these theories. Lieutenant Miller said Mr. Bower and apparently a full law firm will be here once they land at SeaTac. They were made fully aware of the crime scene details from their younger daughter, so there's no hiding it from them."

* * *

When Mr. Bower invaded the large conference room near Lieutenant Nancy Miller's office that afternoon, his five-man legal team circled the table through solemn introductions. Sitting down with the families of victims usually involved fighting to keep from being caught up in their grief. Sitting down with Russell Bower and his attorneys didn't feel like grief. It felt like an interrogation, and we were on the wrong side of the table. I didn't like the intimidation.

"Detective, we want you to ensure that this case remains on the front burner," the senior attorney said at the end of his outline of the family's expectations. I wasn't sure if applying the wrong rank to Lieutenant Miller was intentional or accidental, but she let it slide. "You will have the full cooperation of my clients, but we will be running our own campaign to make sure the person responsible for Olivia's death is caught and prosecuted."

"We appreciate your passion for your clients and this tragedy." Lieutenant Miller stepped cautiously into defense. She'd been through enough of these conversations to master the politely firm response. "But we need to make sure we're able to work the case without undue interference."

"You need to find the person who murdered my daughter." Russell Bower's voice shook as he spoke, his right hand fisted on the table. "I want to know exactly who will be responsible for leading this investigation, and I want that person to know I will demand updates. I will not tolerate her case being ignored."

"Detective Cantwell and I are working this case, sir," Bryan said. "Is there anyone you think could have hurt your daughter? Are there friends that we can talk to?"

"My daughter didn't have friends, Detective," Russell Bower said with a shake of his head. "We did everything we could for Olivia, probably too much, and she was on a path that brought her into some questionable circles. She didn't cultivate friendships as much as she collected fans. My wife never could truly cut her off, and she had . . . a lot of bad decisions and hangers-on. My wife and my daughter know a lot more of the names than I do, but you should start with Zac Peters. He was the most recent loser she tried dating to make me crazy. His own parents threw him out, but my team can get you their information."

It was obvious by the time the meeting ended that keeping Russell Bower off our backs was going to take as much work as our investigation itself. Unlike our swiftly fulfilled requests through Ethan for Dana's detailed records, the process was going to be more drawn out for twenty-one-year-old Olivia. We needed written requests for her bank account and credit cards, phone records, and school records. Nothing was going unchecked, and nothing was going to be received without the proper paper trail.

Nancy Miller poked her head into the conference room shortly after Sam and Gabe had called it a day. Her blonde hair was in a simple ponytail now, and she'd ditched the fitted red jacket she'd been wearing during our earlier meeting with Mr. Bower. This was the Nancy Miller I was used to: professional and straightforward, without a lot of fuss. The version of her who'd sat down with Russell Bower and his team in a tailored suit and tight chignon was one I saw only when she knew she was playing defense. "Have we made any progress?"

"We've asked for all of Olivia's records, and Shannon submitted a request to the forensic lab to expedite the reports for her and Dana Mayhew so we can compare them to Sarah Goodall. The request was received, but they didn't give him a time frame," I answered.

"I talked to Agent MacAllan this morning," Bryan added. "He's up-to-date, with a bit about the Greek stuff, and is ready to help when we're ready."

Miller feigned a smile that didn't match the concern in her brown eyes. It was never easy to consider needing outsiders on a case. "All right, once we get the info for Zac Peters, we need to get him in here for a sit-down. We've run into a new issue, though, and you two need to figure it out ASAP. We might have a leak. I've got a voicemail from a reporter asking if we were investigating a cold case because she has an *unnamed source* who says that we're looking at multiple murders."

"We are," I answered, not registering why our boss would be concerned about such a simple question.

"But we weren't yesterday, as far as anyone else knew, and it was left yesterday after I'd left for the day. I need the two of you to figure out who knew we'd made a connection to a cold case before the death of Olivia Bower was discovered, and how any of that information would have ended up with a reporter."

The suggestion that we would have someone on our team leaking any kind of information seemed impossible. I'd worked with these teams my whole career and never considered any of them capable of something like leaking information to the press. I glanced across the table at my partner, and his scowl told me he'd come up with a suspect. He promised to get to the bottom of the issue and waited until Nancy Miller left the room before letting me in on what he was thinking.

"I think we need to talk to your new friend, the helpful professor, and find out who she has spoken to about our cases. This doesn't look good, Cas."

"But why would she say anything to the press? She's trying to help us." The idea created an instant headache. I'd felt so confident in her willingness to help, and in her assurances it would be done discreetly, I'd never considered she would betray us to the media. There was a second possibility I was uncomfortably aware of, and I couldn't even share it with Bryan. My sister. "Did I screw up?"

My partner shook his head, trying to look convincing. "I was right there with you. And a good journalist was going to figure out a possible connection eventually, but we still have to control the narrative. There's too many details to protect at this stage. I'll set up the surveillance schedule on Zac Peters; you need to check in with Professor Darcy."

* * *

A small pang of envy surprised me as I watched couples take advantage of a dry fall evening up and down Pacific Avenue. After talking with the parents of Zac Peters, it took another three days to track down the most recent friend to lend their son a couch. He was a lanky guy in his mid-twenties with an intricate geometric neck tattoo and a small umbrella inked under his left eye. He hadn't let us inside when we stopped by this afternoon but was more than willing to stand on the porch and tell us the places we'd most likely find his freeloading roommate.

"On a normal day, I'd say you had until at least seven or eight PM before he'd be fall-over drunk, but this thing happening to Olivia has him pretty messed up," the roommate said. His top canine teeth were capped in gold and glinted in the sunlight when he spoke. "I don't think he's stopped drinking since he found out she was murdered, and he didn't come back here last night. Zac is a creature of habit when he's drinking, though, so you have a good chance of catching up to him at a place called Thor's on Pacific anytime after seven PM."

Now we were watching the corner of Pacific and Ninth from our unmarked patrol car, waiting for Olivia's most recent boyfriend to show up. Lucky for us, Zac Peters had a distinct look that wasn't going to be hard to spot, but we'd been watching the same door for over an hour, and I was getting fidgety. I wasn't aware of how fidgety until Bryan grabbed my knee from the driver's seat.

"No more coffee," he said. "You're shaking the whole damn car."

It wasn't just a case of boredom that had me stir-crazy. Since the murder of Olivia Bower, I'd been restless, with a constant carousel of distraction anytime I was too still. Before I'd made it to the office today, I'd already fought with Nicky. Meghan had been MIA and wasn't answering my calls, making it impossible to talk to her about our discussion about my cases and who she might have told.

We were comfortable clearing Professor Darcy in the possible leak to the journalist, but the reporter was still leaving voicemails for Lieutenant Miller. So far, none of the news organizations had suggested that there could be more victims of this possible serial killer, but we all feared the details that could be exposed at the expense of our investigation.

"If we sit here much longer, I need to change places with Gabe. I need dinner," I answered. Gabe, his close-shaved head and tattoos visible in a T-shirt, was inside the bar, nursing a tonic water in plain clothes. My partner nodded vigorously at my suggestion, then Sam keyed up his radio.

"Our guy is coming your way, you can't miss him," he said. "Black hoodie, black pants, neon-green hair."

"On my way out," Gabe answered while Bryan and I climbed out of the Charger together. We quick-stepped across the street and caught up to Gabe, who stepped out of the bar and into the way of Zac Peters.

The young man swayed on his feet and put both hands out for balance. "Sorry, my man," he apologized to Gabe. Sam was right behind Zac, and Bryan and I filed in from the other direction. Gabe took the lead for our side.

"Hey, it's Zac, right? Zac Peters?" The young man, obviously intoxicated, didn't answer. "I know you're Zac. I'm Detective Hutchins. We were hoping we could talk to you about Olivia."

"Olivia is dead," the young man slurred. "Did you know that? He killed her. Crazy son of a bitch killed her."

I moved in closer, unsure if he'd said what I thought I'd heard. "Zac, do you know who hurt Olivia?"

He studied me with deep concentration, then sputtered, "You were there. You were on the news, I saw you. You know he murdered her. My Olivia." And with that he broke into sobs, further impairing his ability to stay upright. It took help from both Sam and Gabe to keep the young man from toppling over.

"We're going to need to hold him until he sobers up," I said, and before my partner could agree, Zac Peters did.

"Yes!" he shouted, unsteadying himself again by throwing a fist in the air. "You take me with you, and then I can tell you the guy . . . I can tell you the guy who killed Olivia.

He just took her away, so now we have to . . ." His voice trailed off and he lost his concentration, suddenly glaring at a trio of seagulls squawking overhead.

"Are you willing to come to the police station with us, Zac?" Gabe asked. "Will you hang out and tell us what you know?"

He shook his head, defiant. "I'm willing to talk, yes, but not to you, you weren't there. I'll talk to her, though." He pointed a shaking finger at me, only a few inches from my face. "She knows. She knows I'll help."

* * *

I stood in my front window watching a thick evening fog roll down the street. Headlights from a passing car barely cut through the darkness. I'd been home for hours but still hadn't been able to shake off the day. As soon as we got him back to the office, Zac Peters had announced he was taking a nap, and we'd left him in a holding cell and gone home to wait for the call that he was ready to talk.

A second murder, a cold case I was positive was connected, an absent roommate—all together, it created a knot in my shoulder that I knew would work itself into another headache. That's why I was standing in my front room window watching the fog and dunking Oreos while a frozen fettuccine baked in the oven. I turned for the kitchen as the electronic timer on my oven went off, followed by the stompy paws of my cat, looking for his own dinner.

I put the hot black dish on a plate and slid it across my counter to sit down, and that's when I noticed a pile of mail on the counter. Looking at the bright-pink envelope on a stack of junk mail, I was furious. Meghan still hadn't returned any of my calls, and she had come home and left again with no word.

I sat down at the table and examined the pink envelope that sat on top. My name and address were printed across the front in handwriting that was confusingly familiar, but there was no return address. I ran my pinkie finger under the corner of the flap and opened it, the sticky threads of self-adhesive stretching until they snapped. I stared into the envelope, my heart racing, and sucked in a short breath before dumping the contents of the envelope onto my table. I grabbed a pen from my junk drawer and then ran to my bedroom. I found the stash of latex gloves and a bundle of evidence baggies I kept on hand in my work go-bag for emergency situations, then sat back at my table to investigate what I'd received.

The first item was a nearly empty sheet of glittery ladybug stickers in a rainbow of colors. Most of the stickers were missing, and I knew why. Jenna had used them on notes we passed in class, even affixing a few to homework assignments. Along with the stickers was a folded strip of yellow paper. With my gloves on, I unfolded the strip, which had been a full sheet at some point before it was folded, wetted, and torn, like we always did for notes.

Like the front of the envelope, the handwriting on the slip of paper brought up emotions of recognition and bewilderment. My shoulders rolled and my stomach dropped as what I was looking at became clear. It was Jenna's handwriting. Part of it, anyway. The strip of paper was a permission slip that had once been attached to a sheet outlining a field trip to the county courthouse to listen to proceedings. It was a field trip scheduled for the week after she went missing that neither of us made it to. Jenna had written her own name and the date in pink ink, and her dad's masculine signature was in the opposite corner. An added line at the bottom of the page in black ink took my breath away: *WHERE IS JUSTICE FOR JENNA?*

My mother had used her soft voice that day. The voice people use when they have to give terrible news. A quiet tone, as if saying the words softer somehow lessens the pain about to be inflicted. My mother was using that tone, tears welled in her eyes, as she began to repeat what she'd already told me. It wasn't necessary. Not the softness of her tone nor the repeat. Each word had hit me like a stone the first time she'd said them; my mind simply couldn't reconcile what her words together meant.

"Kissy," she started again in a whisper. The nickname was from childhood. Kissy was who I became when others thought I needed to be protected. My twin went from Jamie to James in those same moments, but I was made small. Standing with all of the adults that day, I wanted to be small, small enough to disappear. "They've found Jenna. She's—"

I reached out and clamped my trembling hand over my mother's mouth, my fingers vibrating against her cheek. She took my hand away gently and tried to hold it, but I pulled back. I ran from the room, taking the stairs on my hands and knees because I didn't have the strength to stay upright. Collapsing with a thud against the back of my bedroom door, I dug my heels into the ugly brown carpet I hated so much to keep everyone else from getting in.

"Where are you, loser?" Jenna's voice sang the message she'd left on my answering machine fifteen days before, when I didn't show up to pick her up for a party. *The* party. Everyone who was anyone was going to be there, and we'd actually been invited. We didn't have to show up as crashers this time. Jenna had no idea when she left the message that I'd rolled the rusting 1990 Jeep wannabe that Jamie and I shared, with both of us in it. She didn't know that I'd never meant to ruin our plans. She never would know.

I always did as much as I could to keep my connection to the unsolved murder case of Jenna Sutton on the down-low. Bryan knew that Jenna was my best friend through school until her death. He knew that I'd been secretly collecting my own files and investigating her murder off and on since before joining the department. Lieutenant Miller knew of my connection as well. When our lieutenant was Detective Nancy Miller, she'd worked on Jenna's case. She'd sat in my living room when Jenna was still only a missing person to question sixteen-year-old me about where I thought my best friend might have gone.

I knew where Jenna was *supposed* to go and confessed all of it to the sympathetic detective on our living room couch. Our pretend sleepover plans, the party we expected to be at for the night, the after-party rave people were whispering about at school that we hoped to find our way to. Jenna and I weren't the first teenagers to lie about our weekend plans. Telling our parents we were spending the night at the other's house wasn't even an original scheme. We'd been pulling the same con since middle school to skirt parents we thought were treating us like children.

When Jenna disappeared, Jody and Peter Sutton assumed their youngest daughter was with me and hadn't checked in as a protest for having her cell phone taken away that week. I assumed Jenna was home, ignoring me, after I'd failed to show up for our planned escapade. None were the wiser until I broke down and called her house to tell her about the accident and ask for forgiveness. I was hoping that the bumps, bruises, contusions, and broken wrist would get me some sympathy from my best friend. Instead, her parents sounded all the alarms after learning their daughter was not with me, and none of our lives were ever the same again.

And now this. A pink envelope and two pieces of Jenna's life, mailed to me all these years later. I'd tried to dismiss the fear I felt receiving the swim team photo. It had taken a lot to get out of the state of high alert Jenna's murder first plunged me into, and I didn't want to slip back into those irrational fears. But this was more than a photo. These were Jenna's things. Things she would have had with her in her backpack that I knew had never been found. Things that were with her when she died. The question of justice was a second punch in the gut. Was someone challenging me, or were they taunting me?

I'd always felt responsible for what happened to Jenna, and now someone else was making me responsible, opening the self-inflicted wounds I'd made years ago. That rekindled pain was the reason I pulled out my tote and put the stickers in my binder, alongside the photo. It was the reason I wasn't going to rush to report this mail from a mystery sender. If I brought it up, I wouldn't be allowed to be the one to investigate, as close as I was to the case. Nancy Miller would never let me stay involved with someone targeting me. Especially if that anonymous someone could be Jenna's killer. I would have to keep the weight of our current cases and the chaos of my personal life under control to push solving Jenna's murder back to the top of my list.

7

It took ten hours for Zac Peters to sleep it off enough to talk to us. Specifically, to me. Sobering up actually intensified his insistence that he would only talk to the one he'd seen on the news, and somehow I'd made it into the camera frame at both murders. Solo interrogations weren't something I'd done much of in my first four months as a detective, but I wasn't worried. Zac was harmless, and Bryan and Gabe would be watching the entire thing on the other side of the two-way mirror if things went sideways.

"Are we sure we want to send Cas in there alone?" Sam asked. "I mean, I'm not questioning anything about her skills, but why can't one of us sit in with her?"

"I wasn't smart enough to get on camera," Bryan laughed. "The kid is convinced if he didn't see us on the news, we aren't really working the case."

"Besides," I added, "I've been dealing with my little sister for years. I have an obscene amount of experience with hungover twentysomethings."

I filled two paper cups with sludgy coffee from our break room, filled my pockets with sugar packets and creamer pods, then sat down with Zac in the interrogation room. I put both coffees in front of him and emptied my pocket stash onto the table. He separated out the powdered sweeteners and the half-and-half, added a handful of sugar packets to his cup, then poured in all five flavored creamers.

I started the conversation with sympathy. "I'm sorry about your loss, Zac. I can tell you really cared about Olivia."

"She was the best thing that ever happened to me." He stirred his first coffee, sloshing a small tidal wave in the cup. "We met in rehab. Liv is the whole reason I got sober."

"How long ago were you guys in rehab together?"

He looked sheepishly through his poison-green bangs and dropped his head. "I wasn't a drinker when I went to rehab; I was all about the hard stuff back then. I have two years sober from that."

I smiled and kept my posture relaxed. I knew being able to collect those years meant everything to someone in recovery. He needed to know I wasn't going to hold his current hangover against him. "Two years is good. My brother just hit ten, so I've seen what it takes. Were you with her in rehab over this past summer?"

"Good on your brother, Detective. I've been talking to my sponsor; he's gonna help me out. Me and Liv did rehab two years ago, and she's been my person ever since, but I didn't go this summer. Rehab friends are different than normal-world friends. Olivia knew my lowest lows and still wanted to be my friend; that's what makes them different. They'll always have your back, but they'll call you out on your shit, and that was Liv at the core. She could be a lot, though, and it wasn't always perfect. I used to say she was an M&M—hard shell outside, soft on the inside." His voice trailed off, and he closed his eyes for a few beats before taking a sip of his coffee. "She didn't let that part show much, but it was there."

"When we caught up with you last night, you said you knew who killed Olivia. Do you remember telling us that?"

Zac sat up straighter in his chair and pushed his bangs out of his face. "Yeah, I remember saying it. I didn't see it happen to her, but they always ask that question, you know, when people are killed on TV—'Can you think of anyone who would want to hurt them?'—and this guy immediately came back to me. I don't remember if it was a few weeks ago or maybe a few months ago, I can't always keep my days straight, but Liam would probably know when it happened; she made quite the scene."

"Is Liam the one who had the altercation with Olivia?" I asked, trying to remember if we'd received contact info for anyone named Liam from our records.

"No, no, Liam knew the guy. We were at the bar and Olivia had an audience, but she was kind of in a mood, so I was sitting with Nora, and this guy comes up and starts talking to Liam like they're long-lost friends. Next thing I know, he's hitting on Olivia, and it did not go well for him. She lit him up, embarrassed the hell out of him right there in front of everyone, and then threatened to have him thrown out if he didn't leave. Even I felt bad for the guy."

"What did the guy look like?" I asked, unsure if Zac was going to be able to give me what I needed to turn his disjointed memories into a lead.

"He was a tech bro guy; they all look the same." Zac laughed at his own humor. I pressed for more, pointing out that wasn't a description I could use if we wanted to get the person who killed his friend. "He was a white guy, straight-laced, not really Olivia's type. I can't remember much. Like I said, I think Liam knew who he was, and between you and me, she didn't want to admit it, but the guy shook her up. Like I said, she was softer on the inside than people thought."

"Do you have Liam's number so we can get ahold of him, try to figure out who this guy was?"

Zac laughed and waved his hand dramatically between us. "Nah, man. Liam wasn't my friend. He wasn't even really friends with Liv. I think he was hooking up with one of the Madisons. I know he wasn't there with Nora or Olivia, so probably Madison or Madison, or maybe Savannah, but I don't really know the guy."

I couldn't blame it on Zac, I knew he was trying to help, but I didn't know that his lead was the lead that was going to break the case. Everyone who'd been willing to answer the phone and talk to one of us had a different story about Olivia's public confrontations, and nothing in Zac's story made it stand out over any of the others. Especially not knowing the time frame for his memories. All I could do now was figure out which Madison could direct me to Liam and hope he remembered the night one of his friends tried to hit on Olivia Bower at a bar.

* * *

Zac Peters turned down our offer to give him a ride home, so I settled in with the records we'd received from Olivia Bower's phone. In a cursory review of her contacts, there were three Madisons, a Madyson, and a Maddy, an MJ, an MD, and one simple initial M. There wasn't a Liam in her contacts at all. I started at the top of the M's and started dialing.

The first two Madisons were a miss, but the third confirmed she not only had been recently dating a guy named Liam, she also remembered the night I'd asked about.

"It was at the beginning of last month. I remember because Olivia hadn't been back from California for very long when it happened, and we skipped going out the next night. Something about him seemed to freak her out."

"Can you tell me Liam's full name and how to get ahold of him?" I asked, my pen ready.

"Liam Wakefield. He works at Octavia downtown," Madison said before rattling off the phone number, and I could only laugh when she ended with, "If you talk to him, tell him to call me after."

I tried the number for Liam and was sent directly to voicemail, so I took what information I did have and hit the internet. It didn't take long to find the home page for Octavia Innovations, and while Liam Wakefield wasn't willing to answer my call, the receptionist at his office was. She was also willing to let me know he was in and his calendar showed open for the rest of the afternoon.

* * *

"Did you get any sleep last night? Because you definitely look worse than I do today," Bryan said as we rode the elevator to the ninth-floor office of Liam Wakefield.

"I'm getting as much sleep as the rest of us." I waited in front of the doors and stepped out first when we hit the ninth floor.

The swanky mini-skyrise, with its abundance of marble and glass in the foyer and people in nearly matching dark suits, seemed like exactly the world Russell Bower hoped his daughter would associate with. The contrast between Zac and Liam was apparent, and we hadn't even met Liam yet.

The receptionist called first to give Liam Wakefield a heads-up that we were on our way, and he was waiting for us when the elevator doors opened and led us to his personal office. The young blond guy in a tailored gray suit with a pink dress shirt and floral tie couldn't have been more different from Zac Peters. Zac's green hair, tattoos, and all-black wardrobe meshed with Olivia's dramatic goth style. I was puzzled as to how a buttoned-up guy like Liam had found his way into her circle and optimistic he'd have the missing piece on the guy who'd scared Olivia Bower in a bar a month ago.

Bryan and I turned down his offer of beverages or cookies and got right to business, explaining the confrontation that Zac Peters had described.

"Zac is the guy with green hair, right?" Liam laughed, relaxed in his black leather executive desk chair. "I don't know him or Olivia very well, but I do remember that night. I have kind of a situationship with Madison and she's been friends with Olivia for a long time, so we hang out from time to time. That night, though, I didn't really know the guy Zac's talking about."

"Zac and Madison both seemed to think he knew you," I returned.

"He said we knew each other from a tech convention, but I go to a lot of them, and he wasn't sure which one. I think he just wanted to use it as an in to talk to the hot girl at the table."

My partner had a small notepad and his pen ready before asking what details Liam could give us for the guy who'd tried to crash their party, and I blew out a heavy exhale at his answer, afraid we were careening toward another dead end.

"I think he was probably about my age—I'm twenty-eight. He wasn't shorter than me, so at least five ten, and I think he said his name was Bill or Will, something short."

"You said he thought you guys had met before, maybe at a convention. Would it have been a recent convention, anything that would have been held locally?" I thought maybe, if nothing else, we could narrow it down to an event that would have photos and videos online to comb through. It would be slow and cumbersome, but it would be something.

Liam shook his head and adjusted his tie. He was uncomfortable with our questions even though he didn't seem to have anything to hide. "He started saying something about us having a friend in common, but before he told me anything else, Olivia asked him who he was. I didn't hear what he said to her, but whatever it was had her trippin'. She told him to leave or she'd have him thrown out. That part was typical Olivia: She could be a princess, and people tend to do what she says. He definitely believed her, because he dipped at that point."

I followed Bryan's lead when he stood up and dropped my business card on Liam's desk. "If there is anything you might remember about him, let us know."

He nodded and stood up to shake hands, as if we'd just finished a business deal. "Sorry it wasn't much help, Detectives. I hope you catch whoever did this to Olivia—it's pretty sick—but I don't know that I'm going to be any help. I didn't even recognize the guy that night."

I was defeated, and it showed as we made it back to the elevator for the lobby. I leaned against the elevator wall with a huff. Bryan warned me often about getting my hopes up, and I'd failed to heed that warning today. There was no justification for the weight I'd given to Zac's lead in finding a suspect. Stepping back from it, I could see it as Liam did—a stranger looking to get close to a girl at a bar—and for what it seemed to be, a dead end.

8

The first thing I noticed were the crickets. There was so much to take in under the artificial glow of the streetlight, but it was the crickets I couldn't look away from. The pile of dead bugs was at the bare feet of a dead woman at Point Defiance Park. She was posed on her back, with a sheer yellow cloth draped over her otherwise naked body. Under the faint light the severe purple bruising around her throat stood out against her pale skin. Her arms, both painted from her fingertips to her elbows with a rosy-pink body paint, were stretched above her head to the east and to the streetlight above her. And of course, there were the crickets at her feet.

She'd been discovered on a running trail that snaked along the waterfront before dawn, and this time someone saw him. The young witness was standing with Lieutenant Miller and an EMT a few yards away, wearing the shell shock stare of someone who has witnessed death. He'd arrived before the park opened, expecting to be alone running in the morning darkness. As he rounded a corner, bringing him closer to the waterfront, he saw a figure in dark clothing and a black baseball cap unfurl a piece of cloth under the streetlight about thirty yards ahead. As soon as the person saw him, they bolted. When he made it to the streetlight, he discovered the cloth was covering a body.

"What the hell is this?" Nancy Miller asked after handing the witness off to the EMTs so they could deal with the symptoms of shock that were setting in. "Our first murder was almost a year ago; now we're looking at three in twelve days?"

I watched while a new member of our team of crime scene technicians snapped photos behind the lieutenant. The boldness of the scene jumped off the sidewalk at me. This was completely exposed. He'd intended for this victim to be found by the public, leaving her overnight in a busy park where the details of his not-so-cryptic iconology would be seen by many at sunrise. Where it wouldn't be possible for us to hide it behind the walls of the police station. And with a time frame that was undoubtedly going to lead to panic in the city. But he'd messed up. Someone else had been there.

There was a feeling of something unfinished with what we were looking at. Her painted arms were posed above her head, but the sheer yellow cloth covering her body wasn't perfect. One breast was nearly exposed, and it had rippled unevenly over her legs. The dead crickets were in a rounded mound, as if they'd first been in a large bowl and then tipped upside down—like a ring mold used by a chef. But a crown of roses was on the sidewalk a few feet from the body, possibly dropped by our suspect as he ran from the witness. There was also a long length of rope left at the base of the streetlight along with a terra-cotta pitcher. He'd been interrupted.

"We're still playing catch-up on trying to put a suspect together after the last two," I said, wishing for an answer that didn't sound so helpless. "How big of a jump did our suspect get?"

Nancy Miller checked the smartwatch that never left her wrist. "The call was received by dispatch at three twelve AM, so we're twenty-seven minutes behind him right now. Witness said he ran into the woods, and we've got units making the loop on Five Mile Drive, but there's a lot of ground to cover here."

"He didn't get her all the way here on foot," I said. "There had to have been a vehicle."

"We need to do as much as we can to keep all details away from the press." Lieutenant Miller pulled on the zipper of her black parka as we were blasted with a cold wind off the water. "I've got Sam setting up the press area to keep them corralled."

Bryan bounced from one foot to the other in anticipation. "We need to set up barricades, keep people out of this part of the park, and fan out. If we can figure out how he got her in here, maybe there will be some cameras on the streets we can utilize."

Flashlights in hand, Bryan and I, accompanied by members of our patrol unit, including some who had been called out on overtime to assist, searched the park on foot. I spaced myself out, keeping my partner in my line of sight as we took our search into the woods and the beginning of dawn surrounded us, with still over an hour until sunrise hit. As we walked through the trees in the dark, we found no one. By the time we'd made our way back out, we were in the overflow parking for a zoo that should be empty, but one vehicle was in the farthest corner of the lot, in the dark.

I pointed my direction to Bryan, and in an abundance of caution, we approached the dark-blue compact with our guns drawn.

A quick scan with our flashlights revealed the interior of the car was empty, and Bryan pulled on the handle for the driver's door. It popped open, the car chirping repeatedly to signal the keys were in the ignition. I opened the other door and reached into the glove box for any paperwork I could find. Receipts and random drive-through napkins were in the mix along with a vehicle registration for a woman named Maggie Cannon, who had a Tacoma address not far from the park.

"The car is registered to Maggie Cannon." I read the name out loud for my partner. Without access to my own computer, I called in to our dispatch center to have them run the vehicle against stolen-vehicle reports and check the name of the owner for a copy of her driver's license photo.

"Found something." Gabe's voice crackled over our radios. "I'm just under the footbridge over Five Mile. There's a garden wagon down here with a few of those dead crickets in it."

Bryan turned in a circle, trying to get his bearings. "The bridge is that way, right?"

"Yeah, back by the way we came," I answered, peering into the car. The only thing up front was a used Starbucks cup and a blue pack of gum. The car was relatively clean, and the back seat was nearly spotless.

"Stay with the car; I'm going to go check out what Gabe's got. Our guy wasn't hoofin' in with all his props and a body through those trees without help."

While my partner jogged away from the parking lot, my phone started pinging with texts from our dispatcher. The car had not been reported stolen. There were no wants or warrants on Maggie Cannon. Lastly, I received the digital image of a thirty-year-old brunette with a bright smile, and my heart dropped. We were no longer in the dark about who our victim was. I was texting the name to Lieutenant Miller to ask her to send someone my way to tape off the scene when I caught the colored lights of a TV camera across the parking lot. The young reporter was on her phone until she realized I'd caught sight of her.

I requested more officers my way and asked our lieutenant for permission to arrest journalists as I moved as far away from the victim's vehicle as I dared go. Sam answered first, letting me know he was almost to me with a second crime scene team.

Nancy Miller responded tersely. *Let's try to avoid arresting the press, but get them to the area they're supposed to be in.*

I shouted instructions to the reporter in the grass, and she and her cameraman turned back the way they'd come. My insincere threats to cuff her were punctuated by the red and blue lights from Sam's unmarked car.

* * *

By the time parents got kids off to school that morning, the words none of us wanted to hear had been spoken aloud by every news anchor in western Washington: *serial killer.* They'd hinted for the breakfast hour broadcast that police were cordoning off portions of a popular park and that the early-morning discovery could be related to the recent collection of murders in the city.

Those of us who grew up in the Pacific Northwest in the nineties had been raised by those who grew up here in the seventies and eighties. They'd experienced all the big names in serial killers and boogeymen. They'd eaten dinner to newscasts about young girls taken from parks and beaches, from bikes on their way home from school, or murdered in their own apartments.

They'd gone to bed with unsettled fear and raised their own kids on horror stories about taking candy from strangers in box vans or looking for missing puppies. When the new millennium came along, the boogeyman went virtual and serial killers surrendered their media spotlight to airport security concerns and mass shootings, but the press was ready and willing to report the new danger in our midst, and calls trickled in from families and loved ones of missing women, eager to confirm they weren't the ones who would need to identify a body.

The mood around the station was sullen when we returned from the crime scene, and Bryan was straight-out snippy after we discovered TV cameras had managed to catch both of us entering the park for the morning broadcast. We huddled in our corner of the office, recording what we'd collected from the crime scene, and prepared for our initial sit-downs for the morning. First, we were going to talk to Cole MacAllan, then we were going to talk again with our witness, who was still rattled by his grisly discovery.

I jolted at the sudden noise of my desk phone ringing, breaking me away from the digital photos of our early-morning murder.

"There's a Special Agent MacAllan up here asking for you," Lori, our bubbly receptionist with shellacked hair and a vast assortment of chunky-heeled ankle boots, said when I answered.

"I'll be right there. Can you let Lieutenant Miller know he's here?"

"Will do. And go ahead and take your time," she continued in a hoarse whisper. "I haven't had anything this good to look at in a long time, and he's wearing jeans."

I shook my head as she laughed over the phone, unexpectedly grateful for her brightness in my otherwise horrific morning. "Sorry, I don't think it's good to keep the FBI waiting, even the good-looking ones."

Special Agent Cole MacAllan was focused on his cell phone when I made it to the front desk, texting with two thumbs. "Morning, Detective Cantwell."

"It's definitely been a morning," I said.

"Bryan told me you were assigned the initial on the first murder case, and I wanted to talk to you before we sit down with your top brass. I hate when joining forces gets presented like a hostile takeover. We do plan on working this case *with you*, not around you."

"I'm not worried about takeovers or who's getting credit," I said. "We just need all the help we can get catching up with this guy."

Cole followed me to a conference room, where Bryan and Nancy Miller were both waiting. With the four of us around the table, Cole started the questions.

"Are you still convinced on this Greek thing Bryan was telling me about?"

"Even more so now than we were before," I answered. "I'll let you know as soon as I get confirmation from our mythology expert on this latest victim. In the meantime, the car has been towed to the forensics lot, and Shannon O'Mara from the ME's office wants to talk to us, if you want to sit in on that, and then we'll go from there."

We answered the call from Shannon and listened to the details he could give us so far. The manner of death matched our other victims. The approximate time of death—between nine PM and two AM—was also in line with our other victims. Then he dropped a new detail that had our collective heads spinning.

"So, like I said, it's a strong sample," Shannon said. Bryan looked at me, hoping I would respond first.

"You sure it wasn't an assault?" I asked for the second time.

"I've done this for a long time, Cassidy. There's nothing here that says there was an assault. If there's a boyfriend out there, I would get ahold of him. We can either clear him or make him a suspect."

"That doesn't line up with your other crimes, so what are the chances that this one isn't related?" Cole asked.

Bryan objected faster than I could. "You saw the crime scene; it's connected."

"That part is for you guys to figure out—you're the detectives," Shannon continued. "What I can tell you is that she was probably killed a bit earlier than your other victims, closer to the nine PM mark than to when you found her, and she was with someone intimately very close to the time of death. We have a good sample if you can find a suspect to match."

We ended the call with Shannon's bombshell and gave Cole a few minutes to review the photos we had of what was now a total of four murders.

"We have the paperwork to get us into Maggie Cannon's apartment, and I've already arranged for my crew to meet us there." Cole pressed at his temples in thought. "I don't know what any of this is yet. It's official that we're joining forces, especially with how much this is picking up speed. Starting tomorrow you'll both be stationed at my office. I hope neither of you became detectives thinking you'd have weekends off. Right now we need to find out who Maggie Cannon was."

* * *

Cole followed Bryan and me to the fourth-floor apartment of our newest victim while Lieutenant Miller took on the unenviable task of notifying Maggie Cannon's family of her death. Her building was a hotel-style complex, with at least twenty doors in an enclosed hallway and an elevator at either end. The apartment of our victim was eerily quiet despite the team of evidence technicians taking photos and smearing surfaces with fingerprint powder.

The living room was filled with an IKEA sofa and entertainment center. A rug of mismatched patchwork squares covered a vinyl floor meant to look like wood planks. The small kitchen was an open space in the opposite corner of the room, with a sliding glass door leading to a balcony in the middle of the two spaces. The white walls were covered with multiple decorative mirrors of different sizes and shapes and an array of framed photos—various candid shots of smiling faces, almost all of them including the pretty, dark-haired woman we'd found this morning.

"What are your thoughts?" Cole asked, watching as I opened and closed the blue metal door, on which hung a *Welcome* wreath in the shape of a peace sign circling a brass peephole.

"This is the only way in, and there's no damage to it. He didn't kick the door in, and we're four floors up, so no one was scaling the exterior of the building to get in here. The neighbors are close, apartment walls are thin, so this is a risky spot for him to strike."

"So maybe he didn't catch up to her here."

"I don't know." I wandered into the kitchen area, where Bryan had opened cupboards under the sink and pulled out a small black garbage can. "No liner?"

My partner shook his head. "Garbage bag has been taken and not replaced, and someone ran the dishwasher with place settings for two."

I let out a heavy breath and circled the living room again. An old broom handle was wedged in the base of the sliding glass door—the original single girl's security system. "We are sure that Sarah Goodall was our first victim at the end of last year. He pushed in a kitchen window at her place and managed to do it without getting noticed. We know he used the back door at Dana Mayhew's, either coming in or going out or both. We had flower petals and marks that look like they were made by someone wearing gloves on the door. He went in the back gate at the Bower house, walking in the flower beds that were against the house to avoid lights and the cameras on the house. He doesn't have any of that protection here."

Cole followed my train of thought with a nod. "And that could indicate our victim let him in."

"Which means she might have known him." I went past a bathroom decorated with neon-colored fish to the bedroom at the end of the hall.

The room was large for a single-bedroom apartment, and against the far wall was a queen-size white canopy bed with sheer white curtains tied back at each side. I imagined there was a frilly duvet with matching sheets to go along with the dozen or so pink and purple decorative pillows under the window, but the mattress had been stripped of all its linens.

"Damn," Bryan said, opening the door for the closet containing a stackable washer and dryer. Both were empty.

"He was here. This is where he killed her." If the cold case of Jenna Sutton had taught me anything, it was the importance of having your crime scene. With what could be done with modern forensic science, even cleaned scenes like this one could yield clues. Hairs, prints, or fluids missed by the naked eye could be brought to life with sprays and powders. Maggie Cannon was still gone, but knowing where he'd killed her gave me more hope we could find the person responsible.

9

The insignia on the front of the four-story building didn't do a lot to declare it belonged to the FBI, but once we were inside, the signs were there in the form of a massive security checkpoint at the front desk. A blonde receptionist with black-framed glasses checked us in and provided us with our own limited-access key cards that allowed us to activate elevators and some of the doors in the building. The check-in process included verification and copies of our personal identification and work identification plus a quick photo session for our temporary badges.

On a normal day, this type of morning delay would have Bryan climbing the walls, but my partner was uncharacteristically chipper this morning, in stark contrast to me trying to deal with being in a new environment without my morning espresso.

"This is going to suck. I miss my old desk already."

"You'll survive," Bryan said. He picked up the paper file box we'd brought with us and whistled on our way to the elevator.

"Why are you okay with this?"

"I'm okay with everything today. Ana confirmed we get to buy pink stuff this time around, and I don't have to sleep on the couch anymore." Bryan was beaming. "If the worst part of the day is that I have to cram myself into some shittastic pretend office at FBI headquarters for a few weeks, bring it on."

"Weeks? I envy your confidence," I said as the elevator doors closed us in.

"Why are you so grouchy about this?"

I rolled my eyes at my own drama as we reached our floor. "Still can't get ahold of Meghan. She's been to my house while I was at work, and she sent one text that she's 'assisting at a yoga retreat' until tomorrow and no response since."

"Let's hope it's one of those silent retreats, then."

We were greeted on the third floor by Eric Halman, Cole's right-hand man. He was the opposite of Bryan and Cole. He was tall and thin, with blond hair, and handsome in a personal-accountant kind of way. He seemed much too lighthearted for his actual career choice. Nothing about Eric said cop. Eric was good at what he did, though, and easy to be around.

We followed him as he snaked through the office, past a few open cubicles, to a large conference room equipped with a whiteboard and projector screen as well as a long glass table with seating for twelve. My partner settled our files at one end of the table, then quickly removed a few of the chairs to give each of us more elbow room.

"Cole will be down in a few minutes," Eric said, settling into one of the white leather chairs. "Phoenix will be joining the investigation once Cole decides to let him back in the building. Everyone else will be available as needed, but we'll be the core team."

"Phoenix get himself benched again?" Bryan asked. Agent Phoenix Rhys was well known for the clashes he had with his boss. I'd interacted with him a handful of times, though, and his case record was impressive.

"He got himself banished this time," Eric said with a laugh. "Cole's had him on lockdown at his house for a few days until they could handle being around each other again. All over his stupid dog. He is supposed to be in tomorrow for his first day back, and he's promised to be on his best behavior to help out."

"We'll take whatever help we can get," Bryan said as Cole entered the newly converted office space. He took a seat at the head of the table and opened his laptop to connect to the wall-mounted TV at the end of the table. The blue screen we'd all grown accustomed to popped up, and we waited to connect with Professor Amelia Darcy.

"Speaking of getting help, before we sign in with the professor, I'll be up front and let you know we did our own little background check on her. Doesn't look like she has any other experience with law enforcement, but she looks clean," Eric said.

I nodded in agreement to cover my momentary panic that he was going to disagree with my vetting, and secret revetting, of the professor. There was no doubt in my mind that Amelia Darcy was not our leak, but to ease her own fears, even Lieutenant Miller had made a follow-up call and come to the same conclusion. The professor had no desire to make a name for herself on this case—for her teenage sons' sake, she didn't want to be publicly associated with the murders at all. Her motivation was purely a desire to help, and a bit of curiosity at how her expertise could be used.

THE MYTH MAKER

Once Eric approved the connection, Professor Darcy appeared on the big screen, again from her office at the university. Her long hair was twisted up, this time held in place by a silver-snake hair stick, the same University mug in front of her.

"Good morning, Detectives. Although I do wish it wasn't necessary for us to talk again so soon. I understand you have more details you'd like me to analyze, and I'm assuming it's related to the news story from this morning?"

"Yes, and thank you for talking with us," I said, and I introduced her to the two new faces on the call. "I think the iconography used today was as blatant as our last case. If you're ready, I'm just going to ask you about a few specific details, without photos today."

"Of course. Tell me what you have."

I studied the image of the body under the yellow cloth in front of me, not wanting to get any of it wrong and not wanting to give too much of it away. "Can you tell us if there is a goddess in the mythology depicted with red arms, or having anything to do with killing crickets?"

The silver snake in her hair bobbed as the professor nodded, flipping through pages in another one of her books. She put the book up on its edge with the pages in front of her chest so we could see them. On one page was the image of a piece of pottery depicting a winged woman standing between two winged horses. The colors in the vase were monotone—the figures in a gold hue, the background dark. At first glance, I saw nothing that matched what we'd seen this morning, and Cole's brows stitched together; he was not yet convinced. On the opposite page, in an exaggerated script, was printed *Eos, Goddess of the Dawn*. That page brought Cole to attention.

"Eos was the sister of Helios, the god of the sun, and Selene, goddess of the moon. She was responsible for opening the gates to allow her siblings to take their positions in the sky and was similar to Aphrodite in her love or lust for men."

"That makes the early morning make sense," Cole said.

"Definitely." Professor Darcy closed the book and opened another but did not move it to our view. "The rosy arms are from the Homeric Hymn to Helius, but in later works she's defined as simply rosy fingered. She's also usually described as having wings and wearing a saffron-colored gown."

Bryan rocked back in his seat. "Saffron would be yellow, right?"

"If your victim was wearing yellow and had red arms, I would say that is in line with Eos. As for the crickets, the mythology is actually about the creation of cicadas, although I imagine crickets are easier to come by. I've raised two boys, and we've bought plenty of crickets as food for one type of critter or another." She paused to take a quick sip from her tea. "The stories from Olympus are a lot more daytime soaps than loving deities, and the cicadas represent one of those soap stories. Eos was cursed by Aphrodite because they were both in love with Ares, and the curse was that Eos would always be falling in love with younger men and many of her stories involve her lovers. One of those was a young Trojan, and Eos was so attached to him that she begged Zeus to make him immortal. Her wish was granted but with a catch. She'd failed to ask for him to be eternally youthful, so he aged like a regular human, but couldn't die. After his old age made it impossible for them to travel together, Eos turned her lover into a cicada so she could keep him with her always. Ancient

Greeks used their story to explain why you hear cicadas chirping in the early morning."

"I think that is pretty clear on who this morning's victim is meant to represent," I said.

"Detective, before we go, I just want to mention one thing that occurred to me this morning about the goddesses we've talked about. Like I said, these stories, whether we're talking about Greek or Norse or Sumerian, there was a lot of drama and infighting in many of these myths. I obviously don't know anything about your victims in real life, but I know these goddesses and their myths quite well. There's crossover and competition within these four in multiple directions. I figured it was worth mentioning in case it gives you another part of the story to explore."

"So you're saying these goddesses all interact with one another in the mythology?"

"Yes. Athena competed against Aphrodite for the golden apple, and she tried to take Circe's child. Aphrodite cursed Eos. Eos was the aunt of Circe. It might not be relevant, but I have a few more study guides I can send to you just in case there is anything to the ways they intersect with one another."

* * *

"Is there anywhere we've found where these women come together?" Cole asked after we disconnected the video call.

I shook my head and shuffled the photos in front of me back into their folder. "There's nothing we've been able to find between the first two, and we're still trying to track down people who knew Olivia Bower. Her dad warned us that she ran with a difficult crowd, and just getting people to return phone calls has been hard. Honestly, I don't know if the three of them have much in common that would have brought them together."

Although they'd lived in the same vicinity, Sarah Goodall and Dana Mayhew had not had many obvious opportunities to cross paths. Sarah was only twenty-four, new to the area, and by all accounts an introverted homebody happiest in her first-grade classroom. Even though that put her in the same age range as Olivia Bower, their lifestyles left little chance for overlap.

Dana was almost thirty, married, and working at a successful real estate office. People had two different views of the woman our killer declared the fairest: beautiful and friendly or beautiful and flirtatious. Maggie Cannon was similar in age and single, according to her distraught family, but we didn't know enough yet to see if she fit with any of the others. Throwing the party-girl college dropout with a no-limit credit card into our mix didn't help bring anything together.

"I should have Maggie's full phone records in the next few hours, and Eric's perfected the process of mapping cell towers, so we can start looking at all four women and how they traveled around the city," Cole said, wasting no time in getting started. "We won't have the full autopsy report or the findings from the car for a while. We'll mix it up a bit today, and Bryan and Eric can work some of the names you guys have pending from the tip line. The family suggested we talk to Maggie's friend, and I think she might be more comfortable with Cassidy, so we'll work that one together."

* * *

Being paired up with Cole felt like being under a spotlight, a reminder of my status as the newbie on the case or in the field altogether. I should have expected it, but the attention made me squirm as we drove to the salon Maggie had worked at with her best friend. According to her family, she'd spent most of her time either at work or with her friends from work. They felt that if anyone was going to know what had been going on in her life most recently, her coworkers would be the best place to start.

The mood inside Luxe Salon was melancholy, in contrast to the bright design of the space. Crystal-covered pendant lights hung above framed gold mirrors at each station, and an antique dresser, painted pink and gold, served as the front desk, with drawers pulled forward slightly to display a collection of handmade bags and jewelry for sale. A few stylists were working away, quiet chitter-chatter floating between them and their clients. A chestnut-haired stylist with a short, curvy shape and heavily lashed brown eyes turned her attention to us when bells on the door chimed our arrival.

"Can I help you?" She slid her scissors into her apron and greeted us.

"I'm Special Agent MacAllan; this is Detective Cantwell. We're looking for Lindsey Jessop."

"I'm Lindsey."

"We were hoping we could speak with you about Maggie?"

She tried to force a smile, but her eyes were already tearing. "I'm almost finished with my client. If you can give me about five minutes, I'll be right with you."

Cole and I waited in the product-lined reception area while the young woman finished her client's blowout, then the three of us went to a stockroom that doubled as a break room to talk privately.

"We're sorry about your loss," Cole started, the apology scripted and automatic although sincere.

"How long have you known Maggie?" I asked.

"We've been friends since high school. We went through cosmetology school together and then came here after we got our licenses. We both bought in as co-owners here two years ago."

"Can you tell us if Maggie was dating anyone?"

Lindsey chuckled softly. "Maggie was always dating someone. She was gorgeous and funny, so guys followed her around like puppies half the time. She wasn't seeing anyone serious, though."

"Do you know the names of the guys who were following her around lately?" I pressed on.

She wiped at her eyes fiercely with the back of her sleeve, fighting for emotional control. "There were a few recent dates with her ex, Josh, and there was some new guy named Sean. She was all giddy about him, talking about how hot he was, but I don't know much else about him. She'd just started talking to him."

"What can you tell us about Josh?" Cole asked.

"He would be the last person to hurt Maggie," Lindsey answered immediately. "Josh has been in love with her since we were freshmen in high school. She didn't go out with him until last year. She thought they were better as friends, but . . . well, she was willing to lead him on if it meant not being alone. She didn't like to be single for too long, and Josh kept giving in to her back-and-forth nonsense because he really wanted things to work out for them."

"The new guy, Sean, how long has she been talking to him?" I asked.

"Only the past few weeks. She ran every morning around five AM, and she met him while they were both running on one of the trails she goes to. I know they'd only run together a few times, but I got the impression that she was waiting for him to suggest more. She stopped talking to me about him, though, so I don't know if that happened." Lindsey looked away to brush rolling tears off her cheeks. "I would blame it on the fact that I recently got dumped, but I told her I thought she was being cruel to Josh and that she should grow up with the rest of us and stop playing around like we were all still sixteen. I might have used more colorful language than that."

I gave a sympathetic nod. "When did that happen?"

"Last Saturday. She stood Josh up again to go barhopping with some of the girls here, then was gushing about trying to get this Sean guy to agree to dinner, and I kind of snapped. Josh and I are friends too. I didn't like seeing him get hurt over and over, but she stopped talking to me after that. I had to tell Josh she was ignoring both of us because of me, and that's how we ended things. Fighting over some stupid new guy that doesn't even matter now, and I don't get to tell her I'm sorry."

Cole and I sat quietly while she gave in to her tears. I knew we weren't going to get much more from her now that the grief had taken hold. Lindsey Jessop was dealing with a pain I recognized more than I wanted to let on. Grief was allowed in a different space when you were only the friend, but the guilt was sometimes heavier. The self-imposed torture that would follow her into her dreams was a connection between the two of us I wished we didn't now share.

We were able to get phone numbers for Josh from Lindsey, then quietly made our way out of the salon to give her time to recover from our visit.

"Someone has to know more about this new guy she was talking to," Cole muttered as we pulled into traffic covered in another coat of autumn drizzle.

"Not really." I sounded as contrary as I felt. "It doesn't sound like there was anything real with the new guy. I'm sure Lindsey knew as much, or more, as anyone else did. My younger sister is constantly meeting new people, going out with new people. I never even know the names of half of them. I know how he picked her, though."

"The boyfriends?" Cole guessed.

"Running at the crack of dawn every day is what made her Eos. Our killer caught Maggie Cannon bringing out the sun."

"And that makes her goddess number four."

I nodded a silent confirmation. "And possibly the first of the four to know him before he killed her."

That small detail—that Maggie Cannon was running with a new guy named Sean and was hoping to ask him out—couldn't be ignored. Not with the information Shannon had given us after the initial examination and the state of her apartment. Not only had she caught his attention, but our killer had possibly caught the attention of Maggie Cannon, and that added another level of threat to the scenario. If these women were getting to know him, he wasn't someone they were afraid of, and nothing was more frightening than an unassuming boogeyman.

* * *

"How did the meeting with the girlfriend go?" Eric asked when we sat down back at the office. He was looking at a map of the city with multiple red pinpoints on his laptop while Bryan worked across from him on his own computer.

"We need to find a mystery man Maggie Cannon was running with recently," I answered. "It shouldn't be too hard; we have no idea where they ran together, no physical description beyond that he was hot, and only the first name Sean."

"That sounds like the same success I had." Eric stretched, then slid a report sheet across the table to his boss. "One of her neighbors called about a guy in their building who sounded appealing. He's got a record, one violent assault against a girlfriend a few years ago, which means there were probably plenty more, but he's definitely not our guy. He broke his right hand two weeks ago in a bar fight. It's in a cast up to his elbow, so strangling anyone would have been impossible. I'm sure if we sat on the guy for a while, he'd do something we could arrest him for, but he didn't kill Maggie Cannon."

"How did your interview go?" I asked Bryan, bringing up my work email.

"I sat down with a guy Maggie dated off and on at the beginning of the year. Both of her brothers were insistent that we needed to look at the guy, but it doesn't seem like there's anything concrete. He's got a pretty reliable work alibi, and I get the feeling the family just didn't like him dating Maggie because he's kind of a tool."

"Should we give the press the suspect description of a flirty man, possibly named Sean, who at least pretends he likes to run, and see what we come back with?" My question was only somewhat sarcastic.

Cole laughed hard. "That would be the Ted description all over again, and that wasn't too successful in the seventies, so I think we'll keep that description to ourselves and see what else we can find first."

Eric hit a few keys on his laptop and pointed a small remote at the projector screen, bringing his screen into view like a classroom display. "I started on a deep dive into the cell movements of our first three victims. They were hitting cell towers all over the city on a regular basis except for Olivia Bower. Did the family mention if she's got a new phone recently?"

"Not initially," Bryan answered. "They weren't very forthcoming with much at the beginning, but you'll notice when you dig in that there's not a lot of activity for the summer. She was at what the family called a counseling retreat at a rehab center in California for June and July. She'd just returned and reconnected with her local friends before she was murdered."

"That clears that up," Eric said. "Your second victim, Mayhew, seems to have been spending a lot of time lately specifically around the glass museum, so I reached out to them about any surveillance videos they might have. Of all of them, the first vic was the least active. Her phone on most days is pinging either near her home or the school she worked at; not a lot of movement with her."

"Her friends from the school said she was a homebody. They could talk her into socializing on occasion, but I noticed she did a lot of online food orders and such. The glass museum is near the café that Dana was meeting her lover at during the workday," I said. "Is there a way we can use the cell towers to narrow down which running trails Maggie Cannon used? All we know is it was early in the morning."

"Once I get my hands on her info, I should be able to map that out if she had her phone with her when she ran," Eric confirmed.

"Make that one the priority," Cole said. "I want to get people on those running trails as soon as we can now that we know she's been telling people she met someone down there. If she ran with this guy enough to get his name and tell her friends about him, there might be someone out there who knows who he is."

"Or we might run into him," Bryan said. "Wouldn't that be a fun break?"

Adapting

He was alone in the dark, rubbing his naked feet on silk sheets, waiting for the next sunrise. Even though he could not feel them, he knew his collection was still there, safe in his hiding place below. The setback of the previous morning and the painful reminders on his right hand took him back to his recent failures. The two failures had thrown him off his game, and his slipups could have cost him the game entirely. He was sure he'd recovered adequately, but it was going to alter the next moves.

The first setback was because of The Asshole. The Asshole worked on the same floor, somehow in the same department, even though he was nowhere near as qualified. The Asshole had creeped up behind him after she'd sent one of her workday selfies and snatched his phone out of his hand like a schoolyard bully. "She's way too hot to be talking to you," he'd joked before giving the phone back. But The Asshole had seen her photo—studied it, even—so he had to be taken out of the game. He never knew what hit him. Best of all, The Asshole couldn't see her on the news and try to cause him more grief.

THE MYTH MAKER

He hadn't been prepared for her. She had forced his hand. He said no when she invited him over for dinner after their first run, but curiosity got the better of him. Weakness. He wanted to scope out her apartment, get his real plan in motion, but she had gotten in his head. She gave him her number. She sent him selfies—her getting ready for a run without him. Her getting ready for work. Her with friends at a bar. He knew the games she played and should have known to be more careful with her. Instead, he'd accepted her next invite for dinner.

She'd met him at her door in a filmy white dress with a pale-pink cardigan over her shoulders. The dress wasn't right for the season. She was wearing it for him. She was wearing it because it showed her curves and the fleshy tops of her breasts through the low neckline. He should have made an excuse then to leave. What else was the point of having a sick, elderly mother if you didn't exploit it from time to time? But he didn't do that. He went in, and it felt like a setup as soon as he stepped inside.

After a mediocre chicken pasta and too much of her cheap white wine, they were entangled on the leather couch in her living room. Her sweater on the floor was soon joined by delicate lace underthings. She was forward and confident, touching him in ways he could not resist. A woman used to getting her way. She was naked and his shirt was missing by the time they made their way to her bed. Before he could slow things down, she'd made easy work of his jeans, and once they were skin to skin, he could not stop. He asked himself in that moment why he hadn't given in to this part of the others.

He knew why now. Being intimate with her jumbled his brain. Her girlish wiles broke his concentration and self-control. He had allowed her to ruin everything. He'd lost himself in it all. The touch of her fingers, the heat of their bodies together in such carnal ways, her real self shining through. He didn't notice what had happened until it was too late. He didn't realize his hands had moved from her waist to her breasts, to her throat. The empty look in her eyes when he finished startled him back to reality.

It wasn't quite time. He had what he needed to bring out her true form, but it wasn't supposed to be tonight. He was afraid of lingering in the apartment, but he had to clean up. Erase as much as he could of himself. He cleaned up and made a few runs to his car, knowing he was running out of time. Finding a way to get her unnoticed out of her apartment was a big risk. He did not like taking chances like this. Chances made him nervous; that's why he liked sticking to his plans. He worked better that way.

He was able to escape with her concealed in what looked like an armful of bedding, down two flights of stairs, then ducking onto the second floor to take the elevator to the parking garage. No gates, no security would allow him to come back for his own car when he was done, and he got to the park right on time. He had such a grand plan. The vision he'd imagined of her on the streetlight, appearing to hold the light in her hands, had been a dream for ages, but that was the first part of his plan to go awry. The unexpected runner was the next.

He'd escaped from the park and was out of sight when he saw the first set of red and blue lights. He was back home and in the shower before he realized his fatal mistake. At first, it made him retch violently, then he rushed into a rage, smashing the bathroom mirror. The blood from his shredded knuckles smeared across the cracked glass and the white granite countertop. They would find her, and when they did, they would find his presence as well. This could ruin everything, and he knew it.

The evening news warned him the police were bringing in the FBI, and they were searching for him. One particularly brash reporter was almost accusatory, raising questions about police transparency and cold cases, but he doubted they truly understood how far ahead of them he was. By the time they caught up to him—if they caught up to him—he would already be on to the next level, long gone. He'd already had another win with his butterfly, and he'd found the next. She might even be the last. The work of the Fates had brought them together, and he had very little time to waste to finish the game. The thought made him smile as he moved his hand under the sheets against skin and silk, feeling his excitement build. He was going to have her soon.

10

I was dripping rivulets of water, and my wet feet had already created a puddle on my bathroom tile. I held tight to the purple-striped towel wrapped around me with one hand and wrung my wet hair into the sink with the other, momentarily ignoring my sister. Meghan absentmindedly brushed through her yellow hair with my paddle brush. "When I said I needed to talk to you and it was urgent, I meant three days ago, not first thing in the morning as I'm getting out of the shower."

"The kind of retreat this was, we didn't have access to our phones much. I got to check mine once a day to check for emergencies."

"I said it was an emergency in three different texts," I said through tight teeth, trying not to lose my cool with my sister this early in the morning.

"Yeah, but no one else in the family was texting me about emergencies, and Mom texted to let me know I still had things in my room she wants to make her sewing room, so I figured it was just a roomie emergency and we could talk when I got back, which is now."

"You came home and brought in the mail," I argued.

"And you weren't here," she argued back. "I needed some more clothes."

I'd planned to do this professionally. To sit down in front of my little sister and very diplomatically ask her if she had spoken to anyone at all about what she saw in my kitchen and what I'd discussed with her during my own lapse in judgment. But that was before. Before our growing body count. Before our growing list of losses and dead ends. Before I'd gone to bed after yet another news broadcast hinted we were hiding things, and before I'd stepped out of my shower to find my sister at my vanity, finishing off the last bite of a pink-frosted cookie and sorting through my makeup.

"My emergencies are the ones that count, Megs. I don't send you emergency texts, ever, but this was an emergency, and I needed you to call me back." My voice lilted a little higher and a little louder by the end of the sentence than I'd intended. Meghan set my brush down and stepped back from the vanity.

"Okay, I'm sorry I didn't call you back. What's the emergency?"

"I need you to answer me with the complete truth, Megs. It is really important that you tell me the truth."

"Oh my gosh, Kissy, just tell me."

"I'm serious." I folded the edge of my towel over itself and stepped into my closet to get dressed in what I'd already set out for the morning. After shimmying into my slacks and pulling my arms into my collared shirt, I leaned against the opposite end of my vanity from where Meghan had returned to brushing her hair.

"I need to know if you talked to anyone about what you saw in my kitchen regarding my investigation."

Meghan went from an obvious pout to lips nearly disappearing in a straight line—a look stolen from our mother and perfected by my little sister when controlling her anger. "Who would I tell?"

"That's what I need to know. I need to know if you mentioned it to anyone at all. Hell, even if you told Mom or Jamie. I need to know if you've said anything about the case to anyone."

"No!" Meghan shrieked, and dropped my brush onto the counter for dramatic effect. "I told you I wouldn't talk to anyone, and I haven't. You made me promise."

"I know you promised. I also know I told you more than I should have, and there's a chance some things have been leaked to the news that you might have bigger insight into because of our conversation, and I just need to—"

My little sister put a hand up at me and closed her eyes tightly, moving her mouth as she counted to three. The counting was something my mom had taught us as kids, but I was fairly certain only my sister and I still used it. Her voice quivered when she spoke and wrenched my heart. "I can't believe you don't trust me to keep a secret. I didn't even tell Sebastian during my private release session, and that shit you see on a regular basis is stuff that everyone should release. I don't know why you would think I'd blab about it, though. I didn't even engage with Professor Gentry when he wanted to talk about your call. I just told him I didn't know any details, you'd just asked for someone who knew humanities. It was dumb, but it was all I could think of. And I thought of it without telling him about any of the pictures of dead girls or the other weird shit like apples or feathers or whatever. I just played dumb, like people expect me to."

"Megs, I never said you were dumb, and I never want you to play dumb. I just have to make sure that whenever this leak gets figured out, it isn't going to fall on you and me." Her lips got tighter and thinner, nothing but a fine line, but she didn't storm out. Standing there with her, my next question became obvious. "When did Professor Gentry try to talk to you about the case?"

"The day after I gave you his name." She softened slightly. "He just asked me what I thought about the cases you were working on, and I said something about you having a hard job."

Professor Gentry. A link I'd overlooked when focusing on our good professor. We'd involved Gentry in so little, I hadn't considered him a suspect, but if he was asking around, maybe he'd found an in, even if it wasn't through my little sister. The question was why.

"Is my interrogation over?" Meghan pouted melodramatically.

"This wasn't an interrogation, Megs. I needed to know, and now I do."

"I'm going back to bed." She started for the door, then turned over her shoulder for her own quick dig. "The only secret I've blabbed about is letting Jamie know you're working on your murder books again."

Her revelation delivered the desired sting, but I let it go. My current case was still top of the list, above anything in my totes, like mystery mail still waiting to be figured out, and I owed it to Meghan to let her land a hit. Hurrying through my morning routine, I kept it to a simple Dutch braid and a layer of mascara while trying to figure out where on the priority list I was going to have to put Professor Gentry.

*   *   *

I arrived to find a further transformed workspace at the FBI headquarters. Cole's ninja IT group had added a bank of phones, two printers, and additional cables and hookups for laptops across the glass table. Bryan was scheduled to start late so he could take Ana to a doctor's appointment, and Cole was locked away in his office in yet another meeting with Russell Bower's legal team. Eric abandoned me without explanation shortly after I arrived, so I tackled the task of organizing the barrage of overnight calls to the tip line that had been left for me. We each had our own list to follow up on, and my list currently totaled sixty-five.

I started by looking for duplicates and was fully engrossed in matching numbers and jumped when I realized Phoenix had joined me in our glass-walled office.

"Anything good yet?" Phoenix dropped a green canvas messenger bag into the seat next to his.

"Uh, no. Not unless you count the thirty-seven calls from the same woman who is absolutely convinced her ex is responsible for the murder in the park," I answered. "I've already cleared him."

"You beat me in here by fifteen minutes and you're already clearing suspects?"

"I can't take too much credit. The guy had the decency to get himself arrested for a probation violation two months ago; the county jail has been hosting him ever since."

Phoenix chuckled, standing in front of the glass wall where I'd put our goddess profiles on display. "You should call her back and give her the good news."

"I've got a stack of names for you too. These are just some old cases and old suspects they thought could be checked against the FBI records, see if you guys have anything we don't." I coolly slid the short stack his way with a smile to hide my guilt. As a general rule, I hadn't roped anyone else into my side work into Jenna's case, but I was making a small exception here. It was possible that the unsolved case of Jenna Sutton would one day be related to another murder, so the comparison wasn't harmful. And the timing of the items being sent to me was making them feel even more targeted. If anyone was going to understand smudging the line a little, it would be Phoenix.

Phoenix Rhys was one member of Cole's team that I knew well. Before joining the homicide team, I'd done a small run with narcotics, and Phoenix had been intricately involved in one of our busts. He was a few inches over six feet tall, with eyes the color of faded denim and dirty-blond hair that was currently longer than what I was used to seeing on an FBI agent. There was an edgy electricity to his demeanor that told you to stay on your toes when he was around.

Why Cole had pulled him into this case, considering he was best known for his undercover work, remained a secret, but tidbits of his history with Cole's team had long been part of the rumor mill. Phoenix hadn't scored as high on the *Hire me* scale as the FBI wanted, actually coming closer to the *You might arrest me one day* side of things. Nevertheless, Cole had seen something he liked and brought Phoenix over to his team. Since hiring him, Cole had found himself having to fight to keep him employed on a few occasions. *Sometimes reckless but always useful* was how he'd been described.

I started into the next name from the tip line, entering the data for a sixty-year-old man with a home address in Fife, and absently listened to the one-word responses a call to Phoenix's cell elicited.

"Looks like it's you and me; you ready to go?" Phoenix asked when he hung up.

"Go where?"

"We're getting a heads-up on a new call that might be related. I'm saying *might* because no one is on scene yet, so we'll know for sure once we get there. Someone else can run backgrounds on those tips—I need you with me so grab your stuff and I'll grab keys."

Phoenix came back with his black nylon FBI jacket, which made him look somewhat more official, and we headed down to the underground parking garage. I climbed into the standard-issue black Ford Explorer, and we pulled out into midmorning traffic. As he made the first right turn with what would almost pass as a rolling stop, I noticed a certain familiarity to the SUV. More than being the same make, same color, it was identical—from the gear bag on the floor in the back seat to the black Little Trees air freshener hanging from the steering column—to Cole's vehicle.

"This is your SUV, right?"

Phoenix's eyes lit up with a grin. "For now."

"Please tell me you did not just steal Cole's car."

"He knows I'll give it back. I'm on my bike today, and you drive a toy. We needed a loaner."

"The agency doesn't give you your own vehicle? I thought all you suits got your own cars."

"They used to, but it got to be too expensive."

"You've wrecked that many?"

He laughed again. "There's been a few. But to be fair, one of them was hit while it was parked, and the fourth one got caught up in some cross fire, also not my fault. I've been undercover so much that Cole convinced them to give me a discount at the impound yard before auction and let me provide my own ride. Thanks to him I got a killer deal on a seized Ducati, and Cole drives me around when I'm here. It's my attempt to save the bureau money."

"Does he know we have it?"

"It's for official business; he'll get over it. He always does. Besides, if this is another one, me taking his car will be the least of Cole's concerns."

"My first homicide case with the FBI, and we stole Cole's car." I pushed my head deep into the headrest. I now had to add car theft to setting up my own requests for information from the FBI and hiding mail possibly related to a cold case.

* * *

Derek North was on the perfectly manicured front lawn of a stately redbrick Tudor home with a dark-haired man in red hospital scrubs under a khaki trench. The man's face was pale, and his eyes had the glassy appearance that remains after tears have stopped, making it easy to guess he was the husband.

"You must have been close. I just called for you," Derek said after he led the husband across the yard and left him in the care of a second patrol officer. Derek took the lead and walked Phoenix and me into the house.

"We got a call at our office," Phoenix said. "Someone else thinks this is probably related."

"Oh, it's definitely yours." Derek shook his head. "Two in two days. This guy you're chasing is one sick psycho, Cassidy."

We followed Derek through the main hall to the back bedroom. "The victim is Felicity Benson. She's a nurse. Her husband is a doctor. He works a night shift at the ER; she works days at the same hospital. His shift ran long this morning, and he expected her to be gone before he got home, but he found her in here. He said it scared him too much to check her vitals, so she's exactly like he found her. Everything is still intact."

"Intact?" The patrolman's word choice created an instant panic in my stomach.

"You'll see."

Pink scrubs were folded on the marble top of a large wooden dresser by the bedroom door, and Felicity Benson's short black hair was still damp from her shower. She was sitting up with her legs straight out in front of her, her head slightly turned and her arms skewed awkwardly at her sides. I could tell she was not a tall woman—only an inch or two over five feet. She was of average build with an olive complexion interrupted by an aged red scar on the right side of her abdomen.

Felicity Benson was naked with the exception of a pair of massive wings. They rose from behind each shoulder, no less than three feet high, and seemed to connect to a length of gold cording that was wrapped under her arms and around her throat several times, deep bruising showing at its edges. The cord was unmistakable after the number of times we'd reviewed our earlier crime scenes over the past week and a half. It was identical to the gold cord used in the murder of Sarah Goodall.

Twigs of various thicknesses and colors were twisted and woven together with more of the cord, forming the obvious structure of butterfly wings. The top portion of the wing frame was larger than the second, lower-wing section. I estimated no less than six dozen white roses had been interlaced with the twigs, outlining the entire wing structure. Smaller, four-petal flowers I didn't have a name for were tucked between the roses, and a bunch of them had been twisted to make a crown resting above her eyes, which had changed to a bluish opaque color after death.

"What the hell?" Phoenix exclaimed. "First it's goddesses, now it's fairies? Who's next, Cas, Cinderella?"

My stomach tied itself in knots as I shook my head. "I have no idea." And I didn't. The research I'd done on the collection of goddesses and ancient mythology our killer was recreating hadn't included fairies so far.

"I can show you how he got in," Derek said. He led us back down the main hall to a brightly decorated living room with sliding glass doors that opened onto the backyard. "We found the sliding door open when we got here. Her husband said that she isn't always good about remembering to lock all the doors, but she'd never leave one open."

Phoenix grabbed his cell phone from his jacket pocket. "Cole's going to want Danni and her team in here immediately."

Careful to keep my hands to myself, I inspected the glass door and inched out into the backyard. The yard was not only fenced but landscaped to maximize privacy with ancient-looking madrona trees, Douglas firs, and several red and purple rhododendrons. On the north side of the yard, a wooden gate under a vine-covered arch was ajar. At the side of the patio, just to the right of the door, a concrete pad was littered in tree trimmings, discarded leaves, and white rose petals. Not deterred from nearly being caught at the park, our killer had taken the time to construct the wings here, at the murder scene. He knew he had time. I went back inside and caught two eyes full of a camera flash from one of our crime scene techs working around the sliding door.

"He made those wings here," I said to Phoenix, blinking away flashbulb orbs. "He spent time here. Even after what just happened at the park, he's not worried about getting caught."

"I talked to Cole to let him know the husband is on his way to him. He and Eric can manage that part," Phoenix said. "We have somewhere else to be."

"Where are we going?" I asked, following him back outside to our borrowed ride.

"We both know what the husband is going to give us. We'll let Eric take his statement. He's better at dealing with families than I am anyway. Danni will kick us out if we stick around here too long and get in the way of her team." He steered the SUV onto the narrow residential street. "The ID badge on the bathroom door was for St. Anne's hospital. We're going there."

After making the quick drive to the hospital, Phoenix parked outside the emergency department entrance, creating a parking spot up front for the Explorer. I followed him to the nurses' desk, trying to keep up with his quick stride.

"Hey you!" A busty nurse with red-and-blonde spiky hair came out from behind the desk and met Phoenix with an enthusiastic hug. "We haven't seen you around for a while."

"Not being here is a good thing, isn't it?" Phoenix offered a lopsided smile. "Gillian, this is Detective Cantwell. This is Gillian Nash. Gillian used to work with my little brother."

"We miss having your brother around, but they are frustrating guys to do after-hours with," Gillian said to me with an exaggerated sigh. "The other one's already taken, and this one never will be. I know you didn't come down here to say hello to your favorite nurses, so what's up?"

"We're here on business. I need to talk to someone who can talk to me about Felicity Benson."

"Felicity is one of our angel nurses in the PICU. She's not in any trouble, is she?"

"Gilli, she's been murdered."

The color drained from Gillian Nash's cheeks, and her eyes filled with tears. Phoenix's tenderness as he put a protective arm around her shoulders surprised me. A sensitive side hadn't been part of the package I'd imagined for him. "C'mon, we can't do this here. Is there someone we can talk to about her?"

"I'll take you up to Dr. Weatherly's office. She heads the pediatric nurses, including Felicity." We followed the distressed nurse down a hallway bustling with activity to a closed door. "She should be able to tell you anything you need to know about Felicity. Is it all right if I tell the others? People are going to want to know. We're going to need to find a way to help Neil."

"Maybe wait until we leave?" Phoenix suggested, opening a solid-wood door after a quick knock. "Give us a chance to do what we need to do first and ask people to keep it low." Gillian nodded and headed back to the elevator in the calm but hurried way nurses always seem to have about them.

"Can I help you?" Dr. Corrine Weatherly stood up from her desk full of file folders. I guessed she was nearing sixty, with short gray curls and round-rimmed glasses.

"Hello, Dr. Weatherly. I'm Agent Rhys with the FBI; this is Detective Cantwell with Tacoma PD. We were told we could talk to you about Felicity Benson."

"Felicity is one of my nurses," she answered stiffly. She motioned to the two chairs opposite her at the dark-wood desk, and Phoenix and I sat.

"We never like having these conversations," I started.

"Don't try to tell me she's involved in anything illegal. I won't believe it." The doctor cut me off defensively.

"No, that's not why we're here. She's been murdered."

"Oh my god." She fell back into the high-backed chair with the blow. "Does Neil know? Is Neil okay?"

"He's at our office now. Were you expecting Felicity in today?" Phoenix continued the questions.

"She was coming in late, after an appointment for the baby. What is Neil going to do with the baby?"

I shot Phoenix a look, and his wide-eyed response confirmed he was at the same point of confusion. Felicity Benson didn't appear pregnant, and there certainly hadn't been a baby at the house when we left. "We weren't made aware the Bensons have a baby," I said.

"They don't have the baby yet. Look, Felicity had more than her fair share of grief. People always say that karma gives you what you deserve, and she used to joke that she must have been a real bitch in a past life, because that girl had been through it all.

"They couldn't have kids, so they've been trying to adopt. They finally connected with a mother who is due with a little boy in two months. Felicity was going to an appointment with her this morning, then she was coming in."

"You said she's been through a lot. Is there anything, anyone, from her life that we should be looking at?"

"It wasn't like she ran away from the mob or anything. Felicity and her two sisters had it tough as kids. Their mom suffered an accidental overdose and died when Felicity was five. The girls ended up in the system. The older sister bounced around in her dad's family, and Felicity and her younger sister went into foster care for a few years until they were finally adopted together.

"At sixteen, she went into kidney failure and needed a transplant, and there's been other medical problems since then. Still, she got herself through nursing school, and she's amazing at what she does. She's close with her younger sister. I know there's been some drama with her older sister but not murder-worthy drama. Things started looking up a bit when she married Neil. She always called him her knight in shining armor, but they've still had some ups and downs. The news about the baby was the high note this year."

"Have there been any strange incidents at the hospital? Has Felicity or anyone else brought up any concerns about suspicious people?"

"As a matter of fact, there was something that happened last week, but it wasn't with Felicity. One of the other nurses, Angie, stopped a guy she didn't recognize. The guy told her he was lost, but she said there was something about him that made her call security."

The news of a report to security made me sit up straighter in my seat. "Is there someone we can talk to about the security report and maybe get some video footage?"

"The guy took off before they could catch up to him, but I could get hospital security up here to talk to you about what they do have."

"That would be great," Phoenix said. "Is there another office we could commandeer for a little bit, somewhere private we can talk one-on-one with your staff?"

"I'll open a conference room for you and have Angie meet you there first. We want to help however we can.

Felicity and Neil are a big part of our hospital family here." Dr. Weatherly escorted us a few doors down to a small conference room set up classroom-style. She left us to get settled and went to call for Angie Reynolds. Phoenix pushed two of the tables together, with chairs on either side, and we waited.

When Angie Reynolds joined us, she was already struggling through tears after being told of Felicity Benson's death. Angie was thirty-four, the same age as our latest victim, and had started at the hospital shortly after Felicity. They were close enough friends that they occasionally spent time together outside of work and carpooled once in a while. "I can't believe this is real. It's not fair," she said between quiet sobs.

"We were hoping you could tell us the details about the incident from last week that made you call security to the pediatric wing," I started.

"Yes, it was sometime at the beginning of last week. Tuesday, I think. He circled past the nurses' station two or three times, so I finally stopped him and asked if he needed help. He was kind of off; I'm not sure how else to explain it. He wouldn't really look at me when I stopped him and said he realized he was on the wrong floor. There was something about him that didn't sit right, so I called Blake, our security guard for this floor, to catch up to him."

"Could you describe him to a sketch artist?" Phoenix asked.

"Beyond telling you he had brown hair and a hat, I'm not sure I could. I only saw him for a minute a week ago. I see so many people, and I've never been good with faces."

After convincing Angie to come down to the FBI office to work on a sketch, we met with seven other nurses who worked closely with Felicity Benson. No one had heard her talking about anything recently beyond picking out baby names and nursery themes. We said goodbye to Dr. Weatherly as word of the murder started to spread through the hospital.

"So, is your brother a doctor or a nurse?" I asked as we started our drive back.

"He's a trauma nurse. He started with the Army and then got out, followed me here from Kansas, and made his way to working in the ER."

"A trauma nurse and an FBI agent. Your parents must be proud."

"You'd have to know my parents. We're their biggest nightmares." Phoenix laughed without going into further detail.

11

Angie Reynolds met with Cole and a sketch artist, but as she'd warned, she didn't have enough memories to describe the man she'd been spooked by the week before. After all the normal tricks and prompts, we were dismayed to see at the end of it all that she'd recreated Phoenix in a baseball cap. The recordings Cole received from the limited security cameras around the hospital were also proving to be a bust.

The security office confirmed they'd gone over their footage the day Angie filed her complaint. The recordings from the hospital showed a man in a black baseball cap with a blurred dark logo walking away from Angie toward the elevator with his hands in his pockets. He managed to keep his head down or his back to the security cameras, blocking every view of his face.

"The guy at the park was wearing a black baseball cap," I said when the video ended.

The collective mood in the room was urgent and frustrated, and everyone was focused on figuring out the handcrafted fairy wings that were left for us. As the guys in the room talked over my head, I made myself another cup of coffee and pulled out the reference books Professor Darcy had written that I'd been lugging around in my bag for days. I'd reached out to her already, but the email had come back with an out-of-office message and she hadn't yet returned my call, and I was determined to find the link. I shut out the noise around me and focused on my research to learn which goddess Felicity Benson had eerily become.

My fingers scanned over pages of descriptors and symbology, searching for anything that matched the details at our latest crime scene. My own internal pressure to come up with the answer and not let this case stall prompted a shortcut. I flipped through the book, stopping at every page with a photo. Toward the back of the professor's guide, I found her. A demure seated figure carved from marble by an Italian sculptor, with a delicate pair of butterfly wings.

"She's not a fairy," I exclaimed, throwing my hands in the air with a small sense of victory. I would email the professor to check my work, but I was sure I was right. "They're butterfly wings. He's using Felicity Benson as Psyche, and reading all of this... he knows her, guys. This isn't a connection he could make physically or by catching on to a running habit. He had to know about her life."

"Tell us Psyche's story," Bryan said, pouring his own cup of coffee from the machine that had been set up in the corner.

"Psyche was a mortal, and Cupid fell in love with her."

Phoenix's eyebrows lifted. "Cupid, like the baby in a diaper with a bow and arrow?"

"Not quite. Cupid as in the son of Aphrodite."

"Aphrodite with the golden apple; I know that one," he said. "Are you saying Felicity is connected to Dana Mayhew?"

"Professor Darcy pointed out that, so far, all of our goddesses can be connected to one another in the mythology. I think that the goddess personas are connected for him, even if the actual women are not."

"So you're not suggesting that Dana and Felicity are connected?" Bryan said.

I shook my head at my partner, continuing to scan the pages that told the story of Psyche. "We haven't found any links between our women to think they had personal connections in the real world. I think it's possible the guy is working from a connected storyline we're not picking up and that's why the goddesses all intersect. This one, though—this is the most personal connection he's made yet."

I had the attention of all four guys in the room as I read to them from Professor Darcy's book. Psyche caught the attention of Cupid, but Aphrodite, his mother, didn't want him to be with a mortal. She decided she would allow their marriage only if Psyche could survive a set of four quests, believing all of them to be impossible for a human to survive, but against the odds she did. The god Zeus married the pair when the trials were completed, and Psyche was gifted butterfly wings.

There was a weighted silence in the room when I finished giving the details of Psyche's mythology, and Cole stood up and went to the wall with our previous mythology breakdowns. "Does this guy think he's Zeus?"

"I don't think that's far off." Eric spoke up from his end of the table.

"We know that Felicity went through a lot to become who she was, but our killer would have to know about her life. He would have to know Felicity Benson survived her own personal trials before marrying the man of her dreams, because he's using those personal trials as her clues."

Cole ran fingers through his graying dark hair. "We've assumed he started something romantic, at least on the surface, with Maggie, but that doesn't fit with Felicity. He's had a different type of interaction with her, is what you're saying? Most of her hardships were in childhood; maybe he's connected that way?"

"He's gotten to know at least something of her," I answered. "It could be someone she was in foster care with or went to school with."

"Or someone who has a Facebook account," Bryan said. "Private lives went out the window when we all accepted social media. People put their lives out there these days for everyone to see. She accepts one questionable friend request online, and this guy would have access to everything she's ever posted. He has run into her somehow, no doubt, but we're assuming there is a personal connection because of Maggie, and I'm not feelin' it with this one."

"You certainly know how to kill the mood." Phoenix rearranged the spread of still photos created from the hospital security footage. "We need to go back to the husband, show him these photos, and find out what circles were aware of her childhood and her medical history. If he knows there's a connection with that personal knowledge, he'll let go of the idea that everyone loved her and think of someone who maybe loved her too much. Or resented her. Someone who looks like he's about six foot and wears baseball caps."

"No need," I sighed. "Bryan is right. All you have to do is search the web and you've got it all." I turned my laptop around for the guys to see what my quick fingers had discovered. An online employee spotlight included in the hospital e-newsletter featured a "Staff Member of the Month" for August: Felicity Benson.

The spotlight outlined her ongoing connection with some of her foster siblings, her support for organ donation programs after her own medical scare, and her excitement over finally becoming a mom. There were even photos of our victim with her arms around two fellow nurses outside the hospital's pediatric intensive care unit.

"Does this narrow it down to hospital people, at least?" Eric asked. "It's not like he could have typed *find me Psyche in Tacoma* and come up with Felicity Benson's name. The guy had to know who he was looking for to find her."

"This goes out to employees at the hospital, its affiliated clinics, and members, which includes everyone who has ever been a patient at the hospital or any of their clinics," I answered, seeing no hope in using that list to find our suspect in a black baseball cap.

12

I sat across the desk from Lieutenant Miller, trying like a kid in the principal's office not to fidget. I'd left the fishbowl at the FBI office, already nervous about the sit-down that I'd been called to. My timing was terrible. It had been forty-eight hours since the fifth murder, and we were beyond the point of anyone pretending all five cases weren't related. Collectively, we were holding our breath in fear that the next was coming soon and we hadn't come any closer to stopping the killer.

As desperate as we were to find the suspect in the black baseball cap, scouring the smattering of security cameras for the routes into and away from Point Defiance Park the night Maggie Cannon was killed had revealed nothing to us. However her car got there that night, it hadn't been driven past the available cameras. We'd spent the day working the tip line, making little progress in trying to determine who to look at first in the new spattering of suspects. And now I'd thrown something else onto Nancy Miller's desk: I was the one who'd caused our leak to the press.

The suspicion was there after I'd confronted Meghan about spilling our secrets. I'd left that exchange out of my quick report to my lieutenant, but I did explain that I'd asked Meghan for a contact for her mythology teacher once I'd decided we were missing the iconology from the crime scenes. I'd also left Cole out of my disclosure, waiting to see what Nancy Miller decided to do with me.

Now she was sitting in front of me, reading through my written explanation of how I thought the idea of a cold case being related to our current murders had made its way to the press. She blew out her thin cheeks with a huff when she finished and put my letter in front of her. "This is a theory at this point, right?"

I shrugged my shoulders, unsure that I could get away with calling it just a theory. It had only taken me going back to my original correspondence with the professor to see where the screwup was. *Crime scenes.* I hadn't given him any specific details, but I had thrown in that *s*. I'd made the email about crime scenes, plural, at a time no one else knew I thought we were looking at two. The fact that he'd talked to Meghan the next day and she'd also said he was curious about my *cases* made it clear. The tip-off had, unwittingly, come from me.

"Have you talked to him at all after this email exchange?"

"No," I answered, trying not to slouch in my seat as my boss sat forward, her hands folded on her desk. "I emailed him to see if we could talk; he called me back and said if I was looking at any type of mythology, I should talk to Amelia Darcy because she was a true expert in the field."

"Have you added him to the suspect list?"

"No, I brought him into all of this myself. We haven't looked at him further than that."

"But why not?"

"We haven't had a reason to. Even if I think he's the one who told the press we were looking at more than one murder after Dana was killed, it didn't qualify him for our list."

With an inquisitive stare, she pressed her tongue to the back of her teeth, and she asked again. "Why not? What do we know about Professor Gentry?"

This was a test, there was no mistaking it, and I counted off what I did know about David Gentry silently before giving my answer. My own revelation made me swallow hard, and the truth hit the bottom of my stomach like a cold stone. Nancy Miller tilted her head, watching me catch up to where I believed she'd already gone to. "He works at the same college as Ethan Mayhew and where Olivia was a student, at least for a minute," I started.

"Right, that gives him access to two of our victims. And we can't forget the whole reason you reached out to him." She walked me into the final revelation. Professor David Gentry was also well versed in the world of Greek mythology.

"Shit." I pressed my palm to my forehead and slumped into my seat. "I mean, I reached out to him; what would the chances be that I was reaching out to a killer?"

My lieutenant's smile was sympathetic and knowing. "That's the thing about this job, Cassidy. It doesn't always make sense, and we don't always get it right. Sometimes we don't get it right because we don't get what we need to put the pieces together, but sometimes we don't get it right because we overlook what's in front of us."

"Am I in trouble for this?" My fear was real and my concern was valid. I'd screwed up—there was no getting around it—by giving too much information to an outsider, no matter what my intentions were.

"No, this was just me sitting down with a new detective working a high-profile case. Going forward, though, keep Bryan involved, check in with the others before you clear anyone from being a suspect. The collective mind helps on these cases—extra eyes and all that. It's really hard to work a case alone."

* * *

As I pulled into Nicky's driveway for the dinner I'd agreed to first thing this morning, Lieutenant Miller's words were still rattling around in my head. It was hard to ignore her warning about working cases alone and the double meaning I'd applied to it. I'd been so careful with my work on Jenna's case. I didn't have any reason to believe she knew about my secret mail, but the idea that I hadn't been careful enough with everything else was possible.

I grabbed my overnight bag and stepped through Nicky's front door, hoping I could make the entire evening without any new surprises. The past few weeks had pushed our relationship to the edge, and I knew how much he needed one night without interruption or distraction. Nicky's text had come through first thing this morning, complete with photos, offering to cook me dinner if I agreed to stay the night at his place. Besides looking forward to a night without a roomie, I was still apologizing for canceling his weekend getaway, so I quickly gave in to his terms.

I hit the front door at Nicky's house with my overnight bag in hand and was immediately intoxicated by the aroma of home-cooked food. I had no doubt whatever was waiting for me in his kitchen was going to be head and shoulders above the Special K with yogurt balls and dehydrated strawberries I would have made for myself for the umpteenth night in a row.

"Hey." Nicky greeted me in his kitchen with a spoon in hand and a black dish towel over his shoulder. He wasn't dressed in his usual at-home attire, which consisted mostly of band T-shirts, sweats, and hoodies. Tonight he was wearing dark slacks and an electric-blue sweater over a dress shirt. He was even wearing shoes. His date night look made me feel better about not changing out of my work clothes. "Taste this. I'm going to put it on the winter menu."

"Amazing as always," I praised, swiping a spear of asparagus from the simmering pan of risotto with veggies and mushrooms on the stove. "Definitely better than it all looked in the pictures you sent me."

Nicky cocked an eyebrow. "You didn't like my food porn?"

"I did," I giggled. "I like eating it better than looking at it, though. I'm not seeing the sexy sweet potatoes."

"I had to edit." He wrapped me up in a tight hug. "I did get you dessert, though, so you'll be happy, and I have a surprise for you after dinner."

"What kind of surprise?" I teasingly pulled at the front of the waistband of his pants.

Nicky turned away from me and went back to the developing perfection on the stove. "The kind of surprise that stays a surprise."

"Is it the kind of surprise that includes you without clothes?" I took a seat at the table nestled under the kitchen window and let Nicky serve the risotto he'd prepared with tender filets.

"If you're lucky, I'll add a strip tease later." He sat down with two glasses of wine and put the chilled bottle on the table.

"Promise?"

"We'll have to see how lucky you are."

Nicky ran through a few new ideas for his seasonal menu while we ate, including making our current meal the star, which I agreed would be a popular and profitable move. He also gave me some not-so-helpful advice on how to rid myself of my new roommate, who still had no plans of moving out—such as signing Meghan up at a convent. *Sister Meghan* had a nice ring to it, he insisted.

After dinner, Nicky ushered us into his living room, and once I was seated on the couch, he handed me a large, flat box, humorously wrapped in Rock and Roll Santa paper. "Apologies for the wrapping paper; that's all I had."

I pulled carefully at the corners, not so much to avoid tearing but because I knew it made Nicky crazy when I took my time. When I finally pulled the lid off the box, I couldn't hide my confusion. "What's this?" I asked, putting the two FOR SALE signs and several pages of real estate listings on the coffee table.

For the first time that night, I caught sight of his nerves. Exhaustion, distraction, or probably both had kept me from picking up on it sooner, but there was a tremor in his voice when he answered. "This is a compromise."

"What do you mean it's a compromise?"

"It's a compromise to our living arrangement. I figure the best way to deal with our new schedules is to live together: buy a place that's just ours. I understand why you don't want to live here; I do." He rubbed his hands nervously on his knees. "Parking sucks, and I get that this was *our house* when Stephanie and I were married. Even though I don't think of this place that way, I get why you do. And we both know there's no way for us to both live at your place. It's way too small, and I can't do anything in that closet you call a kitchen."

"You want me to sell my house and call it a compromise?" My brain was instantly flooded with an unexplainable panic.

"I want to sell both of our houses and buy a place together that could be ours. That is the compromise."

"Buying a new place is not a compromise, Nicky. That's huge. I mean, we're not . . . well, we haven't even . . ." Before I could get the *m* word from the back of my throat, Nicky covered the awkwardness for me by pulling a small, black ring box from out of nowhere and held it out with shaking hands.

"Now? You're going to do this now?"

Nicky's face wrinkled in an expression of shock and terror. He tightly closed his fingers around the velvet box. "Truthfully, I had something a little more romantic planned for this, but you weren't available that weekend."

"We haven't even talked about this."

"Yes, we have. We've talked about all of it. I didn't realize I needed to clear a proposal with you first, though. I thought it was still customary for it to be a surprise."

My panic ramped up, washing over me with a stomach-churning heat. He was right. The marriage idea had been tossed around on several occasions, always by Nicky, but I hadn't guessed he was this serious about it. I was waist deep in a miserable murder investigation, with no end in sight. Trying to sell my place, buy a new place, and plan a wedding that would involve dealing with my mother was a lot to add to my schedule. "It isn't that I don't want it," I started cautiously, my eyes closed. "There's so much going on right now. Realtors and wedding planners are the last thing I have time for." I lifted my eyes slightly, wincing at the devastation on Nicky's face. "It would be better if we talked about this after the case is over."

"Do you want to know why that doesn't work for me? After this case, there will be another case and another case after that, and when there isn't a new case, there's Jenna's case. You're always going to be working on a case." Nicky pushed a few wayward curls off his forehead with both hands. He stood up and dropped the ring box on top of the red metal FOR SALE signs, leaving a hollow tink echoing through the silent room. "This is what you do. This is your life, whether I like it or not. You've asked me to understand, and I try, but it can't be like this. If this—us—isn't what you want, you need to tell me the truth. I don't want to waste any more of my time. Or yours. I can't spend forever trying to compete with your job and a dead girl."

"This is about us, Nicky, it's not about Jenna."

"It's all about Jenna. Everything you do is about Jenna," he argued. "The job comes first because Jenna comes first, and I tried to get comfortable with that fact, but I can't. I can't get comfortable with the idea of us not going any further than dinner and sex when we both have the same night off. After two years, I don't think it's unreasonable to say I want more than just a casual thing."

"You know that's not what I think this is." My voice quivered at the sight of his tears. Nicky was intensely emotional, but I wasn't used to seeing him with tears, and knowing I'd caused them shattered me.

"I honestly don't know what you think this is, Cas. I really don't. But I do know I don't want to spend the rest of my life coming last in what's important to you. I can't do this with you right now. I need to drive, get some air. Do me a favor and lock up when you leave."

"Nicky, wait. We need to talk about this." I moved off the couch and reached for his arm, but he pulled away, refusing to look at me.

"I think we've talked enough already." Nicky didn't wait for an answer, slamming the heavy wood door as he left.

Resisting the urge to peek in the black ring box still resting on the sale signs, I listened to him peel out of the driveway. I was not leaving. I didn't want to go back to my place and deal with an inquisitive baby sister. I also didn't want to let Nicky walk away like this. He did not forgive easily, and I'd made a mess of his special moment a second time, whether intentional or not. I was going to have to make up for it.

I gave myself a few minutes to cry it out, then sulked to the bathroom to clean myself up. My eyes were red and puffy, and my face was streaked ugly with mascara. I washed my face and shrugged out of my work clothes, swiped one of Nicky's worn-out T-shirts from his closet, and curled up on the couch to wait him out. He'd come back home eventually.

Nicky had been talking about the long term a lot more lately, and I wanted the stability and attempt at happily-ever-after he was offering. At least I thought I did. We certainly had our issues, and we didn't always fight well, but I thought we'd managed to hammer our relationship into something that worked for us. It wasn't that I didn't love him. I was silly afraid of disrupting what was already working for us just to be able to tell people we were married. Were the husband and wife titles really necessary if we were happy? Was he not happy?

I poured my thoughts and apologies out in a string of texts to Nicky, hoping for any type of response. I wanted to keep trying. I knew he was trying to deal with my schedule change and my job, and we could keep talking about getting married. After an hour of constant messages, I received nothing back. For a fleeting moment I considered calling

Jamie, but I shut the idea down. I couldn't involve him until I knew where Nicky and I stood. Pity party needed or not, it was too early in this new mess I'd created to ask my twin to take sides.

* * *

I woke up in the dark in a fitful sheen of sweat on Nicky's couch. The nightmares that had been relentless recently were playing the end credits as I sat up. I'd spent my sleep running through a dark and dense forest. Jenna was ahead of me, and I struggled to keep up. I was falling farther and farther behind, and then it happened. I caught up to who I was chasing only to discover it was Nicky. A black plume of smoke shot up from the forest floor where Nicky was standing, and he was gone. I screamed until I startled myself out of my sleep.

The only sound I could hear was my own heartbeat in my ears, and the thudding was thankfully fading. I grabbed my cell on the coffee table and was surprised to see it was six thirty AM. I knew I was still alone in the house. Nicky hadn't come home. He also hadn't replied to any of the messages I'd sent before crashing on his couch. Calling in sick was not going to be an option with our current workload, and I knew Bryan wouldn't believe me if I tried, so I dragged my travel bag into the bathroom and forced myself into a shower. I went through the motions of my morning routine and readied myself to fake my way through a day at the office.

I settled into my temporary seat at the table and muttered a round of morning hellos. A rambling message had been left on my voicemail regarding a caller's theory on her neighbor's son's best friend stalking women on running trails, and I had Professor David Gentry at the top of my list. My plan was to stay focused only on the investigation and what was going on in the office for the day and avoid thinking about the mess I'd made of my personal life. I failed miserably at my plan.

Bryan made it to the office fifteen minutes after I got myself started and guessed that something had gone down. As soon as he asked what was wrong, I gave in to tears, which made matters worse. Tears at the office were never okay. He pulled me out of our shared space into an empty meeting room and demanded details.

"I know I joke about him being a pain in the ass, but I thought he was the real deal for you." Bryan sat on the corner of the table, giving me time to pull myself together, an obnoxious smirk on his face. "I cannot believe you told him no."

"I didn't tell him no! He didn't let me finish. Now I don't even know where he is." The squeak in my voice caught me off guard.

"Like it or not, Cas, you told him no. That's how he took it, anyway, and I can't say I would have taken it any different. Jesus H., the guy was trying to give you a ring, and you told him you can't because your caseload is heavy."

I dabbed under my eyes with the wad of tissues Bryan handed me. "I've tried calling Jamie, but he's not answering either."

"Whoa! How bad are you trying to make this?"

"What else am I supposed to do?"

"Jamie and Nicky were friends first. If he goes to your brother, you're going to have to deal with that, but you can't be the one to put Jamie in the middle of your mess and expect that to end well."

I dropped my head onto the table in surrender. I had no idea what the right move was going to be to fix what I'd messed up. "So what do I do?"

"Well, you need to decide if you want to fix it or end it. After you've decided that, show up at his place after work, make him talk it out. As for now, thanks to Cole's plea to the public yesterday, we have loads of new tips and pretty much nothing else, so we can distract you all day long with background checks and phone calls. You won't even have to leave the office. Just throw yourself into the work; that's what the rest of us do."

"According to Nicky, throwing myself into my work is part of the problem," I sniffed.

Bryan gave my shoulder a friendly squeeze. "If you need to take your mind off of Nicky, you could tell your partner why Lieutenant Miller called you to the office yesterday."

"Do you like torturing me?" I sniffled and dabbed my eyes, then wiped my nose with a tissue. "Who told you I was talking to Miller?"

"Gabe saw you," Bryan answered without hesitation. "He wanted to make sure we were still working over here."

I broke down the conversation I'd had with our lieutenant, giving myself all the blame for inadvertently giving away too much information to a stranger and skipping over a possible suspect without trying to protect myself.

"Damn. You weren't the only one who didn't put that together." He rubbed a hand on his freshly clipped hair, taking in the implication of my full confession. "Well, now you know what to focus on today. Just start building your file on whoever this professor really is, and don't worry about Nicky. You guys will be okay; you always are."

* * *

THE MYTH MAKER

By the time five o'clock arrived, I wasn't simply worn out, I was running on empty. To my dismay, I'd made little progress on building a file on David Gentry. The community college professor had no criminal background. The only thing I could find was a speeding ticket from two years earlier. His bio page on the college's website didn't give much info beyond his own education and hobbies, and he had almost nothing on his social media accounts. I left a message for the dean, but as the day went on, I lost hope of getting a call back today.

Ignoring drink offers and the everything-will-work-out pep talks, I shut down my laptop and headed for home. I opted to make it a Ben & Jerry's dinner night, so I made a quick stop at the corner market for what I knew was missing from my freezer. All I wanted was some ice cream that included lots of things covered in chocolate, a bath, and my bed. When I pulled up to a familiar red Toyota truck parked in front of my house, my mood went from sad and sour to all-out annoyed. I was beginning to regret giving any of my family members keys to my place.

I waited until the garage door closed before taking a big breath and getting out of my car. Counting backward from ten, I trudged through the door that led to the kitchen and a purring Freddy, who quickly twisted himself around my feet. Not fooled by the silence in the house, I called out to my brother. Jamie was here, and the ambush was coming. The last thing I wanted to deal with was being criticized in person for how I'd handled the previous night by someone who'd been ignoring my calls.

"In here," he answered from the living room.

I dropped my bag on the counter and opened a pouch of the special wet stuff for Freddy. "Didn't know I was going to have company. I hope you weren't expecting dinner."

"Funny thing; I wasn't expecting company at one o'clock this morning either, yet I got it." Jamie ambled his way into the kitchen and seated himself at my round glass table. Under his hazel eyes, my brother was sporting unusual dark circles that were almost as black as his V-neck. Paired with faded jeans and flip-flops, tonight's look was a casual one for my twin. He put his hands on the table and stretched his lean body forward. "Do you want to tell me your side of what happened last night, because I've already spent hours listening to the other side."

"Nope. I'm not even sure what happened last night, and I don't have the energy to get into it with you." I grabbed my new pint of ice cream with chocolate chip cookie dough and brownie bits, and I popped onto the counter, spoon in hand.

"I'm not going anywhere, so you might as well tell me what happened. Why is my best friend currently passed out on my couch, after keeping the two of us up until morning, in a full drunken rant about all things you? What the hell happened, Cassidy?"

"I said I don't know. I'm sorry he went to you, though."

"Oh, he didn't come to me. I had to go to him. All the way to downtown Seattle at one in the morning. Luckily, a sympathetic bartender cut him off but didn't kick him out. When he passed out there, they called the ICE number on his cell, which I didn't know people actually did, and which happened to be me. They realized it would cost him a fortune to Uber all the way back home, and they didn't want to call the cops. Nicky told everyone at the bar about his cop girlfriend rejecting a marriage proposal, so the guys there felt bad for him and called me instead." Jamie got up to rifle through my fridge, coming out with a can of Coke and frowning at a snack-sized bag of baby carrots. "He was passed out when I got to the bar, and then completely invigorated and pissed off by the time we got back to my place. Cooked us a full breakfast at three AM and explained that my twin sister turned down a marriage proposal before he could even flash the bling. That's exactly how he put it too, about fourteen dozen times, then he passed out again. Well, first he threw up, and then he passed out. It was a great morning."

"That isn't a fair assessment of our evening, actually. I was caught off guard, but I remember saying not right now in the middle of this case. I didn't say I wasn't ever going to marry him. He wouldn't listen to me."

"Admit it, you didn't let him get to the down-on-one-knee part, did you?"

I shook my head, spoon in mouth. The more questions my brother asked, the less I wanted to continue. "I don't know what to do."

Jamie let the bag of carrots drop on the table and sat up straight in his chair. "He was a mess last night, and I'm completely confused and exhausted. If you're not going to tell him, then at least tell me why. I thought you were happy with Nicky."

"I am. I was? I don't even know how to answer that anymore. Like I said, he caught me off guard, and the idea of selling my place and trying to plan a wedding around Mom made my brain spin in my skull. I don't know what's going to happen if he won't talk to me."

"I've been dreading this for a long time," my brother continued. "You are my little sister, my twin, I love you, I would die for you, blah, blah, blah, but Nicky has been my best friend for over ten years. There was shit Nicky saw from me that I still haven't been able to talk to you about. The guy literally saved my life. You have to know that I'm not going to cut things off with him if you do. I have to be able to keep you both. You do know that, right?"

His statement was the truth I'd been hiding from. The history between Nicky and Jamie was the part of the equation I always tried to shut out. The fact that there was so much more at stake than my heart if Nicky and I couldn't make this work, and that was what I was most afraid of. The bond between my brother and my boyfriend was more than a shared love of good food and baseball.

As his roommate, Nicky had stood in the middle of a dark spiral my brother had put himself into while we were in school. At Jamie's darkest point, it was Nicky who'd found him unconscious in their bathroom and taken him for help. And it was Nicky who'd made the calls to me and my parents once Jamie was admitted to the hospital. It was also Nicky who'd given my brother a black eye and nursed his own broken nose after they'd brawled over whether or not Jamie was going to get help for his drinking problem—and other issues—the rest of us had been busy ignoring. Especially me.

I knew that the depth of the drama Nicky had shielded me from in the time leading up to my brother's recovery, and then in the months during, was always going to remain a secret between them. I'd been so wrapped up in still trying to shut out my own trauma that I'd refused to see what my brother was doing to himself, and he refused to let me be part of it. Those months Nicky spent protecting both of us were part of what cemented the connection they shared as friends.

It was their connection I'd feared most when I started dating Nicky, and it was what I worried about most now. Losing Nicky was going to be bad enough. I couldn't handle possibly coming between the two of them. All of those pent-up fears in the middle of my chest burst forward at once with deep sobs and cheek-soaking tears. Jamie was on his feet in a flash with a hug, which only made the tears come harder.

Controlling my breathing and silently berating myself for being a wuss, I pulled the breakdown to a shaky halt. "Do you think I can fix this or not?" I asked into my brother's shoulder.

"I want you to try to if you want to. I have to be honest, though: Nicky was pretty bleak about where he sees things. The two of you are going to have to get honest with each other about what you're both looking for. Did I mention he went through all my emergency smokes?"

I sat up straight and smacked Jamie's chest. "You quit!"

"I said they were for emergencies."

"You quit," I repeated fiercely, selfishly relieved to turn the focus on someone else.

"Relax, Kissy, I didn't offer to mix him bitters and Absolut, just a lighter and some Reds." My brother met my glare, not willing to let me turn things on him.

"Nicky doesn't even smoke."

Jamie cracked the first smile of our conversation. "Sorry, he does now. A lot. I told you: You messed him up last night."

"Should I go see him at your place? Bryan thought if I showed up and forced a conversation, he would have to listen to me," I said around a frozen bit of cookie dough.

"Uh, no, do not take Bryan's advice. The last thing I need is to be stuck with both of you there for the weekend. You should call him and have him meet you here or go back to his place and talk things out in private. I eventually will need to get him off my couch."

"You've been with him all day; you know he's not taking my calls. Neither were you, I might add."

"I've been busy dealing with him. I couldn't deal with both of you at the same time," Jamie said. "Give it a bit and I'll call him; he'll pick up for me. He was out cold when I left, and he hasn't slept much today. Not to mention the killer hangover he's going to have, so let him sleep. Where's Hippie Long Stockings? Let's go get something to eat."

"Megs is working tonight, thankfully, and if you haven't noticed, I am eating." I held out my Ben & Jerry's. "The last thing I want to do right now is go out. I want to put on my comfies, eat the rest of this ice cream, and be miserable until Nicky agrees to talk to me."

"Then tell me you have something here besides carrots and ice cream and we'll stay here. I don't know how you date a chef and live without real food in your house."

"There's a decent pizza place around the corner that delivers. That's about the best I can do." I dropped my spoon in the sink and started through my junk drawer to find the familiar red-and-black pizza menu.

"Oh, I'm also supposed to give you this, but from Mom, not Nicky. She said you're getting mail at her house now?"

A jolt went through me at Jamie's words, but I forced myself to continue looking for the menu. He picked up a small postcard with a crinkled corner from where it lay next to the regular mail I'd left on the counter.

"Pick what you want." I handed the menu to my brother and examined the postcard, finding exactly what I was looking for on the back. Jenna's copied handwriting. The front image was a nondescript waterfront photo with a blue wave rolling onto a sandy shore and a massive piece of driftwood off-center in the shot. On the back was my name and my parents' address this time, with another short message: *YOU SHOULD HAVE BEEN THERE!* The dot of the exclamation mark was a small star, just like Jenna used to do. I wanted to scream, but that would require telling my brother the truth about the postcard, and I wasn't ready for that yet. I wasn't ready to tell anyone that I was being called out for what I'd known was my failure all along, and I was pretty sure I was being called out by a killer. "I think it's someone from school trying to reconnect. Let's call for pizza." I shoved the postcard into my purse, hoping Jamie would let the subject drop, and started feeling around for my phone, but before I could dig it out, my cell started singing. I knew before looking at it who was calling.

"Nicky?" Jamie was hopeful.

I frowned, not wanting to answer. "It's Bryan." I grabbed the phone and hit the touch screen. "Hello?"

"Hey, we have another victim and it's a mess. We need you down here," Bryan growled.

"Where did they find her?"

"We haven't."

"I thought you were calling about another goddess case?"

"I am, but he didn't kill her. The psycho bastard just kidnapped a nineteen-year-old girl from a flower shop."

I pressed my thumb and forefinger to the bridge of my nose. "How do we know this is related to our case?"

"It's him, Cas. The victim and her mom were working together. Mom went into the shop and left her in the greenhouse; when she came back, the daughter was gone. This is the escalation we were afraid of. Cole said call the professor; he wants to see if we can get her to the crime scene. We're not making heads or tails of this one."

"Text me the address and I'll meet you there." Snapping into work mode, I threw the cell back into my bag and rushed to the bathroom to conceal the evidence of my latest crying spree. I added fresh mascara and some lip balm, then grabbed my bag off the counter. Dealing with my exploding love life and the mystery person sending me hate mail was going to have to wait.

"Another case?" Jamie asked, his disappointment clear.

I nodded and tried for a terse smile. "There always will be; just ask Nicky."

13

I pulled my Mini Cooper into the parking lot of Blissful Blooms behind Cole's SUV and caught up with the rest of my new team. The telltale yellow tape hung across the front entrance of the greenhouse, and Bryan and Phoenix stood with their shoulders together, talking low. Cole was at the back door of the main building with an older, dark-haired woman who was trying to hold a bottle of water in quaking hands. I weighed my options and headed for Bryan.

"What do we have?"

"Alayna Keller, nineteen, five three, thin build, long brown hair, brown eyes, pink shirt, jeans, she went missing from the greenhouse." Bryan stopped to check his watch. "She's been gone about forty minutes now."

"Is that mom with Cole?"

Bryan nodded. "Vivian Keller. She was out here working with her daughter on some arrangements. She left for a few minutes to help an employee running the shop, and when she came back, Alayna was gone."

"And we jumped to a kidnapping because?"

"Definite sign of a struggle. I don't know what any of it means, but it's like the whole greenhouse is a possible clue with this goddess business. There's dozens of flowers, and a mess."

Cole left the mother of our victim with Eric and took long, hurried strides to where we were huddled, waiting for Professor Darcy to be brought through the barriers. "Mom says she was inside for less than fifteen minutes. Alayna was working on an arrangement when she went in; the whole place was trashed when she came back out, and daughter was gone."

"I'm sorry, hello? Detective Cantwell?" Professor Darcy shouted from the wrong side of the barricades set up to control traffic. I waved to the patrol officer standing guard to let her through.

Looking around the business lot, I didn't see many places to hide here, but there were several ways in and out. The shops were mostly strung together on both sides of the street, and the flower shop backed up to an alley shared with a residential street. We were completely out of daylight, and the spattering of flashing squad car lights and flashlights hitting the windows created a muted glow to the reflections. Three media vans were on scene, and I could see one eager reporter watching the professor's approach.

"Thanks for coming out, Professor Darcy," Cole said. Everything about his posture and tone said he was in charge, while the professor's hesitant steps and anxiously darting eyes relayed her nerves. "Recreating these goddesses seems to be part of our killer's psychology, and I know we need to understand what he's doing."

"I'm afraid I can't help you with any modern-day psychology, but I can tell you that he's familiar with the stories of these goddesses. The details that have been shared with me so far have been pretty spot-on."

"In the previous cases we've had a body, and the clues have been left with the body, but we don't have that tonight, and I want to see if you can look at this crime scene and tell us if anything connects it to the others. I need to know if we are possibly looking at something unrelated." Cole smoothed fingers across the stress lines of his forehead. "I can't afford to be wrong."

A sigh of relief escaped as Professor Darcy put one hand over her heart, and I realized I hadn't been clear about the type of crime scene she was being called to. She'd come to help, prepared for anything, even a body. "I can tell you what I see and leave the psychology up to you."

A blast of cold air hit us as we walked into the greenhouse, and a cooling unit made a strained rattling sound. The scene was chaos, with entire shelves of flowers knocked to the ground. The table that our victim had been working at was tipped on its side, glass shards from a vase crushed beneath it. Roses had been the main flower used by our killer, appearing at the murder scenes of Dana Mayhew and Maggie Cannon and in the wings left with Felicity Benson, but there were multitudes of flowers here now and no way to know what was important.

Professor Darcy immediately went to a pile of flowers on the ground, near the back wall of the greenhouse, and we followed.

"We have collected samples, but we don't know what the dark stuff is," Cole said. The substance was thick and sticky looking, with a dark, glossy red color, almost black. It had been poured on the floor and splashed in an arch across the wall. "We can tell you it's not blood."

The professor pulled up the bottom of her long wool coat and bent down to study the puddle on the ground. Before any of us could react to stop her, she dabbed one finger into the sticky substance, smelled it, and then touched the tip of her tongue to the remnants on her finger. None of us said a thing, but the shared look of shock was obvious on all of us. Professor Darcy's hands covered her face in immediate embarrassment, and she took a giant step back.

"I . . . I don't know why I just did that," she stammered, her eyes wide and darting between the four of us watching. "Have to admit, I've never been to a crime scene before, but I'm pretty sure that is pomegranate molasses. I use it all the time. Can you tell me if the woman who was working has a daughter?"

"If I said yes, what would that mean?" Cole asked cautiously.

"One of the better-known myths, Agent MacAllan, is the story of Persephone. Persephone was taken to the underworld by Hades and hidden away from her mother, Demeter. She was the goddess of agriculture and of the harvest. When she couldn't find her daughter, she refused to let anything on earth grow during her time of despair. That could be represented by the dead flowers that have been thrown into the mix."

I studied the pile of dead blooms and realized that, while the greenhouse was filled with a variety of flowers, the mound of dead flowers was almost exclusively wilted roses with a bright-white-and-yellow daffodil at the top of the pile.

Professor Darcy was studying the daffodil, trying to conceal the type of smile that happens when you've solved a puzzle. "Oh, there's even a narcissus." She was nearly whispering. "Persephone was drawn to pick a narcissus flower, and when she got close to it, the earth cracked open so Hades could bring her into the underworld. He was the god of the dead, but he fell in love with Persephone and built beautiful gardens in the underworld to make Persephone happy and achieve his main goal—he wanted her to fall in love with him—and over time she did. Demeter was still determined to get her back, though, so she had to go to Zeus, and it came down to what Persephone wanted, which was to stay with Hades."

I almost didn't want to ask my only question. "Did Demeter ever get her daughter back?"

"In a way," she answered. "Zeus split the difference, and Persephone spent half the year on earth and half the year in the underworld, based on the number of pomegranate seeds she'd eaten in the underworld. Every time Persephone returned to Hades, Demeter would make everything die. It was how they explained the change in seasons."

My partner momentarily turned his back to the rest of us, hands on his head. "Our guy just moved from murder to kidnapping," he said.

I nodded a grim agreement. "This isn't a ransom; this guy thinks he's a god."

* * *

"No surprise, we didn't come up with anything good by way of physical evidence overnight," Cole began from his spot at the head of the table as I nursed a mug of sugary coffee. We'd gotten an especially early start. "I've already talked to the boyfriend this morning. He called on my way in. They've organized family and friends and they're going to be out in force with missing-person flyers today, and they'll be working with our liaisons to make a full statement to the press."

"Jordan turned over her laptop and a tablet they both used, but we don't know what happened with her phone," Eric said. "It's not on, no idea if she still has it, but we've also still not found Maggie Cannon's phone either. We did put out a possible vehicle description, if you count white four-door as a valid description."

"We might know how he found Alayna," I said. "A few weeks ago, Vivian Keller started a print ad campaign showing her and Alayna and their flower shop, and I think he picked Alayna from that. With the aspects of the Persephone myth the professor shared, I don't think this is going to be a ransom. In the myth, Hades doesn't want Persephone to leave the underworld, and I don't think he's going to murder five women, kidnap a sixth, and then just let her go in six months."

"How many pomegranate seeds do you think are in a bottle of molasses?" Phoenix asked rhetorically. He hadn't taken the time to shave this morning, and the five o'clock shadow he was wearing made him look even less cop-like.

"I am going to need so much more coffee before I can process that for you," I snipped. Cole's brows shot up, but my partner, much more accustomed to my occasional early-morning struggles, snickered.

"You can get more coffee," Cole said to me. "And do it on the way to Vivian Keller's house. I want you to make contact out there. Alayna's cousin is her closest friend, and she spent the night with her aunt. I told her to expect you this morning. Talk to her, find out a little more about Alayna's day-to-day, check on how mom's doing."

There was no chance to argue against my new solo assignment, but meeting with the victim's family alone made me uneasy. Cole put Bryan and Eric together back at the crime scene to help lead the canvassing. Pheonix was sticking close to the office, away from cameras, to follow up on the information we received from the tech guys.

The emotions moving through the Keller house were hauntingly familiar, and I couldn't help but connect with the recognizable fear. Vivian Keller was sleeping when I arrived, with the help of some strong medication, and was being protected by her sister and her niece, Tara. Jordan, Alayna's boyfriend, was already at the command center wanting to help by the time I arrived at the house. I accepted the floral-printed mug of coffee that was offered, and we gathered around the kitchen table. Tara immediately took control of the conversation.

"I don't understand why someone would take Alayna. She doesn't go out much. Most of her time is spent in class or with Jordan," she said. "How did anyone even know she was out there in the greenhouse? It doesn't make any sense to me."

"We believe it's possible the person who took her was watching her prior to yesterday. You and your cousin talk often, right?"

"Basically every day. We're going through for the same major, and we have two classes together during the week. Sometimes we get together to study, but we chat through Messenger when we're not together."

"Has she mentioned anything to you about anyone paying too much attention to her? Any out-of-the-ordinary contact with strangers she might have mentioned in passing but didn't mention to anyone else?"

"No. Most of our conversations lately have been about a class project she was struggling with and her trying to get used to not living at her mom's house anymore. She moved in with Jordan about a month ago, and it's been an adjustment for her and my aunt. It's always been just the two of them."

"Nothing seemed off over the past few weeks other than that new adjustment?"

Tara let her gaze drift past me, momentarily lost in her own memories. "Honestly, I don't know if Alayna would have noticed if there was. She's a little, well . . . flighty, and she spends a lot of time in her own head. I was walking with her a few weeks ago, and she walked right into a crosswalk sign. She was so involved in the story she was telling me she didn't even see it until she hit it with her face. If someone was watching her and didn't come up and tap her on the forehead, she wouldn't even notice."

"Your aunt is going to need a lot of support from you guys in the coming days. If there's anything you think of, anything anyone else remembers she might have mentioned, please let us know right away. We'll be in contact with you all throughout this process, and we'll keep you involved. But you never know what's going to solve a case, so any little memory that comes up, share it. It could be what finds her."

I said goodbye to Tara and the few other family members already milling around, then left, unsettled. I walked out with no more information than what I'd walked in with. What I did carry out with me was a familiar fear and loss and uncertainty that matched what I'd been carrying myself for years. I hadn't been able to resolve my grief, but I was determined to limit theirs.

* * *

The state of our fishbowl office space was chaotic when I returned at Cole's request, and Phoenix was the only occupant. He was at his laptop, sheets of paper covering the glass surface in a close perimeter around him, with everything stretched to just within his reach. Some of the papers I'd added at the beginning, which included phone lists and bank records for our victims, had been pulled from their rows, leaving random open spaces on the glass walls like windows. He didn't look up when I closed the door behind me.

"I'm glad you're back; I could use some help," Phoenix said.

"Did you find something?" I shrugged out of my jacket and took a seat next to him. The screen on his laptop was crowded with images of laughing teenagers, and I realized some of the photos were of Alayna Keller; others were of her boyfriend, Jordan.

"Combing socials?"

"Yep. There's way too many cameras for me to be on scene right now, according to the boss, so he assigned me this, and told me to give you this when you got back." He handed me a pink Post-it with the login for the memorial page that friends had set up after the murder of Sarah Goodall. "You and your professor have convinced him that we've missed some sort of intersection with the victims. I'm working on the most recent, you can start with the first, and we'll meet in the middle. We're trying to catch any connection between them—photos at the same events or restaurants, that kind of thing."

"This is going to require more coffee." I filled my mug with the drip maker that had appeared with the last equipment update and logged in to the Facebook page memorializing the short life of Sarah Goodall—Athena to our killer. She was five years older than our youngest victim, Alayna Keller, and four years older than Olivia Bower, but she looked younger than both. She had round cheeks, and her auburn hair was cut in a textured pixie. After scrolling through pages of messages from friends and loved ones, I came across the last post made by Sarah herself. That's when I realized the memorial page was Sarah's own page, renamed after her death. Two other social media accounts were available, but no one had taken responsibility for keeping those going. Both had last posts near the day of Sarah's death.

The last post was of a collection of paper plate snowmen and the caption "Getting ready for winter with my kiddos!"

"Alayna posts so many photos of herself online. So many." Phoenix kicked his feet out under the table and leaned back into his chair. "I don't know if there's anywhere in the city she hasn't taken a picture of herself."

The posts from Sarah Goodall were different across all three of her social media accounts that I was combing through. Rather than a collection of selfies or meals, there were photos of her loom projects and shots of her classroom each time she updated for a holiday or lesson theme. Her online world was almost entirely her two loves—her weaving and her classroom.

"Do you think he's done?" I asked. It was the question that had been running laps in my mind since the night before. Going from murder to kidnapping was a switch I hadn't seen coming, and I didn't think I was alone.

Phoenix shrugged. "Eric is the one with the psych degree, but I'd say no. I know what your myths say about the goddess he's got Alayna Keller playing, but I don't think those Patty Hearst scenarios are all that easy to pull off. Cole's not breathing right either, and that's always a reliable clue you'll start to pick up on."

I nodded, not wanting to agree. It was an unsettling conclusion to make, that only if Alayna Keller stayed with her captor would the killing stop. And for how long? I continued to scroll through photos of kid crafts and geometric wall tapestries, until something caught my attention in one of the few photos Sarah had posted of herself. An autumn photo, one hand wrapped around a to-go coffee cup, her head tilted to a smiling blonde next to her. *Pumpkin time!* she'd written with the photo, tagging a young woman named Jessica, the friend who'd taken over the page, on the post. I knew what I was looking at, but to be sure, I grabbed one of the evidence photos off the glass wall behind Phoenix.

"What do you have?"

I opened the photos tab of her page and scrolled, looking for just the photos of Sarah, and I was able to find it again. Opening both photos, I turned my laptop screen toward Phoenix. "See anything?"

He studied the photos, eyebrows raised, and then he kicked back with a whistle. "That's your gold apple."

"It looks like the same ring, right?" I held the photo up against the zoomed-in image of Sarah's hand wrapped around her coffee, and the small apple ring was there on her right ring finger. I'd never seen Sarah in person, but I had seen the ring. The small size I'd thought would fit a pinkie was actually worn on her ring finger, indicating how petite the young woman with the Tinker Bell haircut actually was.

"We need to talk to her," Phoenix said, tapping his finger under the image of the second woman in the photo. "Who is she?"

"Jessica Pembrook. She's also a teacher at Hillside Elementary School."

"Then that's where we're going. Let's go." Phoenix jumped up, excited to have a new destination.

"Just like that?"

"I can't sit in this office all day, and she might be able to tell us about the ring. She's the one close enough to be maintaining her memories; she's going to know about the ring."

"And if there was an engraving." I caught up to his thought process out loud.

"Exactly. You can drive this time; Cole took my ride."

* * *

We caught the attention of a hall monitor as soon as we entered the elementary school and were led to the office of the principal, who was none too happy to see a police detective and FBI agent, unannounced, at his desk.

Mr. Howl, the principal, was a bald man with a gray mustache and Coke-bottle glasses. He straightened his tie after giving us a chance to introduce ourselves. "I appreciate that you're doing your jobs, Detectives, but a little heads-up would have been helpful in getting classrooms covered if you need to speak to teachers."

I spoke up first. "We only need to speak with Jessica Pembrook, and it is an urgent matter, so we were hoping we could just interrupt her day for a moment. It shouldn't take long."

"I'm lucky with the teachers I have here. Our school is very much a family, and Sarah's murder was unlike anything else we've had to weather together. Of course I'll call Miss Pembrook down, but I just ask that you be discreet while you're here. A police presence in the building can make some of our kids nervous."

Rather than finding us an alternate space, Principal Howl had us meet Jessica Pembrook in his office, and the rekindled sadness for her murdered friend was immediate. "Sorry," she sniffed, and she accepted the tissue box Principal Howl offered. "It's still hard, thinking about what happened to Sarah."

I nodded with sympathy more personal than the young teacher understood. "I want to ask you about a ring that Sarah wore. It's the one in this photo." I put the printout of the coffee post on the desk, and Jessica took it in her hands.

"Her mom bought it for her when Sarah accepted the job up here and moved from Oregon." Gently, she put a hand on the image of her lost friend. "It says *Beautiful* inside the band. Sarah wore it pretty much every day. She didn't have the heart to tell her mom when she lost it."

"Do you remember when she lost it?" Phoenix asked. It wasn't the scenario we'd come in with. Both of us were betting that if we confirmed Sarah's ring was the one found in Dana Mayhew's mouth, our guy would've taken it the night he killed Sarah.

Jessica nodded while grabbing a second tissue. "I was with her; it was last year on Halloween night. One of those companies that hosts trivia nights hosted a spooky pub crawl, and about three stops in, she realized it was gone. She was so upset about it that we actually tried to backtrack a bit, but we didn't find it."

* * *

"Halloween," Phoenix muttered, folding himself into the passenger seat of my Mini Cooper. "What day was she murdered?"

"December seventh." Frustrated, I smacked my palms on the top of my steering wheel. "We know he had the ring because he left it with Dana, and I don't believe in coincidence enough to believe he isn't the one responsible for Sarah losing it." There was no denying it now. Whoever our killer was, he was able to get close to these women, maybe even intimately close, without raising fears. These women played into his game while he remained invisible.

When I finally got home, I was relieved to see that Meghan was gone and I'd be able to get into my case binders again without her nosing through them. I dragged one bin into my living room, turned on the TV, and then my phone rang.

"How are you doing?" Jamie asked.

"Exhausted, but I'm all right."

"Have you talked to Nicky? He didn't show up to work out this morning."

"Even if he was taking my calls, which he's not, I didn't get home until after two AM and I was back to work before seven AM. I don't exactly have time to indulge him in this tantrum he's throwing."

"Ouch."

"Whatever. He started it," I said on an exhale.

"I guess you haven't had a chance to talk to Meghan today either." Even over the phone I could hear my brother's cocky smile, and I hated him for it.

"No, I have not talked to Meghan. What has she done now?"

"She's giving Mom a heart attack, and it's all your fault. Mom called me about an hour ago to find out what I know about Meg's new life plan you've helped her decide on."

I groaned too loudly. "That one I know I had nothing to do with. She's been staying with me, but I barely have time to see her, and I haven't butted into her current life plan other than to tell her she couldn't smoke weed in my house. I am off the hook for any new life plan she's put together."

"I'm so glad I get to be the one who gets to tell you this," Jamie laughed. "Last night our darling baby sister let Mom and Dad know, in person, that she's going to apply for the police academy. She claims you helped her make that decision."

"Oh, for hell's sake! I never talked to her about joining the damn academy. I definitely never told her anything that would make her think I thought she should be a cop."

"Well, for the sake of the rest of us, you might want to find some time to talk to her about it before someone unleashes Meghan on the world with a gun."

"Why is it always on me to save her? Everyone acts like I can talk her out of any of these ideas she comes up with. The girl walked to Canada for her graduation, joined a circus and a cult in the last two years—I can't keep her from doing anything. I will talk to her once I have a free minute, but if she's signed up by then, it's out of my hands. Currently dealing with a kidnapping and five murders you might have heard about, and it hasn't left me with much spare time."

"Try to find the time to talk to her, and keep me posted. I'll let you know if I hear from Nicky," my brother offered.

"That's not necessary," I sighed, not sure if it was hurt, self-pity, or pure exhaustion that was pushing me to the verge of tears again, but I had to pull it to a stop. "Nicky is a big boy. I figure if he wants to fix things, he'll call me. If he doesn't, he won't."

I disconnected the call and pushed the conversation to the back of my mind, going back to my priority. The postcard with Jenna's handwriting. We'd been running nonstop with no time for my side investigation of why someone was trying to bring me into Jenna's case. I felt my way through the pocket I was sure I'd stashed the postcard in, but it wasn't there. Frantic, I tipped my bag upside down on top of the lid on the rubber tote, spreading the contents. ChapSticks, loose change, and multiple hair ties were mixed in with the standard purse fare, but the postcard was gone.

I ran to my garage and pulled the doors open on my car, sliding both seats all the way back, using my phone as a flashlight. A stick of gum and a full punch card for coffee were all I could find. I knew I'd put it in my bag when Jamie gave it to me. I knew it was still there when I arrived at the Blissful Blooms flower shop, where I'd moved it from the main pocket to the interior pocket because I thought it would be safer. Now it was gone.

14

The image of a convenience store counter flickered on the large screen at one end of the conference room. At the three-second mark, a dark-haired girl in the video made her way through the door. She glanced quickly at the clerk and then deliberately at the camera positioned over his head. No one made a sound as the camera lost track of the young woman in the oversized jacket. The time clock at the bottom of the screen ticked off twenty-six seconds before she came back in frame with drinks in her arms: two bottles of water, an energy drink, and a canned tea.

She put her four drinks on the counter, waited for her purchase to be rung up, and then handed the clerk a twenty-dollar bill from her jacket pocket. She took the change and the receipt, waited for him to place the drinks into a bag, and then left. There was no audio, but the clerk had confirmed she'd only muttered a thank-you at the end of the transaction. She didn't seem scared; she didn't plead for help. She simply paid for the drinks and walked back out into the night.

"Anyone need to see that again?" Cole finally asked the silent room. The image of Alayna Keller walking away from the store was still visible in the glass of the double doors. When no one needed to see the footage again, Eric flipped the lights back on. "The clerk who called this in didn't realize she was a missing person until after, but we've watched it a few times, and I think it's agreed it's Alayna."

"The jacket she has on doesn't look like it's hers, but there's a lighter shirt underneath. Pink shirt, blue jeans, black Vans. Everything matches to say it's Alayna." Eric said.

"Alayna was taken at four forty-five PM. That gas station is only about twenty minutes away from the flower shop, but she isn't there until after ten thirty PM. There's no way to know where they were in between, but she seems unharmed."

"It has to be said," Bryan started grimly. "Is there a chance at all that she left on her own? She's a bright girl, maybe a little overwhelmed with school and boyfriend and trying to help out her single mom. Maybe she met someone else and had some crazy, romanticized idea about running away from it all."

"I think you're reaching," I said.

"I think he watches too much Lifetime channel," Phoenix chided.

Bryan grinned, an experienced player at the game of devil's advocate. "Why didn't she ask for help? Why did he let her go in there alone? You can't tell me Stockholm syndrome took effect in five hours."

"I don't know why. He's obviously got something he's using to control her, even if it's just controlling her emotionally, but we know she wasn't in on this. No one outside of this room knows about the Greek connection. Those dead flowers in pomegranate syrup? There's no way to not connect that. Whoever took her is our guy." The lab work on the sticky substance matched what Professor Darcy had said it would be—pomegranate molasses—completing the connection to the Persephone myth.

"What do we do with this, then?" Bryan asked. "Do we show her mom? Give it to the press? How far do we want to go with it?"

"I'm going to have her mom look at it." Cole rubbed absentmindedly at the back of his neck. "I don't think we're wrong, but I want to have a positive ID. I'm not ready to release it to the media. For now, I've given you all your next assignments, so I'll leave you to it. I'm going back to the house to meet with Ms. Keller and show her this footage."

I looked over the address of the motel Bryan and I were headed to, relieved to be paired up with my partner again. I wasn't hopeful about our assignment, though. A motel clerk had called in that she believed she'd seen Alayna and an unknown male in a white four-door sedan this morning. She offered to give us a receipt, but the motel didn't have surveillance cameras, and they didn't have a plate number for the car.

* * *

"Rise and shine, sleepyhead," Bryan teased, shaking my knee. I opened my eyes to see we were parked in front of the Sweet Dreams Motel.

"After this, I obviously need more coffee." I retied my ponytail, made a quick swipe under my puffy eyes, and pulled my cherry lip balm out of my pocket for a refresh.

"Eesh. I am not seeing many sweet dreams happening here," Bryan said as we walked up to the dilapidated office.

"It's no Holiday Inn, that's for sure."

The office was attached to a small house for the on-site manager. To the right of the office was the two-floor motel strip, twelve rooms per floor. Each of the buildings was finished in a dingy white stucco with bright crayon-blue trim. The doors and all the metal railings were painted in the identical shade of blue, as were the curbing, the four garbage cans, and a scattering of concrete flowerpots on the main strip that were currently filled with nothing more than neglected dirt.

I followed my partner into the office, trying to swallow my yawn as we walked through the glass door. Bryan rang the old-fashioned brass bell sitting in the middle of the counter. A faraway door slammed shut, then a woman in a worn pink housecoat came padding through the office door.

"You looking for by the day or by the hour?" the woman asked with a smoker's rasp. She was heavyset, with a bustline twice as big around as her wide hips.

Bryan didn't miss a beat. "Neither. We're with the police, ma'am. Did you call about a possible sighting of a kidnapped girl?"

"Heavens no!" The woman roared with laughter. "I'm Edna. It was my crazy twin who called you folks. I'll grab Esther for ya; she's just finishin' up some pancakes."

I shot my partner a wide-eyed glance. Hearing Edna refer to her sister as the crazy twin made me question the necessity of following up on *every* lead. My hopes were growing dimmer by the second. A few minutes later we were greeted by a second, equally round, equally busty woman, not wearing a bra under her Tweety Bird nightshirt. After a second glance, I could tell she also wasn't wearing any teeth. I'd guessed the twins were around seventy, but admittedly, the missing teeth could be adding a few years to my estimate.

"Hello, Officers," the round woman rumbled. "I'm Esther Forsberg. I'm the one who saw that young girl on the news waiting in that car this morning. I didn't see her when he checked in, but he was checking in late. I saw her this morning, though, waiting in the white car just like they said on the news. The young man she was with was very polite. I got his receipt right here, paid in cash." She handed Bryan a pink carbon copy with a scribble at the bottom that resembled artwork on his desk from his three-year-old.

"What name did he give you when he checked in, Ms. Forsberg?" He asked.

Esther pulled out a three-ring binder and flipped it open with a thud on the counter. She ran a chubby finger, tipped with a bright-red press-on nail, down the list of names and stopped at the third from the bottom. "I guess it was a scribble here too."

"You don't require your customers give you names when they check in?" Bryan's earlier sunny mood was fading.

"We note the names if they're paying with credit cards, just to cover ourselves, but we don't actually see a lot of those." Esther let out a husky cackle and slapped a hand on the chipped Formica counter. "Officers, Edna and I see a lot of returning customers, and they tend to be couples who would rather us not jot down their personal info for our record books. We're in no position to judge others, seeing how frisky we were in our younger days, so we choose to look the other way here at the Sweet Dreams Motel."

I stifled a giggle at the vision of the frisky Forsberg twins that my imagination threw at me. "Miss Forsberg, has the room they were staying in been cleaned yet?"

"Oh, no. We don't start cleaning until after breakfast to give guests time to clear out before we start making noise. Would you like to take a look at room twelve?"

"Definitely."

She hesitated. "Do you need a warrant for that before I let you in?"

"No," I answered quickly. "They've checked out; we're in the clear with your permission."

Esther pulled a key from the pegboard behind her and shuffled past Bryan and me to the door. I followed our barefoot escort to room twelve, at the very end of the bottom floor, farthest from the manager's office. Bryan stopped at our car and popped the trunk to grab our kit of basic crime scene supplies. Esther unlocked the room and moved to step inside before I blocked her.

"Thank you, Miss Forsberg. We'll bring the key back as soon as we're done with the room," I said, allowing Bryan to slip in around me.

"Well, all right, but can you keep a low profile while you're here? I don't want to scare away our other guests."

"We'll try not to be noticed," I said, closing the door.

The motel room was as dingy on the inside as it was on the outside. At one point the walls had been white, but they wore a drab yellow tinge now, and the carpet was a full-pile blue shag. A single queen-size bed sat in the middle of the room, and a TV console encased in wood that rivaled what my grandparents once owned stood against the opposite wall. In the corner of that wall, near the ceiling, were three holes. If forced to wager a guess, I'd have said they were bullet holes.

"I'll check this side, you check that side," Bryan instructed. He tossed me a pair of black latex gloves and snapped on his own pair before flipping on the light in the bathroom. "He was a very polite motel guest. He's folded the bedding up out there, and he's folded the used towels in here. Looks like he took the garbage with him too."

"He even stripped the pillowcases. Everything about this room says suspicious," I replied as I lifted the aged mattress. "I know there's more important things, but all I'm thinking about right now is bedbugs."

My partner laughed from the bathroom, and I made my way to the other side of the bed. I pulled the corner up with my flashlight in the other hand. As I pulled the mattress away from the box spring, a crinkled slip of paper caught my eye. I scooped it up and stood in the doorway of the bathroom, waiting for my partner to acknowledge me.

"What did you find?"

"The receipt from the gas station for the drinks Alayna bought." It was all there: the gas station logo, the correct time stamp, and charges for four beverages. "She left this like Gretel leaving breadcrumbs. We need Cole's team down here to process this room."

"That took guts and more than a little bit of faith someone would find it. Seems like a stretch to say she hid it intentionally. Maybe he lost track of it."

"He took the bathroom garbage with him, Bry. This was her. It was her only way to say *I was here*. This was her bit of hope."

Cole's team spent roughly two hours at the Sweet Dreams Motel, much to the chagrin of the Fosberg twins. Esther and Edna were quite vocal about the problems such a heavy police presence would have on their reputation for being discreet. Cole apologized lightheartedly and tried to appease them by promising the motel wouldn't be mentioned in any news reports. Garbage cans outside were emptied; the bedding was removed and bagged, as were the still-damp towels from the bathroom.

Cole brought his sketch artist to the scene—the same artist who had created a composite of Phoenix with Angie Reynolds—and he had more success with the second attempt. It didn't take long for Esther to describe the man she said had paid cash for two nights and checked out with Alayna Keller waiting in his car. The new composite depicted a smiling man with wide-set eyes and dark, short hair. He didn't necessarily resemble Phoenix now, but I wasn't convinced the generic sketch was going to help us narrow down our search.

"That's exactly why you need to make up with Nicky," my partner said as we pulled away from the motel behind Cole's crew.

"Why?"

"So that thirty years from now you're not running a hooker motel with Jamie and missing all your teeth." Bryan laughed when I punched him playfully in the arm. "I'm just sayin'! You should reconsider marrying him."

* * *

Cole called for a meeting in the fishbowl after our search of the Sweet Dreams, and Bryan and I gathered around the table with Eric to wait for him. Phoenix was noticeably absent. When Cole finally joined us twenty minutes late for his own meeting, he tossed a small stack of papers in the middle of the table and took a seat.

"I spent the last hour getting my ass shredded by everyone higher up than me in this office and yours." That Cole managed to say it with a smile made me think he'd enjoyed at least part of the confrontation. "I'm going to be doing another press conference later today, and there is still debate going because I'm dead set against it, but we may be showing the gas station footage. We also have the new timeline that Cassidy discovered for our first victim." Cole waved his hand in my direction like a band conductor.

"The apple ring we found with Dana Mayhew originally belonged to our first victim, Sarah Goodall," I said. "It was a gift from her mother, and she lost it last year during a pub crawl with friends on Halloween. So we can assume he was watching her from Halloween until the seventh of December."

"With as fast as he escalated, he had to be watching more than one of them at a time," Phoenix added.

"What's with these?" Bryan grabbed the stack of papers Cole had brought with him.

"Those are your new schedules going forward. The ones in charge want to say this is a 24/7 operation and mean it, but we can't run all of you into the ground. This means we're going to start a rotating night shift with a core group of teams working the goddess cases and nothing else."

After scanning the schedule, Bryan dropped his head back with a groan. "Looks like we switch to nights next weekend," he said to me. "Ana is going to kill me."

"Sorry." Cole was sincere. "We've been ordered to do more and use less, so we're cutting back on staffing as well. We'll have our original crew here, alternating with a crew made up of guys from your office that Sam Tennyson is going to lead. We'll rotate off nights in a few weeks and switch with that group. The only way out of the shift work is to ask to be let off the case. There won't be any repercussions for anyone who wants out."

Bryan shook his head and answered for the three of us at the table. "We'll make it work."

A night shift wasn't going to make it any easier to work on things with Nicky, who so far was still refusing to talk to me, although I was trying to get him to agree to coffee. It would also leave me at home more often with my new roommate, who was working afternoons at a bakery and striking out in her attempts at finding a different living arrangement.

* * *

I had my nose in my phone, responding to a message from Lieutenant Miller regarding David Gentry. She'd reviewed my earlier message regarding his lack of anything that made him suspicious and had added him to the list of suspects Gabe was going to be handling. I was deflated by the message; being removed from part of a case because of my own error was a hard pill to swallow. I stepped into the elevator alone, and then Phoenix grabbed the door and jumped inside.

"Glad I caught up to you," he said, adjusting the strap of his messenger bag on his shoulder. "We've cleared out most of those files you gave me to check on, but we've been going so hard I haven't had a chance to talk to you about the last one."

"Oh, yeah, I kind of thought we'd cleared them," I fibbed, afraid I knew which case he wanted to talk about. I'd known when I did it that throwing in a request for what information the FBI might have on the murder of Jenna Sutton was risky.

The side glance I got from Phoenix was a clear indication he didn't believe me, but I kept a stone face. He chuckled quietly and followed me out of the elevator, through the main doors, and unexpectedly to my parking space in the parking structure. "I'm going to be straight with you, Cas; one of those cases would have raised some flags if I ran it, and then Cole would want to check in with me and check in with you, and I figured neither of us needed that right now, but I wanted to let you know."

I could feel the heat spread from my neck to the tips of my ears. I dropped my own bag on the hood of my car, scrambling for a response that wasn't going to sound like I had done . . . exactly what he thought I'd done. "What kind of flag would be put on a cold case?" I deflected.

He shrugged, an inquisitive crease in the corner of his blue eyes. "All right, not so much an official flag as an internal flag that goes off when I'm about to do something that is going to get attention. It comes from experience. I know about the Jenna Sutton case. I've known since the first undercover thing I did with you guys. It was part of my own research on who I was working with."

I put both hands to my forehead and smoothed back my hair with an exhale. "What does that even mean? Are you telling me the FBI runs background checks before working with the PD?"

"No." He offered a sly smile and a bit of a laugh. "It's nothing official, ever. When I'm undercover, I just like to know who I'm dealing with, and I asked around. Your partner told me about your connection to Jenna way back when." He shifted his stance and relaxed his shoulders, trying to ease my discomfort. "Was there something that came up in these cases that felt connected?"

Shaking my head, I trained my gaze on the toes of my shoes. I could keep it simple, I could lie, but instead, when I started speaking, I told Phoenix my secrets. "No, nothing in Jenna's case matches the goddesses. But . . ." I ground the toe of my shoe into the concrete, delaying what I was going to say next. "Someone recently mailed me some things, things I think might have been Jenna's."

My admission caught his attention and he stiffened, stuffing both hands in the front pocket of his black-and-red motorcycle jacket. "Recently, in line with this case?"

"I thought at first, maybe. I got the first one . . ."

"Hold up, first one? You've received multiples?"

I bit the inside of my cheeks and nodded. I could feel the heat at the back of my ears, immediately questioning my decision to loop him all the way in. "Three. I got the first one the night we responded to Dana Mayhew's murder, but it was actually left a few days earlier at my parents' house. I don't think it's related to what we're working on, but I think the person sending it to me knows what happened to Jenna."

"Cas, have you turned any of this over to your side yet?" He had a familiar tone to his question, much like how Bryan sounded whenever he thought I was making things harder for myself.

"Not yet, but listen, whoever is sending these things wants me to figure this out, and I need the chance to do it. If I give it over . . ." I couldn't finish the thought out loud. Phoenix turned his back on me for a split second, then back.

"Do you have any suspects in mind?"

"None."

He nodded a few times, choosing his words carefully. "I know people think otherwise, but I'm not out here getting away with as much as people think I do. I might push things, but Cole keeps me around for a reason. I'll give you time for now, until we can catch our breath again, *but* if anything else happens, if you think you've made a break, then you have to say something. Don't go rogue on this."

I waited until Phoenix pulled out of the parking garage on his black-on-black motorcycle before I pulled out into traffic. My chest was tight, and my hands trembled on my steering wheel. My head was spinning, trying to understand my own motivations in sharing all my secrets. Secrets I hadn't shared with my partner, my boyfriend, or my twin. Even though they all thought they knew where I was with Jenna's case, it was Phoenix calling me out on it that got me to break. I knew he'd give me the chance to figure it out, but he made it clear I was running out of time.

Adjusting

A wave of guilt crashed over him as he stared at her sitting stiffly at the end of the couch. Her bare legs were tucked underneath her, her arms folded tightly across her chest. She was not warming up to him as much as he'd hoped, but she had at least stopped with the tears. The bruises certainly hadn't started the week off right, but he'd warned her. That was what he told himself now as they watched TV together in tense silence. He had warned her plenty. What could she possibly expect if she continued to fight him?

He'd dreaded Monday morning's arrival, and getting her to her dayroom had proved as difficult as he feared. It was cold out that early in the morning, so he'd allowed her to dress in the yoga pants and purple fleece he'd taken from Aphrodite, as well as a pair of thick wool socks. Her shape was different, making the fleece top not as snug as he'd expected, but she made do.

He realized his error as soon as they stepped out of the main house. Without her nakedness to keep her vulnerable in the elements, and with the hiking socks providing enough protection to make her brave, she broke free and took off down the gravel driveway as soon as they stepped off the back porch. But he was bigger and stronger and faster than she was, and it didn't take much to catch up to her.

The gravel scraped up her hands and knees, tearing a hole in the thin fabric of the stretchy pants. His anger resulted in an additional dark bruise under her left eye. He hated seeing her like this, bruised and sullen. He wanted her to be sunny and feisty. He wanted her to understand what he was trying to do for her. Instead, she'd forced him to return her to the house for the chains. He'd intended to leave her free in the day cell, but she forced him to leave her without enough slack to even get off the cot. He was not going to risk having her rush him when he came to collect her after work. She would have to earn his trust back, he explained.

She'd lost her urge to fight when he refused to give her clothes on their second morning at the safe house. He made her make the walk naked, and her nakedness took away her bravery. Now they sat—the silence interrupted only by the laugh track for a show neither watched—and she refused to look at him. His gut told him she'd picked up on his frame of mind during dinner. He guessed that was partly to blame for why she was folded up so tight.

He couldn't stop his heart, though, and his heart wanted certain things. She was his, he loved her, and he was going to make her see that. He had the rest of his collection safe in its hiding place. His beauties who had given in to their fate nestled safely away for him forever. All except Eos. He hadn't been prepared for her. Eos had tried to change the rules of the game, and he should have known to be more careful in dealing with someone known to be so cunning.

Maybe it was the Fates that had made him pivot in the greenhouse. They'd revealed the true identity of the beauty hiding there in plain sight for all the world to see. No one was paying attention to her, though. No one worthy of her, at least. Lesser players had missed it, but not him. With her milky complexion and thick chestnut hair, he knew who he had found. His redemption. He had her now, his Persephone. He would make her see the truth, but if he couldn't, there were still more out there. His game would continue.

15

"You should all have an email about two guys they didn't get a chance to look into today that Sam thinks need to be a priority. We also have an update about someone Cassidy raised concerns about." Cole started our first night shift with a surprise I wasn't prepared for. "Gabe Hutchins has been digging into a professor that was spoken to early on in the investigation. He's been cleared of any involvement in our murders or the kidnapping, but as expected, he was the one who leaked early info to the reporter with channel seven. Guy's going through a divorce and thought he could make some money."

"So, that's it, David Gentry is off the list?" The news was a rush of relief.

"Yes, we're clearing the good professor. The guys on the priority list you've got need your full attention tonight."

I rooted through my email to find the suspect files from Sam. A local man with a long rap sheet had piqued the interest of at least one anonymous caller, who thought he deserved a look.

"Do you consume anything else?" Cole teased as I stirred sugar and powdered creamer into my first refill of coffee.

"It's like oxygen to me. I blame my mother."

"I thought people turned to alcohol because of their mothers."

"Off duty there's a red wine habit I also share with my siblings," I laughed. "My mom starts and ends every day with coffee. It's always brewing at her house, so I blame her. She blames her Swedish genes."

"How do you sleep?"

I shrugged. "That's what the red wine is for."

Thirty minutes later I'd exhausted my computer search on the suspect suggested by Sam. The man—Michael Gold—had a criminal background that included voyeurism and lewdness charges, and his offenses spanned years.

His age and most recent mug shot from a year ago showed a thirty-six-year-old man who vaguely resembled the suspect sketch we'd gathered from the Forsberg twins. His state criminal file showed Michael Gold had been a participant in the parole system until nine months ago. He'd been released last summer, five months before the murder of Sarah Goodall. I decided to reach out to the Adult Probation and Parole officer who had been stuck with his file all three times to see what information we could get on our latest suspect.

"Anything good?" Bryan asked.

"This guy Sam left for us did a few stints as a parolee," I said as I finished off my email to the probation officer, Anthony Nguyen.

"Is he still part of the system?"

I shook my head. "Released for the third time in August last year. This is his last mug shot." I flipped my laptop around so Bryan could study the image, and Phoenix rolled closer for his own look. Both guys squinted through their examination of my glowing screen.

"Similar," Bryan agreed. "But our sketch is similar to about one-third of the male population."

I was in the middle of agreeing when my cell lit up with a number I didn't recognize.

"I'm looking for Detective Cantwell." A husky voice came over the line.

"I'm Detective Cantwell."

"Hey, this is Anthony Nguyen with APP. You just sent me an email."

"I didn't expect to hear from you this soon."

"I figured if you're asking about Gold, there must be a reason, and it's probably not for a jaywalking case."

"No, it's not jaywalking. We're working on the kidnapping of a nineteen-year-old and five additional murders."

"Shit." Nguyen let a heavy sigh come through the line, and I guessed he was regretting having checked his email this late after all. "I watch the news; I know what case you're working. Where are you guys?"

"We're at the FBI office right now, but we can come to you if that's easier at this hour," I offered. "You understand why we want to rush this."

"I told them last time not to release the sick motherfucker... Uh, sorry. Truth is he's twisted, Detective. Sick and twisted. If you want to come to me, I can tell you what I can about Michael Gold."

"Lovely. We'll be to you within the hour, if that works for you."

"I'll meet you there."

I hung up and shoved Bryan's chair with excitement. This was a real possible lead. "We need to go down to his office at the county building. There might actually be something with this one."

* * *

Bryan, Phoenix, and I sat in Anthony Nguyen's cluttered office, waiting for his aged desktop computer to come to life. The overwhelming smell of tobacco suggested Anthony wasn't a staunch believer in the building's no-smoking policy. He was a gray-haired, compact man, with thick shoulders and heavy lines around his dark eyes. He put out three manila file pockets—each jammed to capacity—and started his introduction of Michael Gold.

"He never missed a check-in," Anthony explained. "His parents and an older sister constantly vouched for him. Between them, he always had a stable address to use, and he was smart enough to stay there for as long as he was being checked on. The SOB is smart too. He never had a problem getting a job, usually with daddy's help." He paused to take a sip off a water bottle. "Even with all their help, he was still one of the cases that scared me most."

"What stood out that couldn't keep him in the system?" Phoenix asked.

"Like I told Detective Cantwell, Gold is twisted. There's something way off with how he thinks, particularly about women, and I'm not surprised that someone would call him in as a possible on this after what I've learned tonight about your case. I suggested at least extended monitoring before his last release, but the court cut him loose."

I flipped through a case report from the most recent file. "What was he doing the last time you were assigned to him?"

"He started a job at a headhunter office his dad's friend runs. He was hired to do simple administrative work, though he bragged to me about moving up to work with the clients. I won't deny it either—he can be charming as hell, and he doesn't look like Shrek. You've seen his pictures. He cleans himself up, puts on some expensive clothes from his parents, and no one would ever guess he's a perv."

"A new Bundy?" I asked.

Nguyen shook his head. "He's never been nailed for anything violent, but I wouldn't be surprised if he was your guy, I'll say that."

"Was he grabbed for flashing his man bits each time?" Bryan asked.

"That was for the first two, and I had him for a few months for each. The second time they added thirty days in jail, then six months with me. The last time, though, he switched things up. They caught him peeping in an apartment complex, and he'd pocketed some undies. They were sure he'd gotten into some of the units, but no one could prove it, so they couldn't charge it. His girlfriend was always there to alibi him too."

"He has a girlfriend?" I exclaimed.

"He's been off and on with her before, during, and after her marriage. I only met her once, and I can tell you she isn't stable either. Her name is Dawn Westinghouse. Her info is in the second and third files: attractive, thin, dark hair, and absolutely loony. He never lived with her because she has a tenacious ex-husband who kept him from being allowed around their two kids. I always figured it had more to do with spite than protecting his daughters, though. Ms. Westinghouse seems to go for dirtbags."

Phoenix shook his head. "And I'm single."

Anthony laughed. "Dawn fought tooth and nail for him this last time, trying to keep him out of jail. She claimed all along the panties were hers and that he always kept a pair with him as some sort of kink. She didn't care that no one believed her or that they obviously were not her size. No one at the complex he was caught at claimed them either, so they couldn't prove anything other than the peeping. They sentenced him to a hundred and eighty days in jail and then another six months with me. That ended last August, and I haven't seen or heard from him since."

"Did they ever consider that he'd picked up his trophies from a different location?" I asked.

"Oh yeah, they checked other complexes but still couldn't prove anything. They pleaded him out on another voyeurism charge, then passed him back to me, like we were going to fix it. I dreaded having to sit down with him more than any other parolee I've had. He liked trying to shock me, and honestly, I think he's done things we have no idea of yet. Like I said, he's clever as shit, so it's going to take a long time to grab him up for anything that will put him away for the time he deserves. Do you guys have anything besides the phone tip that led you to me?"

I closed the file in front of me with a heavy exhale. "We didn't even get a name from the person calling him in. He resembles one of our sketches, but then again, Phoenix resembles the other sketch. Do you know what kind of car he drives or if he runs the city trails?"

"Running doesn't seem like his scene. He was driving a white four-door Lincoln when he was with me last. Bought it off his dad."

Bryan smacked the desk with both hands, sloshing droplets of water from Nguyen's water bottle onto the paper files. "That's it! We know the guy who took Alayna Keller was in a white four-door, but no one had a better description. We need to start tracking this guy down."

"I hope you guys nail him for something good this time around," Nguyen said with a toothy smile. "It couldn't happen to a more deserving guy."

By the time I left the office in the early morning, there was a formulated plan to track and observe Michael Gold. Cole stayed behind to share our new details with the morning side of our investigative crew. I pulled into my driveway and stared disbelievingly at my brother sipping coffee on my porch. Dressed in black track pants and a gray Mariners hoodie, he was not in his normal off-to-work attire. I guessed he was not on his way to the office, which was nowhere near my house, either. I skipped pulling into the garage and greeted Jamie at the front door.

"What's this all about?" I asked, standing over him.

"I brought you breakfast." He put his coffee down between his feet and pulled the sack open to reveal a selection of doughnuts inside.

"Sorry. A girl can't help but be suspicious when she finds her brother on her porch at seven thirty in the morning."

"I brought you doughnuts."

"I'm even questioning the doughnuts." I sat myself next to him, shivering at the contact with the cold concrete steps and my backside.

"I was working out and figured I would come over and say hi. I know what you're going to be like working nights."

"And?"

Jamie flashed a sly, familiar smile. "Can't that be it?"

"Not with you."

"Stephanie called me last night," he breathed out in a rush. I always bristled at the mention of The Ex who had stayed part of Nicky's life even after their divorce, calling him when she needed things like small loans and big furniture moved. "Nicky fired two people from his kitchen in the last week, and people at the restaurant are freaking out. She wants me to talk to him."

"Is staff management part of your responsibilities as investors in that place?"

"No. We're supposed to hang out and watch it make money. One of the servers knows Steph and sent her an email asking for help. At least one of the waitresses is planning on quitting because his recent tirades are leaving staff members in tears. Brandon's doing his best to manage the place around Nicky, but he's not making any headway against him."

"I'm not following why all of this means you bring me doughnuts."

"He isn't working out anymore, and he's at the restaurant 24/7, so I haven't seen him. I'm worried about where his head is, and Stephanie is panicking that we're going to end up with a financial stake in a restaurant with no one to run it if he keeps going."

"And I'm supposed to care about her?" I gave a half-hearted chuckle and pulled the only maple doughnut from the bag. "He stopped returning my calls, and you told me to leave him be for now, so that's what I've done."

"I might have given you bad advice," my brother admitted.

"I don't think so. I didn't think he would stay this angry, but he's making a bigger deal out of a misunderstanding than I thought he would. I have too much else going on to keep worrying about him."

"You're just going to move on?" Jamie threw his hands up, and I caught a glimpse of the familiar red-and-white soft pack in the front pocket of his hoodie. He smacked my hand away when I reached for the cigarettes. "Hands off. This is not about me. Tell me where you really are with this. Where is *your* head?"

I didn't know what to say. Fighting wasn't abnormal for Nicky and me. We'd had our fair share of clashes through our relationship. He'd stay mad for a night, maybe a weekend, and then we'd reconcile over food and a movie, with neither of us going as far as to give an apology. His reaction to the proposal was different than anything else he'd thrown at me before, and I didn't know how to react. "I don't know where I am. There isn't anything I haven't already said to him, and it's not enough. There isn't anything I can do until Nicky decides to forgive me, but I can't keep begging for that. You do know I've been into it up to my eyeballs, right?"

Jamie took a long swallow of his coffee. He pulled the lid off the paper cup, stuffed the half pack of Marlboros into what remained, then replaced the lid and handed it off to me. "I do know what you're dealing with. The twin senses have been active, and Meghan did tell me you've been having nightmares lately. I know you have a lot going on, but I'm afraid you're giving up on him. I'm flying to LA tonight for a pitch in the morning, but I'll only be there for two days. Keep me posted if anything changes, okay?" Jamie put an arm around my shoulders and kissed the top of my head.

"You'll be the first to hear if he starts talking to me again." I gave my brother a weak attempt at a smile. "Don't hold your breath, though."

The early-morning ambush left me too unsettled for sleep, and finishing off a second doughnut gave me a mild morning sugar rush. I started a desperately needed load of laundry, then planted myself on the couch to surf the TV. The front door woke me briefly—Meghan coming or going; I wasn't awake enough to be sure. I pulled one of the blankets I kept folded at the end of the couch over my head and went back to sleep.

The next time I opened my eyes, the house was dark and quiet. I blinked wildly, focusing on the fact that it was my phone ringing and not my alarm that woke me. "Hello?" I tried to sound convincingly awake.

"Are you off?" The voice was one I hadn't heard for a while and wasn't expecting.

"Um, I'm working nights for a bit, so I haven't gone in yet. Is everything all right?"

"Look, you need to back off using Jamie to get to me," Nicky said.

"I'm not," I snapped sharply. I was fully awake now.

"He's been calling me all day. I told you I need time."

"And I told you he's not calling for me."

"Why else would he call me seven times in the middle of the afternoon and not leave a message?" He was accusatory now. The angry Nicky everyone was being introduced to making an appearance for me.

"Because your ex-wife called and asked him to check in with you about people you've fired and the rest of your staff that want to quit. He hasn't seen you for a bit, so calling would be his next best option. People do that," I blurted out in one breath. I sat up on the couch and rubbed my eyes. "This stupid tantrum you're throwing has been felt by more than just me, so if someone calls you out on it, it's not because I asked them to."

"I fired people who needed it, that's all. I'm working some things out, but it doesn't have anything to do with what's going on at Fleur, and it is none of Stephanie's business," Nicky fired back. "I'm fine."

"I'll be sure to tell her that." My comment was greeted by a cold silence, and I realized that Nicky had hung up. I fought the urge to throw my phone or kick something or call him back so I could hang up on him. I started to call Jamie but changed my mind, figuring this was not an update he needed to hear from me. If Nicky was annoyed that Jamie was calling, Nicky could pick up the phone and tell him himself.

I padded through the dark to my kitchen, wearing Nicky's concert tee and a pair of cutoff sweats. With a start, I came face-to-face with a stranger standing in the middle of my kitchen. I let out a scream, grabbed the half-naked guy wearing only a pair of hip-hugging boxer briefs and a ponytail, twisted his arm behind his back, and threw him face down on the floor.

"Who the hell are you?" I yelled, straddling his back and yanking his arm toward his shoulder.

"Oh, god, please don't shoot me!" the stranger shrieked. I could hear my sister shouting the same plea from the hall. She flipped on the kitchen lights, breathless.

"Please don't hurt him!" Meghan waved her hands over her head, her expression one of pure embarrassment. "I'm sorry, Cas. This is my yoga instructor, Sebastian."

"Nice to meet you," the young man still face down on my kitchen floor stammered.

I relaxed my grip a little, but I didn't let him up. "Do you have your own place to live, Sebastian?"

"Uh, yes. I rent a place above the yoga studio," he said.

"That's all I need to know." I let go of his arm and stood up, leaving the young man hyperventilating on the tile floor. "Oh, and the ice cream is off-limits." Not wanting to know anything else about my sister's new friend, I made my way to my bedroom and locked myself in. I had three hours left to sleep before starting our night shift watching Michael Gold.

16

Search warrants are exceedingly hard to pull off discreetly in busy apartment complexes where all the doors are inside. There was nothing stealthy as we made our way past the leasing office to the elevators in Michael Gold's building. My stomach was in knots, creating enough adrenaline that my body didn't focus on my continued lack of sleep.

Cole and Sam had worked some day-side magic after two days of surveillance and investigation to secure various search warrants. I wasn't sure who'd called in what favors, but we'd gained access to a storage unit as well as Gold's bank accounts twenty-four hours after we started looking into him. The storage locker was a bust, but our suspect's spending got us close enough to convince someone up high we needed to bring him in. Gold's infamy helped.

Our afternoon surveillance said that Gold was home, but after several announcements to get him to open the door, we were forced to go in the hard way. Once we were inside, it was frustratingly obvious the apartment was empty. The emptiness sent Cole into the first legitimate rage I'd witnessed from him since we'd started on the case together.

"Tennyson said they've been sitting on this place all day, and the last report was he'd pulled into the parking garage and gone inside. Where the hell did he go?"

"Not far if his car is still here. We need to wait him out," I said as we assembled inside the doorway. A quick look around the living room and it was clear we were in the home of a stereotypical single man. The front room furnishings consisted of a glass coffee table set in front of a black leather couch and one of the biggest wall-mounted flat-screens I'd ever seen. There were two black media towers on either side of the TV, both loaded with DVDs with campy porn titles I wasn't interested in cataloging.

I followed Bryan and Phoenix down the hall to a small bathroom with no sign of life. A clear plastic shower curtain hung from the rod, and a pile of plain white towels lay on the floor. Next to the bathroom was the main bedroom. A king-size bed with a solid blue duvet sat oddly in the middle of the floor. I pulled the closet open to reveal a few hanging dress shirts along with a tie organizer full of silk ties, all in muted colors, all expensive.

The final door in the hallway was closed but not locked. Without taking much pause, Phoenix opened it and walked through in one fluid motion, with Bryan close behind.

"Ah, shit, don't come in here, Cas," Bryan said, half a second too late.

I rounded the corner and stopped with a screech. Bryan pushed me out of the room, and I planted my butt against the wall with my hands on my knees and my head down. My screeching brought Cole running, and I tried to warn him not to go in. He didn't listen.

"What the hell is that?" I screamed, taking in short angry breaths. Bryan and Phoenix were laughing at my drama on the other side of the wall, but I was too freaked out to care about who was looking.

"There has to be at least a hundred of these suckers in here," Bryan answered. The image of all the glass boxes filled with spiders that lined each wall, floor to ceiling, was still bright behind my eyelids. I knew my partner's estimate was low. Way low.

"Is that a mattress in there?" I asked from my still-bent position.

"Yep," Phoenix shouted back. "And there are some framed photos in here to show its purpose. That parole officer wasn't kidding when he said this guy is twisted."

"Can you handle photos?" Bryan tried to hide his grin, giving away how much fun he was having at my expense. I held out my hand for the small stack of four-by-six glossies, not eager to look through them.

"What the hell?" The stack was shot after shot of naked women, a dark pillowcase over their heads, hands and feet tied, and spiders. Lots of spiders. Most of them appeared to be different types of tarantulas. A few shots were of the women with one or two of the eight-legged monsters strategically placed, while in others they were covered in what I could only guess totaled several dozen. The final shot showcased an exceptionally large creature posed in the center of a bright-pink lotus tattoo on a bare hip. I shivered hard and handed the stack over to Cole.

Bryan laughed again. "I'm guessing this is the girlfriend Nguyen was talking about. Most of the framed photos in there include that tattoo. I bet we could ask the ex-husband to identify it."

"That would be an awesomely awkward conversation." Phoenix snorted from inside the room of horror.

"Why would you do this?" My skin was still crawling, and I spastically brushed the sensation off my arms with a shiver.

"Why are you asking me? None of this goes on in my fantasy world." Bryan was still grinning.

Phoenix stepped out of the room, shaking his head. "I hate to tell you, but there are more of the big ones in the closet, along with some fancy camera equipment and some more—much more—graphic photos."

"I'll take your word for it."

"Does this fit?" Cole asked no one in particular. "I don't know what this is, but I don't know if it fits."

"It fits," I insisted. "Athena created spiders. And I'm guessing this guy knows exactly where to buy crickets. We need to talk to him."

"We need to figure out where the hell he went first," Cole said, frustrated by the surveillance snafu.

"You guys can sit around here and wait for him to come back if you want, but I'm not spending any more time with the creepy-crawlies." I left the lot of them in the apartment and headed back to the lobby to wait. As the shiny chrome doors of the elevator slid open, I found myself instead face-to-face, and alone, with Michael Gold. He registered my recognition, and a look of panic flashed in his eyes. I knew what he was thinking.

"Police!" I shouted, fumbling for the badge that was hanging on my usual chain around my neck. "Don't do it, Gold."

Before I could give any more orders or grab hold of him, Gold bolted for the main doors. I spat out a few choice words as I started after him and shouted details to anyone who wanted to listen on the other end of my radio. My partner's voice came back at once.

"Do not take him alone," Bryan ordered.

I could have backed off. I could have kept sight without approaching, especially given the lack of speed Gold was moving with, but I set out to catch up. My team would be behind me soon enough. I needed to get Gold into an interrogation room. I sprinted down the sidewalk, keeping my eyes on Gold, who was running like someone scared and out of shape. Over my radio, I continued to give new coordinates as Gold crossed the street, not listening to the orders from Bryan that came back to me, ordering me to fall back.

The space between me and the object of my pursuit shrank to a long arm's length, so I took advantage, reached out for the hood of his jacket, and yanked backward. The move didn't have the results I was hoping for. Gold turned on me and stopped, which I hadn't seen coming. I'd expected him to go down.

"You wanna play, sweetheart?" he snarled, and took a swing, and this time it was exactly what I expected. I caught his wrist and pulled, using his own momentum against him. I twisted him into a wrist lock, and he went down, unfortunately taking me with him. Still on my adrenaline high, I scrambled to get my knee between his shoulders and my cuffs from my belt before he could right himself.

"Don't do anything to ruin my day, please," I hissed as he tried to buck against me, screaming overdramatically about pain. I tightened my grip on his little finger and keyed my radio to give my final location, then waited patiently for my backup to arrive.

* * *

"You can't enter a room full of spiders, but you'll take on a big guy alone? I don't get you." Phoenix was laughing as we climbed into the elevator at FBI headquarters.

"You should have waited." Bryan was fuming behind me.

Phoenix nudged me playfully with his elbow. "You did good," he whispered, a smile in his fierce blue eyes.

"It's not an argument of whether or not Cassidy's good." Bryan's voice rumbled with disapproval. "She's good enough to know she doesn't need to take on lunatics on her own to prove anything."

I shot a warning glance to my overprotective partner, who was in annoying-big-brother mode since catching up to me and our suspect. "Bry, I'm all right. I knew I could handle him."

"Your knee is bleeding through your pants," Bryan returned.

Even with the bloody knee, I was all right, and I knew my partner would get over my perceived recklessness before we signed out for the night. One thing he didn't do was hold grudges. I also knew that Bryan's response had more to do with the eight-inch hunting knife I hadn't known was under Michael Gold's jacket than it did with my hurt knee.

When we reached our floor, I broke from the others to clean myself up and change my torn pants. I told Cole I wanted in on the interview with the spider herder. I was determined to see this thread of our investigation through to the end.

"How's the knee?" Cole asked as we prepared for our sit-down with Gold.

"Not as bad as Bryan made it out to be," I fibbed. The sting of the scraped flesh against the bandages was irritating as I kept up with Cole's stride.

We made our way to their bank of interrogation rooms that were wired for video and sound. "Eric processed him in and read him Miranda. He hasn't requested a lawyer yet, so we're going to start. Eric will monitor things on the outside."

On the other side of the gray metal door, Michael Gold was seated at a rectangular metal table, his hands cuffed in front and secured to the tabletop. He'd relaxed since first being arrested and gave us the same look you would a door-to-door salesman. Not interested.

"Hello, Mr. Gold." Cole took a seat directly across from our suspect. I sat down next to Cole with stiff shoulders and images of spiders in my head.

"Agent. Mrs. Agent."

"I'm Special Agent MacAllan, and this is Detective Cantwell with Tacoma PD."

"Yes, the detective and I have met." His voice dripped with sarcasm.

"We've been talking with Anthony Nguyen about you," Cole said.

Gold shook his head with a look of amusement. "Mr. Nguyen is not a fan of mine."

"Do you have many of those?"

"More than you want to know, sweetheart."

"We need to know where you were week before last," Cole continued. "Wednesday, right before five PM?"

"I'm usually at work until then, so I would have to say I was at work, sir."

"We've checked with your employer," I said. "It doesn't seem anyone can say one way or another if you were really there, so tell us why you visited Blissful Blooms floral shop."

"You've been through my place. Do you take me as the type of guy who buys flowers?"

"We don't think you were there for the flowers. You were there for Alayna. Where is she?" Cole pushed.

"I'm sorry, I don't know anyone named Alayna."

"You might call her something else," I said. "Maybe . . . Persephone?"

"I know I'm disappointing you right now, Detective. I've worked with a Lana a few times, and I've spent some time with an Annie, but never an Alayna. I would remember an Alayna, and I would definitely remember a Persephone."

I shook my head, fighting against the repulsion that was rolling through me as a shudder. "What about Athena, then?" I asked, curious to see if the connection to his spiders would get something out of him.

Michael Gold laughed, and the sound sent a shiver through me. "Twisted—that's the way Mr. Nguyen described me, right? It's his favorite adjective for me, and he's not wrong either. I am twisted. What I'm not, though, is crazy, and I don't like prison. I watch the news, and I'm not interested in a vanilla girl that's going to land me in an eight-by-eight cell I have to share with some dumb fuck who misses his mommy. It was very unenjoyable last time."

"Then tell us where you were Wednesday before last at five PM," Cole repeated. His patience had been thin before we started and was hanging by threads now.

"At work. I already answered that one, so let's move on. What else have you got?"

What we had was bank records. Bank records that showed Michael Gold had been much closer to the flower shop in the days before Alayna's kidnapping than he was being honest about. Bank records that a judge had ruled were enough to get us into his house and his car.

Cole's voice was tight as he laid it out for our suspect. "We've got the ATM records. You were across the street from the flower shop that Monday, two days before the kidnapping. We know you know the shop. We know you were there."

"You've really been looking into me for this? I'm offended." Gold gave a Cheshire grin. "I took cash out about two weeks ago, when the internet connection at the pet store was down. They could only take cash, and they had some furry little friends I wanted to bring home to play with. Could it be that Eddie's Exotic Emporium is close to your flower shop? I would like to call my lawyer about now."

"The Exotic Emporium? Do they sell crickets there? I'm guessing you need those for your creepy-crawlies. Is that what you needed the cash for?"

He maintained his smile. "Eddie's is where I went to look at a new Gooty sapphire. They're extremely hard to find, and I absolutely needed one. For crickets, I don't need to go to Eddie's when I've got a Petco right across the street. Gotta keep the little chirpers alive, ya know. And really, I've answered more questions than you deserved, so again, I want my lawyer."

"We'll be watching you," Cole warned. "You do anything I can pull you in for, I will."

"You find me that intriguing, Special Agent MacAllan?" Gold taunted.

"I find you disturbing."

"You don't need to worry about me. My Dawny, she showed me what is out there in the world. All the women I can connect to with the help of the World Wide Web. Women who let me do whatever my twisted little heart desires to satisfy their own twisted little needs. I get what I want, and I never have to worry about prison. So watch me for as long as you need. Learn a few things from me while you're at it. You might get pretty things like this one to follow you around more." He threw his head in my direction.

Cole clenched his jaw for a beat, then let it go. "I don't care if it's for dropping a gum wrapper on the sidewalk.

Every time we have something that we can look at you for, I will have you in this room."

"I look forward to our next meeting, then, Detective." Gold smirked at me with a wink, and I stuffed down the cold shiver that made the hair on the back of my neck stand. "I'll take my lawyer now, thanks."

We left Michael Gold chained to the table for someone else to free and headed down the hall in silence. I trailed Cole into the control room, where Eric was waiting for us. There was a small collection of black-and-white monitors that were mostly blank. The middle screen showed Gold, now relaxing with his head on the table.

"He's got an answer for everything," Eric said as Cole took a seat at the narrow desk.

"I know."

"His parole officer is right: This guy is guilty of something, whether we've caught him for it or not," I said. Even though I was no longer sitting in the room with him, the danger vibe was still burning through me, refusing to be ignored.

"We'll nail him for something eventually, but I don't think he's our guy."

"It's been almost two weeks." I sighed. "If he had her, we'd have found her at his apartment. That's his lair. And if he'd killed her, we'd have her, because he wouldn't miss that opportunity to show us what he'd done."

Cole stood with a stretch. "I haven't talked to Ms. Keller for a few days, so I'm going to check in, because this will make the news, and then I'm going home."

"What do you want to do with Gold?" Eric asked.

"Have PD book him with assault on Cassidy; let his daddy's lawyer play with that for now." The defeat in his voice was catching.

Appeasing

He wasn't sure if she was aware of the significance of the day, but he was going to make it special for her nonetheless. He'd stopped for champagne and flowers and planned on lobster for their celebratory dinner. He would have preferred to take her somewhere fancy to celebrate properly, but she wasn't ready to be with the public yet. He didn't know how long it was going to take for that to happen. He was starting to think it would require a change of scenery.

As much as he liked the freedom at his current office and the seclusion of their current home, the chances were too high that she would be recognized. He had been researching the job market and was sure he could find something on the East Coast. Maine seemed like a nice, quiet option, but he wasn't sure he could deal with the cold. His second choice was Puerto Rico. Maybe a life of sunshine and warm beaches would finally bring a smile to her beautiful face.

He pulled into the long gravel drive and unloaded his groceries onto the kitchen counter. He started the preparations for dinner. He set the flowers in the middle of the table and changed his clothes before retrieving her from her dayroom, ditching his khakis and blue polo for black wool pants and a red cashmere sweater.

Last, he took the surprise he'd bought for her and hung it on the back of the bedroom door. He'd never understood the draw of the silk-and-lace nighties that were so popular with women—nothing was sexier than bare skin, after all—but he hoped it would make an impression on her. He wanted to show her he did have a sweeter side. That was the whole point of the evening: to show her he could do regular boyfriend things.

He trekked his way to the outbuilding that held her during the day and down to the farthest corner of the secret basement to her cell. On some days, she greeted him with cold silence, refusing to speak to him or even look at him for the entire evening. Other days she screamed and called him names. When he opened the steel-enforced door, it was clear that today was going to be a silent-treatment day.

He guided her to the bathroom for a shower, waiting for her to acknowledge the nightie hanging on the door, but she ignored the first gift. Her slight annoyed him, but he pushed his anger down. This was going to be their special night, and she was not going to ruin his efforts.

"You need to wear it; I bought it special for tonight." He gritted the words out between clenched teeth. She stared at him blankly. "Do you know what tonight is?"

"One more day I'm not home." She wasn't playing nice.

"It's our anniversary. It's been one month since I freed you."

Tears started, which was not what he'd hoped for when he planned the evening. "Freed me? You are keeping me prisoner here. You didn't free me."

"I did free you. I'm trying to help you find your true self. I want you to recognize that, Persephone." He struggled to keep his voice even. Shouting would ruin the moment he was trying to create. "I bought you flowers."

"Is that supposed to make me forgive you for what you've done?"

"It's to help us celebrate."

"I don't want to celebrate; I want to go home!" She threw the nightgown at him, and he grabbed her wrist tightly to bring a halt to the tantrum.

"Do not spoil this evening," he warned. "I have made an effort to make a nice evening for us, so take your shower and get dressed." He forced the smile back to his lips and turned her toward the shower. When she finished and pulled the white silk-and-lace gown over her head, he led her to her seat in the kitchen. She tensed but didn't fight him when he fastened her to the shortest length of chain so they could talk about his day while he cooked.

He'd picked up dessert from the fancy patisserie that people kept talking about at the office and set the blackberry tart in front of her. He poured champagne and then put the biggest surprise of the night alongside her dessert plate. The ring sparkled in the open box. It was exquisite, and he didn't wait to point out the perfection of the center diamond and show her the certificate of clarity the jeweler had provided.

The round diamond was almost flawless and a full carat and a half in size. Around it were two weaving rows of small rubies. Twelve rubies total. He'd handpicked each stone to make sure they all shared the same rich, red color. Her reaction to the ring was considerably less than he'd imagined. Rather than the giddy excitement over the jewels he'd anticipated, within a matter of seconds she was in hysterics again.

"Why are you crying?" he demanded. "It's beautiful. It's perfect!"

"I don't want it. I want to go home."

"This has to stop. Why do you have to make me angry?"

"Why do you have to keep me here?" she challenged, the hot tears streaming down her pale cheeks.

"I love you. I love you, and you are going to love me."

Her beautiful face twisted into a hideous grimace, and she continued to sob. "I will never love you."

Her words were his breaking point. Before he knew what he was doing, their dessert plates flew, shattering against the wall behind her. He marched her to the bedroom by the wrist in cold silence. "Why can't you see what I'm doing for us?"

It was dark outside when he finally gained control. He struggled to put the lost moments in order in his mind, unsure how much time had passed since she'd pushed his buttons and he'd ended their celebration. The nightgown he'd picked out so carefully was tattered, and his goddess was bruised but sleeping. He was afraid waking her would result in more fighting, so he decided to let her be. He slipped into a pair of flannel lounge pants and a sweatshirt and sulked into the front room, locking the bedroom door as he went out. He needed time to put his head back together before he gave in to urges he'd regret.

17

My brain began a slow ascent into consciousness, and I tried to grab pieces of my memory while registering movement. My movement. Why was I shaking? There was the office, a bath, a glass of wine, and a review of Jenna's case, and now someone was definitely shaking me. I peeled my eyes open and let out an inadequate scream, trying to coordinate my limbs to a sitting position when I realized I was still on my couch. "What the actual hell, Bryan! How did you get in here?"

"You're kidding, right?" My partner laughed and casually flipped through the top binder I'd fallen asleep looking at. "I've had a key to this place since you moved in, remember? Get up, we gotta go."

"Why are you in my house at . . ." I stole a look at my watch. "Why are you in my living room at four thirty in the morning? What if I wasn't on my couch? What if I was naked? What if I wasn't alone?" I shot the questions off one by one as I stacked my binders back into the open tote on the side of my coffee table.

"I would have gone in your room, I've seen you naked, and I'd know if you weren't sleeping alone." Unfazed, he grabbed my cell phone from the end table and tossed it onto the couch before striding across the hall to the kitchen and flipping on lights. "Apparently *someone* forgot to plug her phone in last night, and our calls have been going to voicemail. How much sleep are you getting? I didn't know you were back to studying your books."

I padded after my partner to the kitchen in the fuzzy socks and oversized sweats I'd put on after the end of our shift. "I'm getting as much sleep as the rest of us," I said. "And Meghan spent the night with a friend, so I was just keeping myself busy. Why are you at my house?"

"Cole got a call from Jordan, who is under the impression that he received a text from Alayna." Bryan filled my coffeepot and selected one of the pods I kept for emergencies. "He's on his way to the kid's apartment, and you and I need to meet him there. Unless you want to sit this one out and actually go to bed?"

"No, I'm not sitting anything out."

"Didn't think so; that's why I'm here. Get dressed, I'll make you a coffee to go."

I scrambled to my closet, clumsily wriggled into a pair of jeans, a white sweater, and a simple pair of black Adidas, then headed to the bathroom to brush my hair, my teeth, and swipe on a least a layer of mascara to open my eyes and fool others enough into thinking I was getting enough sleep. I snagged my phone and my charger on my way out of my room. Bryan was waiting for me at the front door with my red travel mug in his hand.

"It's mostly coffee, splash of milk. You're out of creamer."

"What exactly did we get from Jordan that makes this rally-the-troops credible?" I followed him outside in the cold to our unmarked Charger.

"I don't know that we got anything, but at this point Cole's grabbing on to anything we can. It was a text, that's all I know so far."

"Yesterday was the anniversary, Bry. People are cruel. This could be a hoax."

"Well aware," he said, pulling away from the curb. "We're going to focus on Alayna right now, but we're going to talk about those books. There were three bins in there, partner. You might need to bring me in on how much you're looking at."

I held my mug with both hands for the warmth and slumped further into the cold seat. "We can talk about it later."

* * *

"Glad you could make it," Cole said when Bryan and I met up with him in the parking lot of Jordan's apartment.

"Sorry about that. I'm not sure what happened with my phone." I dropped my eyes sheepishly. Cole knocked, and we heard hurried shuffling on the other side of the door.

Jordan was frantic with energy when he opened the door to the three of us. "It's her. I know it's her." We followed him into the small living space of his apartment, and he pushed his cell phone into my hand.

"It's important to stay calm about this, Jordan, not get our hopes up yet," Cole warned.

"No, it's her. She's sending me a code."

I took the phone and checked the open screen. I read the short message, and then a second time out loud. *Please find me. Sorry about the eggs. Don't respond to this.*

"Sorry about the eggs?" Bryan asked.

Jordan nodded enthusiastically. "That's the code! The day she was taken, she tried to make us breakfast before I went to class. She forgot to add oil and fried the eggs right to the bottom of the pan. That's why I know it's her."

"Maybe you mentioned it to someone, or she did?" I asked. Jordan shook his head.

"It was just us here that morning, and she was joking that she couldn't let her mom find out because she was already not sure Alayna was ready to live on her own. We kidded around about it, but it's not something she would have shared with her mom, and that's where she went after I left. She was here, then she went to spend the day with her mom because she hadn't been around."

"And you don't recognize this number?" Cole took the phone from me for further inspection.

"No. My first thought was to call back, but she told me not to, so I didn't."

"That was the right move," I assured him. I called dispatch and requested history from the phone number but struck out. They'd never received any calls from the number we had.

"Jordan, we're going to take this. I want you to stay here; try to go about your day as normal. If this is from Alayna, she took a great amount of risk getting this out, and we don't want to do anything that will put her in more danger. We're going to track this down; we'll find who sent this to you," Cole said.

"It was her. It was Alayna." Jordan surged with excitement and conviction. "She's still alive, so we have to find her."

He gave us his word he would not contact anyone else until we were sure of what we were dealing with. Before we made it back to our cars, Cole called Phoenix and Eric and instructed them to meet us at the office. "I've got something in mind for now, but if it doesn't work, we'll call everyone else in."

* * *

Phoenix made it to the office right behind the three of us. Unshaven, with his shaggy hair and a black San Francisco Giants T-shirt, he looked like he needed an escort to be in the FBI building. Maybe some cuffs.

The buzz created by the possible break had us all vibrating with eagerness and excitement. Bryan started a pot of much-needed coffee, and Cole filled Phoenix in on the details, not waiting for Eric to arrive. "I've requested everything we've got on the number, but I don't want to wait until business hours to jump through hoops to get the details from the cell companies. I've already cleared with the DA's office that this is an *anything goes* operation, so we're going to make it up as we go." Cole slid Jordan's cell across the table to Phoenix. "That's the number."

Phoenix raised an eyebrow. "What do you want me to do with it?"

"I want you to call it," his boss answered. "We can't just sit on our asses while we wait."

He checked his watch and grinned. "You want me to call our possible kidnapper at five forty-five AM and say what? *Can you give me your address so we can come down, guns blazin', and get that girl you kidnapped*?"

"You're the best liar I've got, man. You'll think of something. We need to know who this guy is."

"In my experience, people don't usually start giving up personal information before dawn to strangers over the phone."

"I've heard you get shit out of some of the best. Find a story and go with it; this is all we've got."

Phoenix pointed a finger at all three of us before hitting send. "No laughing at my performance." A few seconds later his fingers flew out for one of the random ballpoint pens in the middle of the table, and he scribbled in the margin of a piece of scratch paper. "It's just going to voicemail." He hung up and flipped the paper up for the rest of us to see: *Tyson Scott, Psy-Comp Product Development Team* was written out in Phoenix's angled print.

"Holy shit," I exclaimed.

"Get on it," Cole ordered, grabbing up his own cell. "Run the name, the company, anything you can get. I'll be right back." The excitement levels in the room rocketed up.

I was the first one to my laptop and started the search into the name Tyson Scott. Entering his name into the database brought up an immediate hit, and the results stopped me cold. "We've got a report in our system regarding a Tyson Scott, age thirty."

My revelation stopped Cole midstride. "What do you have?" He was a rush of curiosity fringed with panic.

"Lakewood PD issued a BOLO for Tyson Scott. He was listed as a missing person by his girlfriend and his mom after he didn't come home from work last month. They updated the case to a homicide three days later. Looks like he was found inside his own vehicle in a parking structure near his home, possible carjacking. The case is open."

My partner rolled closer to scan my screen over my shoulder. "He went missing three nights before Maggie Cannon was murdered. I don't remember seeing this."

Phoenix kicked his feet up on the table and rubbed his eyes. "We've been focused in on female victims—a guy getting carjacked wasn't going to stand out for any of us right now. It's like we're living with tunnel vision."

I continued my search on Tyson Scott and found my way to the company website for Psy-Comp, a gaming technologies company. The home page included graphics of gold and silver medals celebrating their wins at industry conventions. Under the "News" tab was a headline pinned to the sidebar from the year before about taking gold at a tech convention in Las Vegas. The article included a picture of Tyson Scott and four other employees, each holding a trophy that looked like a computer monitor.

All four men were in their early thirties, the first three in graphic T-shirts and jeans. The last man was dressed in a starched, collared shirt and a pair of pressed-linen pants. He had wide-set eyes and dark hair—attractive in a polished-grad-student way—but something was off about him in the photo. He was smiling, but his eyes were empty. He was out of place in his crisp, expensive clothes, and he was proud of it. The tag on the photo identified him as Will Dunham from Psy-Comp Technologies.

As I skimmed the article, puzzle pieces began falling into place, and I tempered the excitement that had my brain buzzing. I was no longer concerned that I'd been caught sleeping on my couch with my murder books, and I was no longer tired from weeks of little to no sleep. Right now, we were one step closer to catching a killer and, if we moved fast enough, rescuing a nineteen-year-old girl. "The guy we talked to after Zac Peters, Olivia's friend's boyfriend, what was his name again?"

"Liam . . . Liam something," Bryan said.

Phoenix urgently snapped his fingers at the other side of the table, jogging the memory loose. "Wakefield."

"Right!" I jumped up from my seat and paced in thought, waiting for the printer to spit out the copy of the photo. "Liam Wakefield said the guy who approached him at the bar to get closer to Olivia said they knew each other from tech conventions. Seems like too much of a coincidence that we'd have a tech guy cause a scene with one victim and then have a tech guy's phone with our kidnap victim. This is it; this is our guy." I put the printed image in the middle of the table and tried to control my excitement.

"Except we've just established he was dead before Alayna was kidnapped," Cole countered.

"No, not Tyson. Liam said he thought the guy that came up to him at the bar said his name was Will or Bill, and they'd met at a tech convention," I said, tapping my finger above the head of the last man in the photo. The guy with the blank eyes wearing pressed-linen pants. "That is Will Dunham. And the article lists the second-place team as being from Octavia Innovations. That's where we interviewed Liam Wakefield; this guy named Will has been in the same circle as Liam, at least to some degree. We need to show the picture to Zac and Liam, see if either of them can identify him."

Cole squeezed the back of his neck, sorting thoughts. "Holy shit. You really might have just found him."

"Talking to Zac right now is probably not our best bet, even if we can find him, so let's start with Liam," my partner suggested.

Cole assigned Phoenix to dig up more information on William Dunham and confirmed he was going to start calling ahead to our DA to make sure we could get warrants if we were successful at tracking down our new suspect. Bryan and I were going to have a second sit-down with

Liam Wakefield. As with the first attempts, he wasn't answering my calls, so Bryan decided to head straight for the home address we had, betting it would still be too early for him to be at the office yet.

Our gamble paid off. Barely. As we pulled to the curb in front of his newly built, craftsman-style home in the middle of a cul-de-sac, Liam Wakefield's garage door opened, and he stepped around to the back of his black Audi with a briefcase and a duffel bag.

"Good morning, Liam." I waved as we crossed over his lawn to the driveway.

Liam tossed both parcels into the open trunk. "Morning. What can I help you with now, Detectives? I was just on my way to work."

"We wanted to ask you to look at a photo and tell us if you know any of the people in it."

"Yeah, sure, I can do that."

I handed him the printout of the convention photo with the participants' names removed, and he flicked it with the fingers of his other hand after a quick glance. "Oh, wow, are you guys working on Tyson's case too?"

"You did know Tyson Scott?" I asked, shooting an anxious look to my partner.

"Yeah, we used to work together until about two years ago, and we'd still get together for drinks after work now and then. He was a really cool guy."

I stepped back with an excited exhale and asked him to tell us if he recognized anyone else in the photo, then held my breath while he studied the image. A slow realization spread across his face, and he looked quickly between me and my partner. "Holy shit."

"Is that a yes?" Bryan was bouncing on his feet.

"This guy. This is the guy that upset Olivia that night." He pointed to the fourth man in the photo, the one in the button-down shirt and pressed slacks. Will Dunham. "That's him. I didn't register it was Tyson he said we both knew. His name is Will, I think. He was one of the Ascendency guys."

"The *Ascendency* guys? Was that some sort of a club?" I asked.

"Ascendency Games was a start-up that failed. I met Tyson after it all went down, but a bunch of them met through some online channels, some of them already worked together, and they started working on a game together. They thought it was going to be their big break, but it kind of fell apart before the launch, and they all walked away from it and moved on. After a while, Ty finished it off and put it online just for fun, and it took off." He stopped talking to look again at the black-and-white photocopy in his hand. "Two of the original guys threatened to sue him, so he settled with them both for some decent money, but it got ugly first."

"And you think that Will Dunham was one of those two guys?" I asked.

"I know he was. I don't know how I didn't recognize him that night." He trailed off for a moment, eyes trained above Bryan's head, lost in his own thoughts. "This picture is from last year in Vegas, and I was there. Ty spent a lot of time with us because things were still kind of awkward at the new office. He didn't realize he was going to be in the same department as Will when he left to take the job there, but it's a bigger shop, you know? Bigger shop, bigger money, so he was making it work."

"What else can you tell us about Will Dunham?"

Liam shook his head and handed me back the photocopy. "I never really met him. He wasn't interested in hanging out with the rest of us that week in Vegas, and I haven't run into him again, other than that one night with Olivia."

I folded the piece of copy paper and put it in my back pocket, stopping to ask one last question. "What was the name of the game they invented?" His answer rattled around in my brain all the way back to the car, and I waited impatiently for my Google search to bring up the results. A few more thumb taps and I was looking at a full fan page about a video game called *Myth Maker*. It was the only game released by Ascendency Games. There was still a global fan base for the game, which had an eerily familiar storyline. Along with powers and weapons, players collected various goddesses as they bested challengers to ascend to the throne of the gods.

"This is our guy," I said, my head swimming in the reality that we might actually have a lead that could give us what we needed to save Alayna, who, as of a few hours ago, was likely still alive.

"What do you have?"

I handed my partner my cell, and he read through the game description on the screen. Bryan let out a frustrated snort and handed me back my phone. "This bastard thinks he's playing a game."

* * *

We went directly from the home of Liam Wakefield to the office of Psy-Comp. The connections were undeniable. We had Tyson Scott and Will Dunham together. We had Will Dunham identified as the stranger at a bar who'd told Liam

Wakefield they knew each other and said something to upset Olivia Bower enough for her to threaten to have him thrown out. We had Tyson Scott murdered—only three days before Maggie—and we had a kidnapped victim sending SOS messages from Tyson Scott's phone. We knew they were connected, but we needed to know if Tyson was simply a victim of a random crime or if he could have been caught up in our murders.

A cheery young receptionist with a glossy French bob and green-framed glasses greeted us at the front desk. "Um, good morning, welcome to Psy-Comp Technologies, how can I help you?"

I introduced myself and Bryan and asked if we could speak to someone in HR or the manager for Tyson Scott.

The young woman put her hand to her heart at the mention of the dead man's name. "It's so terrible what happened to him. Let me call Lance Baker—he's VP of HR." She tapped the wireless headset she was wearing and dialed a short extension. "I have more detectives here that need to talk to someone about Tyson Scott; are you still handling that?" Getting the answer she needed, she hung up the call and with a forced smile told us Lance Baker would be right with us. "He's the one who spoke with the other cops too," she added.

A few minutes later we were ushered by Lance Baker into one of the only rooms with actual walls on the main floor of Psy-Comp Industries. He was younger than I'd expected him to be, with round cheeks and perfectly tamed blond curls. The box of a room he took us to was constructed in the middle of the building, so the floor-to-ceiling windows on one side looked onto the main floor of the office and a busy cubicle farm. The other three walls were covered in a peel-and-stick mural of outer space. We seated ourselves at the round table that anchored the room, and Lance Baker got straight to asking questions.

"Ella told me you have more questions regarding Tyson Scott? I'm not sure what more I'm going to be able to answer for you."

"Well, actually, I'm Detective Cantwell, and this is my partner, Detective Ramirez. We're with Tacoma PD, not Lakewood, so we're not investigating the actual murder but a possible related crime."

"Oh, wow." He sat up in his seat, his hands working nervously to find a stopping position. "That's terrible. I still can't believe what happened to Tyson. They say it was most likely a robbery—got away with some insignificant stuff, didn't even take his car."

Taking the lead with the questions, I stepped right to the point. "I'm wondering if you can tell us if Tyson Scott and Will Dunham worked together?"

"Tyson and Will?" He leaned his elbows on the table, suddenly uncertain of where our meeting was going. "They both work here—well, Tyson worked here, but Will still does. They're in the same department, but Will is in a position that allows him to mostly work on his own."

"Was there a reason for that setup?" Bryan asked.

"I need to put this delicately, considering the circumstances, but yes, Will rubs people the wrong way, Detectives. Almost always. And yes, Tyson was one of those people; the whole team was on the list of those who've had issues with Will. He doesn't work well with others, so his current position allowed him to just have ownership of a particular project while bigger teams collaborated on other projects."

"If he was that difficult, why keep him around?" I asked.

He shrugged. "Results. Will was complicated, especially for management and HR, but he's undoubtedly one of the best at what he does. In this industry, talent matters, and it sometimes comes with ego. If it brings in money, we'd rather deal with him than lose out to someone else who will."

Bryan shifted beside me, antsy in his seat. "Is Will here now?"

Lance shook his head apologetically. "As of this morning, Will requested an extended leave of absence due to family issues. There's been a lot of complication with his mother since last fall."

I sat straighter in my seat with the news of the call out. "Mr. Baker, we would appreciate it if you could give us the current home address you have for Will Dunham, please." The timing couldn't be more conspicuous—the same morning Alayna risks sending a plea for help, Will calls out at work. My heart was thundering in my ears at the possible significance. Had Alayna been caught? Were we already too late?

The young man's hands flew up in protest. "Are you suggesting that Will might have had something to do with Tyson's murder?"

"Right now, we can only tell you we really need his most recent home address," Bryan answered. "It's pretty damn urgent."

Lance Baker was in shock, silently attempting to process that he might have employed a murderer without knowing the full details of what we believed Will Dunham was responsible for. He rattled off the address for a downtown loft, Bryan read it back to him, and then we showed ourselves out. We needed to find Will Dunham. I was sure of it. And I was terrified what would happen if we didn't find him soon. Calling out without a return date was not a good sign for us or Alayna. We still didn't know what role Tyson Scott had played in all of this, if any, but I was sure we knew who had killed the goddesses and who had taken Alayna.

* * *

The exterior of the building still resembled the original packing company that had existed in earlier days before being turned into the pricy studio apartments Will Dunham lived in. The foyer of the building was styled with acid-stained concrete floors and a bank of brass mailboxes on a long brick wall. No doorman, no security, and of course, no elevator. Together again with Cole and Phoenix, we made our way quickly up the three flights of industrial-style metal stairs to unit 900. Phoenix pulled a compact black kit from the pocket of his cargo pants, and within a matter of seconds the door was open. We stepped in, each avoiding a stack of newspapers piled outside the door, and Bryan flipped on the overhead lighting. The fluorescents flickered to life, illuminating a loft with a big personality.

Multiple abstract canvases in bold reds and blues hung in contrast over a stark-white sofa. Glass cases on either side of the wall-mounted flat-screen showed off a collection of action figures and several comic books set in glass display boxes. Scattered in with the collectibles were a handful of awards—glass prisms, glass disks, some sort of cartoonish-looking gold computer monitor on a block of wood.

A large desk with two monitors and a wall hanging rack with four different computer cases sat where the kitchen table should have been. Next to the shelves of computers were two framed degrees, both from the UCLA Computer Science Department.

"This guy is a geek," Phoenix said.

"This guy is a delusional sociopath," I corrected.

Phoenix laughed. "And a geek."

I grabbed a stack of mail on the kitchen counter. The postmarks were all more than a week old. The poured-concrete countertop was otherwise bare. No dishes in the sink, no trash rotting in the stainless steel garbage can. He wasn't living here, or at least he hadn't been recently. Disheartened but determined, we continued our search.

A king-size bed stood against the south wall opposite the kitchen, closest to the bathroom, concealed by a six-foot screen of frosted glass. I started my part of the search there. The bed was made with a white-and-red-striped down comforter and red silk sheets. Rather than a traditional headboard, a narrow bookcase hung horizontally above the bed and was full of books, mostly hardback and primarily fantasy. In the middle were two different copies of Homer's *Odyssey*—a hardcover and a paperback with a worn spine. His introduction to Circe.

At the far end of the bookcase were a few programming books and battered college textbooks. Then, squeezed against a set of Thor's hammer bookends, my eyes stopped on *Romance for Dummies*. I was caught somewhere between a laugh and a scream over the idea that our guy would be consulting a guidebook to get close to the women who became his victims. Phoenix was more right than I'd given him credit for. The guy was a geek.

After examining Will Dunham's book collection, I went for the most obvious hiding place for anyone who'd grown up with brothers. Trying to disturb as little as possible, I ran my hand between the memory foam mattress and the box spring. At the end of the bed, my fingers struck gold. "Oh. My. Hell."

"What do you have?" my partner yelled from the kitchen.

"It's basically his trophy case." I made my way back to the kitchen with the leather-bound photo album in my hands. As I put the album on the counter, a small stack of Polaroids slipped from between the pages and scattered on the floor. The images of young women frozen in time on the dated squares of film stopped me cold. Bryan collected the fallen photos and shuffled through them.

"These aren't our victims," Bryan said, tossing the stack on the counter. "I don't recognize either of these girls. Looks like these are at least ten years old."

"When, since 1980, have people been carrying around Polaroid cameras?" Phoenix asked.

I opened the binder and displayed the first two pages. The images rivaled those from our own morbid collection of Sarah Goodall. They were all shots unmistakably taken after her death. There were four pages total of Dana Mayhew's body in her trashed living room. The same number of pages were reserved for Olivia Bower, included close-ups of the braided hair. I continued through pages of Felicity Benson, with two photos of the wings before they were attached to her body, and finally the print ad for Blissful Blooms with a smiling Alayna Keller holding an arrangement of red-and-orange gerbera daisies.

"There's no pictures of Maggie," I said as Cole flipped back through the pages a second time.

"We knew Maggie screwed him up. He didn't follow his normal course with her," Phoenix said. "He shattered the mirror in his bathroom. He didn't even clean it up, so we've got dried blood in there we might be able to test against the DNA we already have."

"Why does it keep happening like this? Why can't the bad guy be home when we get here?" Cole muttered. "We know it's him; now we've got to find him."

"If he's got something besides this place, there's going to be records. I don't think he's moving from one motel to the next with a hostage who's been all over the news for a month. He's landed somewhere he feels safe with her, or we would have gotten a call about a body," I said.

"Let's clear this place. We're taking these." Cole pointed to my critical find.

"Now what?" I asked after Cole sent Danni's team to collect the blood samples and check for fingerprints in the open apartment.

"We've expanded the property search to include the entire state, but so far we have no other residences in his name. The only car registered to our Dunham is a 2019 Porsche 911, black in color, so no info on the white four-door we know he was in. I've got a desk guy running checks at area car rentals, but I'm not hopeful he's out there using his real name all over the place."

"So, do we split up again—search out friends and family?"

"We aren't going to find any friends," I said. "We know he's not social at work. He's Mr. GQ in a group photo with a bunch of guys in skater tees. He's got business trophies behind glass like they're Oscars. He believes he's so superior they gave him his own department of one. This guy doesn't have friends. According to the HR guy, though, he is off dealing with a family issue, and there's been a lot of family issues over the past year."

"Family it is, then," Cole agreed. He flipped through a few pages of his notes, doing his best impression of a speed reader. "It looks like we have information on parents; that's about it. Cassidy, you're with me, let's go."

"Go where?" I asked, unsure of why he was calling on me after how we'd started our morning.

"Visit with Psycho's mom. This started as your case, remember? You guys head back in, keep up on what we get from the revised property checks and the rental places. We need someone to get ahold of HR at his office, see what they will give us. And, Bryan, check in on Jordan. Make sure he's still keeping quiet. I don't want to get ambushed by the media because he's let something slip." Cole clicked the door locks for his Explorer. "Call if you find anything that even resembles a possible location for this guy. I'm ready to be done with this game."

Aggravation

After the unsettling events of the previous evening, he struggled to maintain his control through their regular morning routine. The disastrous ending to his carefully planned anniversary celebration kept his teeth on edge throughout the rest of the night. He sat in front of the TV until early morning, paying no attention at all to what was on the screen, just thinking. Plotting. More was needed to get her under control in time for his plan to be completed, and decisions needed to be made. Knowing he had a plan in place would cut some of the stress he was drowning under.

He raced through a cold shower before heading into the bedroom to wake up his Persephone for the day. When he stepped up to help her from the bed, he realized that for the first time he hadn't remembered her constraints in his frustration from the night before. The fact that she had remained obediently in bed without them offered a flicker of hope.

His hopes of a good day were dashed as soon as he got her into the shower. She was holding on to the night before and treated him to a silent tantrum. Her anger was vibrating through her, and she refused to look at him even when ordered. That was the last straw.

"You need to understand something." He stood glowering over her as she tried to brush her teeth. "Last night I tried to make things good for you. I will not continue to put up with you acting like an insufferable child. I will not continue to tolerate ungratefulness." Needing her full attention, he grabbed her petite shoulders and pushed her against the wall. "It's not only you that I have here. Your mother. Your boyfriend. A beautiful cousin who likes to talk about you on TV with her perfect smile. I can take them all."

"Please . . . please leave my family alone," she whimpered.

"Do you want to know about the others who played this game before you? Should I explain the fate you've avoided by being the chosen one?" She didn't respond, but her brown eyes went wide with anticipation. Fear. He hated that there was always the mortal reaction of fear. She wasn't learning.

He wrapped her hair in his fist and walked her into the kitchen, to the familiar constraints bolted to the floor, so he could continue their routine without worrying she would make a move for a butcher knife. She needed breakfast, though. He dropped an English muffin in the toaster and began peeling an orange while watching her in silence. After putting jam on the muffin, he poured a tumbler of milk and put the breakfast down in front of her.

"Do you want to know about the rest of my collection?" He waited for her to answer, irritated that it was only a meek nod. "You were not the first goddess to be discovered by me. That's the first thing you need to comprehend. The others—especially Aphrodite—were all stronger, more powerful than you, but I still chose you for this honor.

"You were supposed to be after Circe. Do you know that? It took me a long time to find you, though. This game was supposed to end with Hera, but you took her place. I'm not sure if the Fates interceded or if it was always supposed to be this way, but you need to understand where you stand with me right now. You need to appreciate what I'm trying to do for us.

"The life I'm trying to give you will be the life you deserve. I will give you everything, but not if you keep fighting me. I will find someone who will accept this gift with grace. There are others out there if it can't be you."

If he could get her to go along with the game, he would be able to give her everything she would ever need. With the extremely pricy new identities he'd been able to secure for William Flowers and his wife, Percy, they'd soon be living the good life on some tropical island in the middle of the Atlantic. He'd buy her a beautiful house as soon as the lawyers could clear the roadblock with his siblings. His lawyers insisted the settlement was close.

Persephone sparked something in him. Something that had flickered but not quite ignited with Eos. There was innocence, but at the same time, she was fierce and strong-willed. He knew he could bring her around if she would only stop the tantrums. He also knew there were others if she refused. He was going to make her understand that one way or another, he was not going to end this game alone. If he was forced to start his search over for Hera, he would. "Tell me you understand my plan."

Her voice was barely above a whisper, and her palpable fear sent him into a rage. "You're going to kill me."

18

We arrived at the address of Will Dunham's mother, and I forced myself into my good-cop smile. The house was a sprawling redbrick ranch. What were once white-painted shutters had peeled and aged to the point of bare gray wood. The front lawn was patchy at best and circled in chain-link, which was being used to wrangle a ragged collection of children's toys and bikes. We were greeted at the front door by a young girl about seven, who led us into the kitchen to meet her "gran," Mary Dunham.

"Mrs. Dunham, we appreciate you being willing to sit down and talk with us about your son," Cole said as we seated ourselves at the honey-oak table. Everything was decorated in mid-eighties Wedgwood blue. Various wood plaques with family-related sayings and tole-painted Pilgrim children adorned the walls, which were covered in wallpaper of perfectly repeating rows of flower-filled baskets. Alphabet magnets scattered their way across the aging fridge, part of the decor for the past thirty years, along with everything else.

"I'm afraid I won't be much help," Mrs. Dunham answered. She had dove-gray curls cut short and was hunched and rounded after raising twelve babies.

"We need to know the last time you saw your son Will."

Confusion spread across Mary Dunham's face. "You mean Sean."

"No, we're looking for Will. We believe he may have information about a crime and might not even be aware of the usefulness," Cole answered. No need telling his mother we thought her son was a psychopath. "We've been to his apartment, but it doesn't seem like he's been home for a few days, and it's urgent that we reach him today. Is there anywhere else he stays or travels to that you're aware of? A girlfriend's house, maybe?"

"Detectives, I'm sure you're looking for Sean. Will is a good boy."

Cole started to answer, but I spoke over him. The fact that Maggie Cannon had been running with a mystery man named Sean suddenly didn't seem to be a coincidence. "What can you tell us about Sean?"

Mary Dunham let out a dramatic sigh to begin. "We haven't seen Sean in many years, not since he was eighteen. He never could do what he was told, and my husband, bless his soul, was forced to make him leave. He was always in trouble then, and I'm sure he's always in trouble still. Troubled souls like Sean tend to stay troubled, you know?"

"And does Will have any contact with his brother?" I asked.

"No. They never did get along. Those two boys were my first babies, and I wanted them to be close as brothers, but it wasn't meant to be. Sean always hated that his younger brother was better than he was at most things, and he got angry with him all the time. We tried to love all our children the same, but Sean made it hard sometimes."

"It could be we're looking for Sean and he's used his brother's name," I improvised. I didn't believe my own words, but it was clear that Mary Dunham looked at her second son through very rosy lenses. "It would be easiest to clear this up with Will. When was the last time you spoke to Will?"

"Well, let's see." Mrs. Dunham thought for a minute, gazing past me out the window over the sink into the still-early morning.

"It was a month ago, Mama." A new voice came from the living room. A tall young woman with ashy-brown curls down to her waist stood in the doorway. I guessed she was about twenty. The girl locked her eyes on me with a focused stare I couldn't ignore.

"Yes, I guess you're right. This is my daughter Misty, and she's right. Will stopped by last month and had dinner with us. It's so hard for him to break away from his work. They keep him so busy with all that computer stuff because there's so much only he knows how to do there, but he tries to see me when he can get away. Will's a good boy." Mrs. Dunham smiled absently.

"Have you taken your pills yet this morning, Mama?" Misty asked. She looked at me and tossed her head slightly toward the front door. She was not just focused, I realized; she was pleading. I also realized Cole had missed her cue. When I followed her gaze, I saw through the window that another woman was outside, lingering just past Cole's SUV.

Mary Dunham was flustered by the question her daughter posed. "I . . . I don't remember right now. I'll have to have you check my bottles."

Eager to find out what was waiting for us outside, I stood from the table and motioned to Cole, who was confused by my sudden need to leave. "It's been nice to meet you, Mrs. Dunham. Please, if you do talk to your son, have him call us so we can talk to him." I held out my business card.

"Thank you. I'm sorry if Sean has done anything too bad. Rotten apples grow even on righteous trees, you know."

Cole followed me to the front door, sliding back into his jacket as we walked. "What are we doing exactly? We didn't get anything yet. We could have talked to that sister."

"Someone else wants to talk to us," I answered quietly. I pushed open the door, and a second woman with the same long curls and the same turned-up nose as Misty was standing by the car. She was in her late twenties, with a small toddler on her hip and a concerned look in her eyes. Cole, for his part, was surprised.

"I'm Detective Cantwell. This is Special Agent MacAllan."

"I'm Bridget. Sean is my brother," the latest sibling introduced herself. The toddler smiled at us, dribbling milk from a sippy cup as her grin widened at Cole.

"So that makes Will your brother as well, right?" I asked.

"Yes, but you need to know that Sean is a good guy, Detective. I don't want you to have the wrong idea about my brothers. If you're looking for someone, it probably is Will, not Sean."

"Your mother made it sound like Sean was estranged from the family."

"Not all of us." Bridget adjusted her toddler to the other hip and continued. "Our parents kicked Sean out when he turned eighteen, but he found ways to check in with some of us. He stayed with a friend's family because they didn't see what our parents saw. If we needed anything, we knew how to get ahold of him. My parents had no idea that any of us still talk to him, and he hasn't come here since being kicked out."

"And Will?" Cole asked.

"Will has a lot of sides to him. My parents thought he walked on water. If he was their only child, my dad would have been just as happy. Our father held certain ... ideals. He believed he was better than most men and he thought that created a lot of enemies in the world, people who wanted to take from him." Bridget shifted the baby again, strained by the toddler's weight. "Will has a genius IQ, Detective, but he shared a lot of my dad's beliefs. For my dad, that meant a lot. He didn't believe in psychology, but if he'd ever been diagnosed, I think my dad was narcissistic and delusional.

"He used religion to feed his delusions more than anything, and the fact that Will went along with Dad's ideas just enforced for him that he was right. Whether or not Will really agreed with Dad or just liked the fact that agreeing kept him in the spotlight didn't matter. I think Will shared a lot of the same self-importance. They thought of themselves as closest to god. The truth is, Will is broken. I don't know how else to describe him. There was always a scary darkness in him, ever since we were little kids."

"Do you see Will often?" I asked.

Bridget laughed, and her short burst made the young girl in her arms giggle as well. "He is the golden child, and he sends checks to show off how well he's doing, but no, we don't see him often. Once a month is asking too much of him. My husband and I are staying here with Mama because she's not doing very well. Alzheimer's. There are twelve of us kids, Detective, and the youngest three are still finishing up in public school. Someone has to be here to take care of things."

"Do you know where he would be if he wasn't staying at his apartment? I can't stress how urgent it is that we find him," I said.

"If he's not at his fancy place, he might be at the farm. My grandfather left it to my dad; my dad passed it on when he died. It's tied up in court between Will and Sean right now, but the rest of us don't go out there."

"Do you have an address for the farm?"

She shook her head and handed me a scrap of paper from her back pocket. "That's Sean's cell. He'll know where the farm is. They took the boys up there regularly when they were growing up, but us girls were never allowed." She flashed us a shy smile. "Like I said, my dad had some odd views on the world. Us girls didn't go up there because he thought we would be in the way. He also said it was best if we couldn't tell the enemies where the place was. That's how he thought about the world; that's what Sean and Will were raised in. Honestly, it didn't hurt my feelings. I never wanted to have to work on the farm. Most of the boys hated it too. They'd come back exhausted and hurting, but Will would come back praising our dad for his prepping."

Cole leaned against the driver's-side door of his SUV. "What is it about the property that's tied up between your brothers right now?"

"Dad talked big about disowning Sean when they kicked him out, and forever after, but he never changed his will. So, when he passed away, the property was still listed as going to his eldest living male child, and as far as biology is concerned, that's Sean. Will wants the property, but Sean is holding out because he wants to sell it. There's a lot of land out there, and Sean wants to share the profits to help take care of Mama. He tries to help when he can, but we're all barely making it ourselves. Will insists he wants to keep the property in the family like our granddad wanted, but it's really that he can't stand the idea of losing anything to Sean."

"Thank you for talking with us. We'll be getting ahold of your brother." I offered Bridget my hand, and she took it.

"Detective, this thing that you're looking for Will for, is it bad?"

"We'll be in touch." I tried for a smile and failed. As much as I knew she wanted more, there wasn't anything more I could give her. Sadly, the Dunham sisters already believed their big brother was capable of troublesome things, and they would get their confirmation of that fear soon enough.

"Of course it's bad, or you wouldn't be here. It's going to be hard on Mama, but I think the rest of us saw something like this coming." Bridget turned herself around and went back to the house. As they made it up the gravel driveway, the little girl cheerfully waved goodbye over her mother's shoulder.

"I'm on it," I said before Cole could give any orders. I dialed Sean Dunham's number, crossing my fingers someone would answer. My heart sank when the phone kicked instantly over to voicemail. The message was the generic automated recording. I left a message for Sean to call me back, adding "as soon as possible" for good measure.

"Keep calling. Or should I turn around? Maybe we can get his address from the sister? Work? We've got to get moving on that farm." Cole slammed his hands hard on the steering wheel in aggravation. "I'm turning around."

"No, no, no. Keep going. We'll get ahold of him," I argued.

Much to my irritation, Cole pulled over to the shoulder and was soon on the phone with Eric. "I need you to pull everything you can find on Sean Dunham. He's going to be tied somewhere to William Dunham. I didn't get a DOB. I need it all by the time we get back. Everyone needs to be ready to move. If you find anything helpful before I get there, call me." Cole shouted his orders, offering no pause for Eric to respond before hanging up and tossing the cell away. A few minutes later, after I persuaded Cole to get back on the road, my own phone started singing.

"Bad news first," Bryan said as soon as I answered. "According to a very nice lady at the cell company, there was no location information available for Tyson Scott's phone since the last time they checked for Lakewood PD. The last registered location is still where his body was found."

"Shit." I knew that had been a longshot, but the defeat still stung.

"The good news is that Sean Dunham is nowhere near as techy as his younger brother, and possibly the last person of our generation to have a listed home line in the twenty-first century."

"You're telling me he has a listed landline?"

"Yep." Bryan chuckled.

"Did you get ahold of him?"

"No, that's the other bad news. I did reach his wife, though. Sean is working on a roofing job, and I'm guessing you and Cole are closer right now than we are. I'll send you the address. She said he won't check his cell until noon when they break for lunch. Getting to him in person is going to be our best shot."

"Got it. Send me the address, and we'll get over there."

There was a pause, and my partner laughed. "Eric wants to know if Cole's stopped screaming yet."

"He's as good as the rest of us," I answered.

In an aggravated silence, Cole plugged the address from Bryan into his SUV's navigation. The neighborhood was a new development, with most houses still under construction. A collection of trucks lined the street, but only one house was getting the final touches of a new roof. Cole parked in front. Five or so guys were scattered across the bare roof, nailing down sheets of tar paper and unpacking rows of shingles.

Cole headed straight for one of the ladders leaning against the front of the house and started climbing.

"Um, am I supposed to follow?" I asked only somewhat sarcastically.

"Be right back," Cole answered over his shoulder. He made his way to the top of the roof and stepped off the ladder. The first step was quickly followed by shouting. After a few exchanges, Cole reappeared on the ladder, followed by a man I could only guess was Sean Dunham.

Cole stepped down, the second man right behind. "Cassidy, Sean Dunham. Mr. Dunham, this is Detective Cantwell."

"Hello," Sean said with obvious confusion. He was only three inches or so above my own five foot five, and he was muscled in the way that men who work with their hands tend to be. With his blue eyes and a few days' worth of dark stubble on his cheeks, there was a resemblance to the pictures of his younger brother, without the overdressed *GQ* element. There was an intricately shaded tattoo snaking up from his right wrist and disappearing under his shirtsleeve. More artwork was visible at the throat of his shirt collar. He was also wearing a black baseball cap strikingly similar to the one the mystery man at the hospital had worn.

"I'm sorry we had to come out here like this, Mr. Dunham," I said. "But your wife told us we wouldn't be able to reach you by phone. It's urgent that we find out where your family farm is. We are looking for your brother Will."

"Funny that I'm not surprised at all that law enforcement is hunting me down to find my brother. What do you need to know about the farm?"

"Do you think it's possible your brother would be staying there?" Cole asked.

"Of course it's possible. We've been fighting over that property for over a year now. He already thinks it's his."

"You haven't been in contact with Will recently, have you?" I asked.

Sean Dunham laughed hoarsely. "No. We make all our contact through our attorneys, which is damn expensive. Lucky for me, my boss got screwed over by family once, and he's hooked me up with his lawyer friend to represent me. If I wasn't getting help there, I would have already been forced to give up, because I can't keep up with Will's finances."

"Can you give us the address for the farm and permission to search it?" I asked.

"Permission sure, search all you want, but it's going to require more than the address and the two of you if he intends on hiding up there," Sean said. He wiped at sweat beaded on his forehead that was forming despite the cool autumn temperatures. "We called it the farm because that's what our granddad called it, but there wasn't actually any farming done up there. My granddad had a few cages of mink for a while, but the property is mostly meant to be a hideout. We're talking about around a hundred acres on a sprawling mountainside, surrounded by thick trees. I think there's a total of sixteen buildings—not sure if that's counting the underground bunkers, though, and there's two of them. Some of the buildings have secret cellars. Seriously, the place is massive."

"If we get the address, we can get the property records pulled for the buildings, but right now we just need someone to tell us how to get there," Cole said.

"You don't get it." Sean adjusted the brim of his cap, trying to conceal his own building frustration. "My granddad and my crazy father were not exactly worried about registering things with the county building inspectors. What they built up there is a compound. It was designed as an intentional maze in case we ever came under attack from the Communists. They started it before us kids were born, and they waited for that damn invasion every day."

My heart tumbled to my toes with Sean's description of what sounded like the perfect playground for someone who wanted to hide. When we first heard about the farm, I'd pictured a quaint farmhouse with grandma-lace curtains in the kitchen and a cow pasture surrounded by trees. I didn't expect a hundred-acre labyrinth tucked into a mountainside, complete with bomb shelters. The news pitched MacAllan right over the edge.

"We're going to need you to come with us," Cole demanded.

"I don't know if you noticed, but I'm kind of in the middle of something here, Detective."

"Special Agent," Cole corrected, taking no time in pulling rank. "Special Agent MacAllan with the FBI, like I said up on the roof. And I don't know if you noticed, Mr. Dunham, but we're kind of in the middle of something as well, and we need your assistance. We need to find your brother *today*."

Sean was not giving in, despite Cole's shift in attitude. "I will write down what I have on the farm, but I can't just walk off my job site and leave my crew here. I wish you the best of luck, *Special Agent*, even more so if it means my brother ends up in jail tonight, but you will have to do what you need with the address. I can't make Will my problem right now."

"Your brother has killed five women, possibly more, and we believe he's holding a nineteen-year-old girl hostage at your farm right now. As of this morning we have reason to believe she was still alive, and we're trying to keep her that way, but he's had her for a month." I shot the words out without warning, and they hit the tough guy hard. Sean bent at the middle with his hands on his knees, fighting for breath. "I'm sorry to throw it at you like that, but we are running out of time. We don't know the circumstances that allowed her to reach out for help, but she did, and the contact connects her directly to your brother. We need you to cooperate with us."

Sean laughed gruffly as he pulled his back straight. Tears were in his eyes, and the color had left his tanned cheeks. "I figured you caught up to him for not paying his taxes or some shit like that." He sucked in a breath.

"We'll give you a ride," Cole returned in a tone I thought anyone would know better than to argue with, but Sean proved me wrong.

"It's okay, I have my truck."

"We'll give you a ride. I need to get you to my office with absolute certainty that you haven't spoken to anyone else by the time we get there."

"Right." Sean gave another nervous laugh. "Like I want to start calling all my friends to tell them the FBI thinks my brother murdered a bunch of women and is holding a teenager hostage on the property we're currently fighting over. Not exactly news you turn into a Facebook status."

"I'm going to give you one chance to choose the ride we've offered or me putting you in cuffs and taking you into custody in front of your crew," Cole said. With a shake of his head, Sean gave in.

19

It was after noon by the time we gathered in the office and finished a quick round of introductions. Jordan's call had come in at four AM, and with eight hours already on our feet, the whole room was haggard, but the mood was electric. Eric laid out the maps of the property we were still referring to as "the farm," and Sean Dunham jumped right in to help tell us what we were looking at.

"This right here is the main driveway." Sean turned his ball cap backward and leaned over the pages with a yellow highlighter from my stash. "The first building at the top of the driveway is going to be the main house. It's your basic one-level with a crawl space under the back porch. There's a living room, kitchen, bathroom, and two bedrooms. It's been easily six months since I've been up there, but Will isn't handy enough to make changes himself, and he's definitely too cheap to bring anyone up there to remodel." Sean turned the paper copy on its side and continued to study. "This building closest to the house is not big. This plan makes them look the same size, but they're not. It's basically a storage shed, and it's full of old tools and equipment that I haven't sold yet, unless he's cleared it out. That is possible. The building after this one is larger, and there's a basement to it. The basement is basically a bomb shelter. One of many."

For fifteen more minutes we sat at the table with Sean as he outlined what he could from his memory of the buildings scattered over what ended up being 109 acres of property in the northern corner of western Washington. Between the spread of the land, the number of the buildings, and the various basements, crawl spaces, and fortified bunkers he outlined, it was painfully obvious to all of us that it was going to be too much for our small team to search.

Cole stepped out to make a call for the response team we knew we needed, and Eric escorted Sean to a more comfortable conference room where he could wait out our search for his brother. He didn't even try to object to Cole's announcement that he wouldn't be allowed to leave. I took the quick break as a chance to grab a much-needed cup of black coffee. Bryan met me at the coffeepot and took a quick glance over his shoulder.

"Is it just me, or have we seen that black hat somewhere before?" he whispered.

"I noticed that when we picked him up. It's a company hat; he wasn't the only guy wearing one."

"What are we really dealing with here, Cas?" he asked, eyebrows raised.

"Right now, I think we're dealing with a pissed-off guy who is cooperating fully with our investigation into his estranged brother."

"Or not. This could be why we couldn't figure out how he was finding all of them, and how he was able to subdue the women so easily. Are we dealing with a tag team?"

"No. That's not a possibility. I talked to his sister, Bry, and his mom. These guys are oil and water. They're not patching up a broken sibling relationship by becoming a serial killer tag team while carrying on a costly court battle over property."

"Stranger things have brought psychopaths together. Maybe it does all run in the family, like the sister told you," Bryan insisted as Cole rejoined our group.

"Parker's team is getting ready and will meet us up there," he said. "GPS says we're over an hour away from the property, so we're still two hours out by the time we all hit the road. I want to quarantine Alayna's family for now, so I'm having them brought here. I want to try to control any type of speculation for the five o'clock news."

As I sat at the table, going over our game plan for our risky entry into a compound with only one way in and one way out, my stomach felt full of epileptic butterflies. We were going to bring an end to this game at last. When I thought we were finally going to be on our way to wrapping it up, Eric came crashing through the office door with a look of panic. "Sean Dunham is gone."

"What do you mean, he's gone?" I was the first to ask.

"As in he is not where I put him. Gone."

"He has to be here somewhere," Cole said. "We brought him here. He doesn't have a vehicle."

"I'm telling you he's not here. I've checked the bathrooms, the open conference room we set up for Alayna's family. He's not here."

"How do we lose someone in a freaking FBI building?" Cole was fuming.

Dread at the realization of what this meant to our operation spread through the room like wildfire. "I've got the home number. I'll call the wife back and see if she's heard from him." Bryan pushed himself away from the table to make the call. He shot me a look, and I knew he was still making a connection between the brothers in his own mind.

"We need to worry about whose side he's on, especially if he's heading up there," Phoenix said.

"He's on our side," I answered.

Eric shook his head. "Phoenix is right. Brothers are brothers. Who knows what we could be looking at if he gets up there first? He may have already tipped off his brother that we're on our way."

I wasn't letting peer pressure persuade me. "No. That family is divided, and the sister made it clear it's been them against Will all along. I'm guessing if he gets up there before we do, it will only be a question of which one is going to be standing when we get there."

"For fun, I called Sean's cell, but it jumped to voicemail, so I called his wife." Bryan shouldered the doorframe. "She talked to him about half an hour ago, and he told her he'd been interrupted on the job site because of some trouble his brother was in. He said he was going back to the job with some of his guys to meet their deadline and would probably be out there all night."

"Do we believe her?" Cole asked.

"I believe that is what he told her, but I don't think she believed he was going to be putting down shingles in the dark."

"Wonderful." I sighed. "We need to get up there now. If Sean confronts his brother, at best we're going to have a hostage situation, at worst a shoot-out."

"You're forgetting one important detail," Cole said to me. I gave him my best *clue me in* stare. "We brought him here. Sean called someone to pick him up. We can't discount the possibility that while he might be dumb enough to go up there without us, he might not be dumb enough to go up there to confront his brother alone."

"I can call his wife again and see if she has any numbers of anyone he'd be working with, but we might need to start looking at a different possibility." Bryan raised an eyebrow at me. I glared.

"What possibility?" Phoenix asked.

"That these brothers aren't at each other's throats like we've been made to believe."

"You're thinking they're working together too? Your partner disagrees, but Eric and I said the same thing."

I tossed my head back in frustration. "They're not working together. I believe the sister; Sean is the good guy."

Phoenix gave me a sideways glance. "The good guy who ran?"

"I'll keep trying to get ahold of him, but I'm not ruling anything out at this point," my partner said.

"Do it on the road," Cole ordered. "Everyone needs to be at the cars in fifteen minutes. Brother or no brother, we've got to head out."

I grabbed my gear bag from its spot in the corner and headed to the solitary ladies' room to change. The jeans and sweater I'd started the morning in were not official enough for this operation. What we planned would require the uniform gear that had thrilled me when I first started my career. I shimmied into the loose-fitting, military-style cargo pants and pulled a long-sleeved shirt that included all the proper identifying patches over my bulletproof vest. I completed my look with my nylon utility belt and black boots. I ran a check of my gear—badge, flashlight, handcuffs, Taser, Glock—then headed out of the room and ran straight into Phoenix.

"You ready for this?" he asked.

"Ready as I'll ever be," I answered, unsuccessful at hiding my nerves. Apprehensions that required a SWAT team were high stress by default. An apprehension that could also lead to a rescue doubled it.

* * *

The butterflies in my stomach switched to overdrive as I slid into the back seat of Cole's familiar SUV with Bryan. Phoenix was riding shotgun, and Eric was riding with a small part of Danni's crew, at Cole's request. Bryan was still working through the short list of contacts Sean's wife was able to give him. He hit pay dirt with the third phone call.

"Guy picked Sean up at your office and drove him back to his truck. He knew nothing about working overtime or exactly why he was at the FBI office. He thought he was just giving him a ride back to his truck. He's still got almost an hour on us. Good news or bad, seems he went up there alone."

Ascension

He couldn't believe the gullibility of the people he worked for. It truly was exhausting sometimes to work for people so dim. He'd called in with a fake emergency involving his poor, ailing mother and left his boss stammering on the phone. He'd convinced him he had time off left that he knew he didn't have. He also knew they were up to their eyeballs with their new product and the scheduled launch was only a few weeks away.

His boss pleaded with him, tried to convince him to at least log in from home, but in the end he won. He still had a job, and if he needed to go back for a few weeks, he could ride up to the twelfth floor and step off the elevator like he hadn't been gone at all. Best of all, he would still be getting paid while they thought he was taking care of Mom.

He needed to get more quality time with Persephone. He needed to get past her walls and make sure she was going to go along with his plan. If he could not convince her of his love and of her true identity in the next three days, he would have to start over. It would be six weeks wasted if he had to start over, and it would require a whole new search. He didn't have the patience for that. Not now. Not after realizing what the end game really needed to be. The end could only be right if he could keep her. Getting her through a crowded airport for their scheduled flight next week would be impossible if she was still trying to ruin him.

He'd put her away and made his emergency call in to work to secure his time off; now he had to go into the trees. He'd hated being out there when he was younger. His dad and his grandfather would take him and his brothers into the thick evergreens to teach them survival. Sean, with his menacing stares, would sulk off and find his way back to the truck first in silence. His younger brother, Patrick, once got so scared running lost through the trees, he'd peed himself, and their grandfather made him sleep outside alone.

Almost every trip out to the farm included tests of some sort orchestrated by his grandfather. The only trips that didn't involve showing off their survival skills were the weekends when they all worked so hard not one of them could have made it out of the trees awake on their feet. Those days of hard labor were the worst for him.

Sean was stupid and Patrick was timid, but they were built for physical labor, with muscular arms and strong legs. Same for his youngest brothers, who never had the same amount of work to keep up with, coming up years into the project. They could all work on the outbuildings and dig the holes for the bunkers from sunup to sundown and still walk straight at the end of the day.

Those were the days he always lagged behind. Those were the days his father showed a touch of disappointment in his favorite son. He loved to brag about Will's brains, but he believed physical strength was required as well to be a real man. Will was told over and over that he needed to be able to work with his hands, not just his head, so he pushed himself to keep up with Sean.

He struggled through each day, usually successful, but he still hated it. As often as he could, he would push Sean's buttons to create a distraction from his own shortcomings. His older brother was always such a hothead. It was never hard to get him with a bit of taunting. Will would sabotage Sean's work to keep things more even. Loosen screws, toss in a bit of dirt he'd dug out, pull wires. There was only one time he took it far enough to regret.

All those years ago, while finishing the bunker closest to the main house, Will messed with the switches and sent a jolt of electricity into his brother strong enough to take him to his knees. Sean retaliated by shooting to his feet and shouldering him to the ground; then Sean ran out and threw the outside bolt, leaving Will locked in, in the dark. It wasn't until morning that his dad came for him and scolded him for letting Sean get the better of him before sending him back to work.

He hated that bunker in particular. It was a cold, damp building that always tended to develop a draft, even underground. The concrete floor had ended up sloped, and the wiring Sean did always had a mind of its own—flickering on and off without warning. It was harsh, but it was going to be the best place for her reprogramming, as far as he could see it. He would deal with his discomfort if it helped break her from the anger she clung to so stubbornly.

There would be no light, no food, no visits from him while she was in there. He was hoping that three days alone would be enough to get her to comply through their flight. If the complete isolation couldn't break her, maybe he would take the flight himself and start over in a new home. The sunny beaches of Puerto Rico would be easier to play in than the dreary Pacific Northwest winter. Many goddesses left themselves exposed and vulnerable in places that sun met sand. He'd found his first two conquests in those conditions.

The dispute over the property was close to over, if he could believe what his nearly worthless attorney was saying. Before he found Persephone, he'd refused to agree to settle with his brother. He wanted to have a place he could hide when he needed to. Eos had changed all of that. After her betrayal, he knew he needed to find a new playground.

With Persephone, he could leave the farm behind, not care if Sean and his welfare-loving siblings shared in his profits, as long as he walked away with the lion's share. The money would set them up on the island with a nice house, nicer than what she'd ever been accustomed to. He'd give her a chance to live like a true goddess.

He stepped back into the main house and rubbed his hands together, shivering. The balmy temperatures of fall were slinking toward winter in a hurry, and for a fleeting moment he worried she would be too cold in her temporary concrete home for the next three days. She'd forced him into this situation, he quickly reminded himself. She'd left him with no other choice.

He rounded the corner through the mudroom and was startled by the clinking sounds of metal links scraping the kitchen floor. He stepped softly, expecting to find Persephone sneaking through the kitchen, somehow freed from her room. Instead, he came face-to-face with the hulking figure of his older brother. Sean's face, tan from a lifetime of laboring in the sun, was wrinkled with confusion. His angry eyes burned into Will.

"What are you doing here?" Will screamed.

Sean let out a bark of laughter that was much more nerves than amusement. "You have balls asking me what I'm doing here, on my own property." He pulled on the collection of chain he held in his hands, the other end attached to the floor under the kitchen table. "What the hell do you have going on up here?"

"I asked you first. Why are you here?" Will repeated. He mentally kicked himself for resorting to the childish-younger-brother role in Sean's presence, but he couldn't control himself. All he could concentrate on was getting Sean out of the house and off the property and keeping him away from any of the refurbished bunkers. He could not let him find her.

"I don't owe you an answer, but if you have to know, I have a buyer for some of the equipment up here to help Bridget with Mom's last ER visit. You need to explain this to me, William." Sean rattled the chain in his grip.

"I don't have to explain anything to you."

"I want you to be straight with me and tell me what this is!"

Without thought, Will took that moment to duck his head and lead with his shoulder, slamming himself into his brother's midsection and grabbing tightly to his waist. That was the first step. He hadn't thought of how to get to step two. Sean landed a hard fist against his ribs and a second blow to the back of his head, attempting to dislodge his attacker. Will held on against the blows and tried to push backward, hoping to get Sean on the ground, but he failed. After a few more hits, Sean threw himself sideways, and Will scrambled to his feet.

"You're not supposed to be here. You're going to ruin everything for me!"

"Tell me what's going on," Sean said again as they circled each other in the small kitchen like gladiators in a ring. "Tell me what you've done. We can fix this. Whatever it is, I will help you fix it."

"The only thing that needs to be fixed is you being here."

"Where is she?"

"I . . . I don't know what you're talking about," Will stammered. He slid closer to the fridge, a frantic plan forming in his mind. The magnetic strip of kitchen knives on the side of the fridge was now within reach. He was unsure of his strategy—he was going to have to act quick—but it was his only way out of this.

"I know you have someone up here. Where is she? This doesn't look like she wants to be here. What have you done this time, William?"

"This is your property. You tell me what's going on," Will shot back.

"No. No. I'm not going down that road with you again. I couldn't prove you did it back in high school, but I know you took my car the night that girl got hurt. I was never there. And this . . . this is all you. Dad's gone, and Mom barely remembers her own name on a bad day. They can't protect you this time. You're going to have to answer for whatever you've done up here, Will, but I can help you turn yourself in."

Sean stepped forward, and Will moved into action, grabbing the closest knife from the strip and lunging forward. His first attempt missed, and Sean jumped back. Will followed, and this time he hit his mark. His brother sank to the floor with a heavy thud, blood rapidly soaking through his shirt. Will realized his mistake instantly, though. He'd let go of the knife.

Sean pulled the blade out of his side and moved quicker than Will imagined his brother could after being stabbed. Sean swung out, and Will felt the blade slash through his pants, below his knee. His flight instinct beat out what little fight he had left. He wasn't going to lose everything because of his asshole brother. He needed to move. He didn't have a choice now. The game was going to have to change again.

20

Our rescue mission ride was painfully slow, even at eighty miles an hour with the red and blue lights hidden in the front grille flashing. When we finally made our way to the long gravel driveway that led to the property, we found Sean's blue work truck parked halfway to the house. The dread intensified its pressure on my chest. Our team split in two at the top of the hill behind the blue truck. Eric and Phoenix followed Parker and his guys to the front door. I followed Bryan and Cole to the back door.

An aged screen door was slamming rhythmically against the wood frame as we approached the back of the house, setting each of us on our toes. Blood on the doorframe caught my eye, and I pointed it out to Bryan. There were more drops across the porch that dropped off at a clearing of wild grasses behind the property. Bryan shook his head at the sight and mouthed to me, "Not good."

"We've got a guy down in here, lot of blood," Phoenix called out.

I stepped through with Bryan right behind me and found Sean Dunham, unconscious, with a wound to his stomach and a large pool of blood under his body. His chest moved in a ragged wheeze.

"He's alive, but not by much." Phoenix continued his evaluation. He grabbed the blood-soaked hole in Sean's shirt and pulled it apart, exposing a deep gash under his ribs. Bryan found a stack of kitchen towels on the counter and threw them to Phoenix. Cole called down to the medical crew hanging back at the bottom of the property to let them know they were needed. If they moved fast enough, they might be able to get Sean out of the mess while he still stood a chance of surviving.

"The house is empty, but she's been up here, no doubt," Eric said.

"He ran as soon as he did this," I said. "Best case is he's still on the property with her. Worst case is he is *gone* gone."

While a few of Parker's crew worked on moving Sean to meet the medics, I took my own chance to search the house. Bryan followed me into the living room, stepping over discarded lengths of chain on the floor. "Are you seeing these?" I asked, kicking at one of the multitudes of large eyebolts sticking out of the floor.

"Unfortunately. They're in the walls too." Bryan pointed above the couch, where two bolts were tucked in under framed prints of pheasants like they belonged there.

"I can't even think about it." I changed course for the short hallway. I peered into the small bedroom, then moved to the master bedroom at the end of the hall. A violent shiver ran down my spine at the sight of the constraints dangling from the carved bedposts. "We're going to have to hit the forest; he's still up here. I feel it."

"You're right," Cole said from the hall. "Parker found Dunham's two cars in the garage out back. We've got a black Porsche and a white Chevy sedan still registered under grandpa's name."

"I guess it's time to get everyone into the trees." I walked with my partner back out the way we'd come in while Cole barked orders.

Bryan and I stayed with Cole, and Phoenix and Eric went together into the trees opposite us toward a small garage Sean had outlined. Two of Parker's team were working to evacuate Sean to the waiting ambulance. Thirty yards into the tree cover, we came upon a small concrete building with a metal door.

"You know it's not going to be this easy," Bryan said as Cole approached the door and pulled it open.

"Not if you jinx it." I drew my gun and prepared to go in, but the adrenaline dropped once we stepped into the empty room. I knew kidnappers with chains on the floor did not keep their victims in unlocked bunkers, but I couldn't dodge the hit of disappointment. In the concrete square of a room was a bare military cot and a frighteningly familiar set of chains.

"She's been in here," I said, pulling up on the chains with the toe of my boot.

"Not exactly comforting," my partner added, hitting each corner of the small space with the beam of his flashlight.

"Well, there's only about a dozen or so more of these little buildings to try to find," Cole said. "Let's move on."

We cleared the space, and Bryan propped the door open behind us. The three of us headed out of the building and trekked into a grassy clearing circled by a canopy of red and gold maple leaves. I was behind Bryan, scanning the ground for any sign that someone had been up here, when I saw it. A rusted pipe sticking up a few inches from the ground, and a second one farther into the trees. I started toward the first pipe, and my boots hit the ground, which gave back a metallic thunk. I stomped again. "I found a door!"

"Serious?" Cole jogged toward me.

"It's a trapdoor in the ground. I'm guessing it was covered up with some of this debris in the not-too-distant past, and I'm also guessing it leads to the underground mazes that Sean said were up here." I kicked the remaining leaves off the door.

A satisfied smile spread across my partner's face.

We drew our weapons, and I stepped back, allowing Bryan to swing open the door.

On the other side was pure darkness. With what daylight was still filtering through the treetops, I could see a line of cinder block at the top of the hole. Bryan stepped first onto what was once a swimming pool ladder, and I was next, with Cole close behind me.

Bryan flashed the bright beam of his LED flashlight to scan our landing point. The walls were rough but reinforced rows of concrete blocks, and the floor was soft dirt. We were quietly debating if we should go left or right or split up and go in both directions when we heard it. The unmistakable sound of a woman's screams. The sound echoed through the overwhelming span of underground tunnels, making it impossible to determine which direction it came from, but we were sure now that Alayna was alive.

The path that led to the right appeared to travel farther into the dark, so we chose to start that way. We followed the darkness, running into a short succession of turns, forcing us deeper into the underground web. I counted six turns in my head, hoping to be able to trace our way back out if we needed to retreat.

The glow of Bryan's flashlight guided us as we moved forward like rats in a crazy maze. We heard a second cry and stopped dead. She was closer. Straining to hear, we ran deeper after her. I tried to shut out the sound of my own breathing rushing loudly in my ears to focus on the sobbing in the distance. Bryan paused, then flinched at something I couldn't see. Without warning, his arm flew backward, slamming me into the concrete wall. "Get down!"

Gunfire crashed through the underground labyrinth. With a string of Spanish curses, my partner slid down the wall in front of me. Even without the blue-tinted LED light he'd been holding, I could see the black stain that trailed after his fall.

"Fuck!" Cole shouted, sweeping his Glock from side to side in front of us. "Cassidy, you okay?"

"It's Bryan. I'm not hit." I dropped to the ground next to Bryan.

"Stay with him. I'm going to find this son of a bitch." No longer in stealth mode, Cole flooded a list of commands into his radio. First came orders for the medical response team to find us and get a helicopter in the air for Bryan's transport. Next was orders to the rest of our search party to rally to our location. After that I lost sight of Cole in the shadows as he pursued Will Dunham. My wounded partner and I were alone.

On my knees, I ripped off my nylon jacket and tried to help Bryan sit upright against the wall. "Where is it, Bry? Where are you hit?" I ran my own light over him, spotting the dampening spot at the shoulder of his dark shirt. It was spreading below his collar, just above his vest on his left side. His eyes locked on mine for a breath and then slammed shut.

"Shit, getting shot hurts," he mumbled. His voice was ragged.

I pushed hard against his shoulder with the cotton liner of my jacket, using my entire weight for pressure. "Please be okay. You have to be okay," I begged.

Bryan let out a faint, shallow laugh. "You need to make me a promise, Cas." His breaths were short and sharp, and he kept his eyes closed while he spoke. "I'm gonna promise to try not to die on you, and you're gonna promise me something."

"Don't you dare pull one of those *if I die* requests on me. We're not going there."

"No, really, you're gonna promise me that you'll tell Ana I want my little girl to be Kathryn, okay? Kathryn, after my grandma. She's been trying to tell me no, so you have to tell her it was my dying wish. Even if I don't die, tell her it was my dying wish. She wants to name the baby Pippa. No Pippa."

"You die on me, and I'll make sure we celebrate baby Pippa every day," I said, relieved by the familiar sarcasm, even if his voice did recede to a whisper.

"I didn't fight it when she named all the boys, but Pippa Ramirez is not my little girl's name." Bryan moaned from deep within his core and reached for my hand, pressing on his shoulder. "This fucking sucks." He hissed sharply at the pain. His breathing slowed, and his grip on my hand relaxed as my partner passed out.

"Shit. Shit. Shit." I patted his cheek quickly, trying to bring him back to me. "C'mon, Bry. You need to stay with me. Try to stay awake until the medics get here, okay? Keep talking to me." This time there was no smart-ass response to my pleas.

Keeping tight pressure on his shoulder, which was growing warmer and wetter as he continued to bleed, I felt the shallow rise and fall of Bryan's chest become slower and weaker. I called out over the radio, requesting ETA for the medical crew Cole had screamed for, and an eternity passed before anyone came back with an answer. They were tracking Bryan's GPS on his phone to our location, but they were still five minutes out.

I shifted on the ground, trying to get more pressure on the bleeding that wasn't letting up. With as much blood as he was losing, I thought five minutes was going to be too long to wait. I tried to monitor Bryan's pulse at his throat and was trying to decide if I could get both of us out of here to avoid waiting underground when I heard the faint sound of sobbing in front of me.

The sound was coming from the same direction the shots had been fired from. The same direction Cole had run off to. If I was right, it meant that either Dunham had doubled back and would be closing in on Bryan and me, or he'd stayed in the same spot and Cole had missed him. The whimpering repeated in soft bursts I couldn't ignore. I was going to have to move.

"Bryan, I really need you to work with me right now," I said in a grave whisper. My heart jumped as he rolled his head, his eyes flickering back to me and then fading away again. I could not deny the concern that he would bleed to death if I left him, but I knew a bigger danger was out there in the dark. Bryan and I would be easy targets with him bleeding on the ground. I also couldn't ignore the danger having Will Dunham close would pose to the medical crew trying to get to my partner. I needed to make sure the whole team remained safe.

As gently as possible, I rolled Bryan from side to side and pulled his arms free from his own jacket. With my bloodied jacket still wadded up and absorbing what was coming out of him at a steady rate, I stuffed it under the collar of his polo shirt. I wound his right jacket sleeve under his arm and across his chest, tying the sleeves together in as tight a knot as I could manage over the lump of my makeshift compress.

My calculations said the medical crew was close now; I could only hope they were close enough to keep my decision from being the wrong one. I explained my plan quickly to Bryan, hoping he could hear me. I convinced myself that either way, he would understand what I was about to do. I pulled my gun from my side and, with my flashlight in my other hand, headed off in the direction the cries were coming from.

I snaked my way down the dark hallway in front of me, taking myself deeper into the heart of the underground tunnel. I didn't have to go far before I caught up to the weeping, followed by a man's voice whispering harsh commands. I crept forward with my gun drawn but killed the light, blinking rapidly to adjust to the sudden darkness.

I was thankful for the dirt floor helping to muffle the sounds of my hurried steps. I cursed myself out silently when my last turn brought me to a dead-end wall, forcing me to backtrack to the last crossroad. I paused at the fork, the tunnel eerily silent, then I saw it. A quick burst of light that went out as fast as it appeared, in the distance to my left. I had him.

I sprinted toward the flash of light and yelled for Dunham to stop, clicking on my own light and steadying my gun. Expectedly, he took off, nearly dragging Alayna behind him into the maze. From what we'd learned from Sean, I knew the brothers had helped construct these tunnels. If I lost sight of him now, he could lose me in the dark, leaving Alayna and Bryan vulnerable. Disoriented, I ran faster, hoping we were running back aboveground and not toward my partner.

My hopes were dashed when the three of us were unexpectedly stopped in a small room at the end of a narrowing path. He'd run us all into a dead end, and his only way out now was behind me. Will spun around, pulling Alayna closer, and I didn't break my eyes away from the small, black handgun he pointed in my direction. This was it. My heart pounded in my ears, and I forced myself to steady my breathing as I came face-to-face with the killer we'd been searching for. The bastard who had just shot my partner. The Myth Maker.

"Put the gun down, Will. Let Alayna come to me and get down on your knees, put your hands behind your head, lace your fingers together." I kept my voice even despite the alarm surging through me.

"She's mine," Dunham shot back, his voice full of terror.

"No, she is not yours. You don't get to keep her." I took a step forward, looking between Alayna and the gun pointed at me. "You lost. She's ours."

"You are not a player here; you don't get to make the rules," Dunham responded, still gripping Alayna's arm tightly. His gun did not waver.

"We've been playing from the start, and we found you. We also found Sean."

"Is he dead?" Dunham was hopeful.

"No. He's the one who told us where you were hiding. He's the reason we found you," I exaggerated. Hoping to rattle him with what we knew about his trophies, I kept going. "We were in your house, Will. Your real house. We have your computers, your books, your photo album. We've got your whole collection locked away, and you are never going to get them back. We won." The hateful glower he gave back was all the confirmation I needed that I was pushing the right buttons. "It was Eos, right? Eos was the one who beat you. Aphrodite was your favorite—you have so many photos of her but none of Eos. She beat you first, and now we beat you, and you didn't even see it coming."

"She did not beat me!" he screamed, and Alayna screamed with him. Against her captor's grip, she sank to the ground, and my heart sank with her as she scooted backward, taking cover behind Dunham rather than moving away. He lowered his gun and paced in a tight circle as I struggled to keep him in my light. "I haven't lost."

"They all helped us beat you. This time you have lost. We have the rest of them, your goddesses. They belong to us now." I strained to get a glimpse of Alayna in the darkness she'd slid into. I needed to get myself between captor and captive, but she continued to cower, which left me with few options. Keeping him talking was going to be the only distraction I had.

He laughed, nervously shifting from one foot to the other, putting him more solidly between Alayna and me. "You don't know what I am, Detective. Your ignorance of my true capabilities is why you'll never win. It's the same ignorance my parents suffered from, my professors, my coworkers. *Tyson.*" He said the last name with a whiny inflection and laughed, flaunting the connection between him and another victim. "None of you understand how powerful I am. You're not in the same league; in fact, you're not even playing the same game. There's no way you're beating me now. You have the prizes left behind from the conquests, but I have what I deserve most. I have her. My goddess is at my side, and she's leaving with me. We will continue, and you will be gone."

My toes curled in my boots toward the ground, trying to steady my stance. "I am not letting you leave with her. You've lost this one."

"I don't lose." Dunham growled and jerked his weapon up. "I don't ever lose."

The cold cement corner lit up with the flash of my gun muzzle as the gunshot echoed in the dark bunker, and my arms jerked with the force of my weapon. As Dunham hit the ground and pain exploded through my leg, I realized it wasn't an echo at all, and the brightness of the flash hadn't been from my own weapon—Dunham had fired at the same time. Alayna let out a piercing scream from the ground, but as I stepped to comfort her, the darkness closed in. I tried to lower myself gracefully to the dirt floor, but my body gave out and I ended up on my backside. Alayna's screams morphed into sobs, and Dunham remained silent and still on the ground. I could hear Phoenix barking directions to the other muffled voices in the corridor. I tried to shout out, but I couldn't manage to make a sound. The last thing to register as I lost hold of it all was pain.

21

The smell of blood and dirt filled my nose, and I blinked, trying to see around the darkness. I was alone, but I didn't want to be, and when I tried to move, I couldn't. My legs were heavy like stone, and my back pressed into the earth beneath me. I screamed out and heard my trembling voice echo back to me. I tried to clear my mind and put back together how I'd gotten to this spot alone, but I couldn't remember. In desperation, I screamed again. This time she appeared.

She reached out and squeezed my hand. Her long dark hair was hanging straight over her shoulders, and she knelt next to me in the dirt. "Shhh."

"We've been looking for you," I said. I was trying to force the memories back into my brain, but I was sure I was looking for her. I was sure I'd been looking for her for a long time.

"I thought we were going to the party," she said, her voice only slightly more than a whisper in the dark. "You never showed, Cassi. What are you doing way out here now?" She looked up into the darkness. Cedars and Douglas firs circled us like a regiment of towering sentinels.

Tears pooled in my eyes, and I remembered pain. Pain in my legs. Pain in my wrist. Guilt. "Jamie needed a ride, and then he gave me the wrong address, so I got lost. When I finally found him, I was running so late, and I was going too fast." My sobs caught in my throat. "I wrecked the car, and we went to the hospital. I tried to get there, but I was too late; you were already gone. I don't know where you went. I don't know how I got here."

Jenna sat back on her heels and pulled her hands inside the sleeves of her black knit sweater, hugging her knees. It was *my* black knit sweater, not hers. I remembered that now. It was a hand-me-down from my older sister, with an uneven line of pink thread in the sleeve where I'd tried to mend a snag. It was my favorite sweater. We'd traded at school so she could wear it to the party, and then she never gave it back. She never came back. "You're out here because of me," she said.

"No, it wasn't your fault. I was driving too fast," I cried. "I looked for you, but I didn't know where you were."

"We're supposed to be best friends, thick as thieves, remember? You need to find me." The sadness in her voice broke me, and I reached for her, but as I grabbed her hand, then her sleeve, each part of her began to swirl into mist until she was gone, and once again I screamed.

"Cassidy? Are you all right? Do you want me to get the nurse?" a once-familiar voice asked as the heaviness of the nightmare slipped off me. My eyes slammed open despite the weight of my eyelids and struggled to take in all things at once. The unfamiliar blue walls and beeping machines of a hospital room came into focus as well as the face of Nicky, sitting in a plastic chair next to the bed, his eyes glossy and tired.

I tried to push myself up against the raised hospital bed, and a tingly jolt traveled from my right hip to my toes. "Where's Bryan?"

"He's in surgery and is going to pull through, but other than that, Lieutenant Miller wasn't willing to tell me much, and I'm not supposed to ask you any questions about what happened."

"I need to get down to where Bryan is," I said, wincing through an attempt to wiggle into a better position. The effort made me painfully aware something was off with my head, and Nicky put a trembling hand on my shoulder to steady me in place.

"They had to sedate you pretty good to get you here, so they said things might be a little fuzzy when you wake up. Just stay put, okay?"

Whatever I'd been given to knock me out had left me with a jumble of images, and they played in flashes when I closed my eyes. Bryan bleeding through his shirt in the underground tunnel we'd chased Will Dunham through. Alayna Keller, screaming in time with the image of a muzzle flash. I had shaky memories of half walking, half being carried out of the tunnels by Phoenix but couldn't remember who had hold of Alayna. I didn't remember how we'd gotten Bryan aboveground, but a paramedic with a blonde ponytail was straddling his chest. There was a piece of a memory of fighting against Phoenix, who used his body to block me from getting to my partner. I couldn't put the whole sequence together yet, but I was pretty sure I took a swing, and I might have connected, my shock at that moment manifesting as anger. And, as always, there was Jenna in my sweater, pleading for my help. The image that wasn't connecting was Nicky in the hospital room with me, and that disconnect pushed me back against the flat hospital pillows. Nicky was the piece that didn't fit. It had been a month since he'd shut me out, that part I was clear on, and him being here now was not fitting into place with the other memories flooding me. "Wait, why are you here?"

Nicky flinched at my question as he stood from the chair, stuffing both hands in the front pockets of his faded jeans. "Apparently, I'm still your emergency contact at work. I was going to call Jamie once I knew what to tell him."

"Updating paperwork hasn't been a priority lately, but I'm sorry they called you down here if you don't . . . want to be here. You could have just called Jamie."

"It's fine; we both know he'd go straight to panic and need a ride anyway. All they told me was that there was an incident and you were injured. I didn't even know about Bryan until I got here about thirty minutes ago. I didn't want to call him until I knew what was going on," Nicky said. "Jamie and I are still friends, even if you and I aren't together."

His words stung, and I wanted to sting him back. "Well, isn't my brother lucky."

"I'm gonna give you a pass on that one because you got shot tonight." Nicky pulled himself into his worn leather jacket with a shrug, the distance between us falling back into place. "They want you to stay the night, and I hope you will, but I'll text your brother because I know you probably won't."

I started to speak and found myself suddenly trying to hold back tears that wanted to escape. It wasn't the time or the place to talk about us, but it had been a month since he'd been willing to talk to me at all, and I didn't want to lose the only chance I might get. I started again. "Don't leave yet, Nicky. You're here; can't we talk? I don't know what you need me to do. I've tried to say sorry for that night, but I don't know how to fix this."

He exhaled slowly, his thumb and forefinger pinching tightly on the bridge of his nose, unsuccessfully hiding his own new tears. "I've thought about that a lot these past few weeks, what we could do different to make this work, and I don't think we should try."

An unexpected pain crushed through me like a bulldozer through my chest. I had only used open-ended descriptions of our situation to this point. *Nicky isn't talking to me. I'm waiting for him to get over it. I don't know what we're doing yet.* Never had I let myself entertain the idea that he would officially end things this time. End us. Even with a month of being apart, I'd fooled myself into believing that once this case was over, I'd be able to go back to the normal life we had before.

"I'm sorry. It's just that . . . Well, I kind of got the feeling that I'm not what you want."

"That's not fair." It came out a whimper. "You never even gave me a chance to talk things through."

"I didn't think it was fair either." He let go of a half laugh before taking my hand and slowly threading our fingers together, letting them rest on the warm hospital blanket. "I've always wanted more from this than you have. I don't think you're being honest with yourself about it."

"Nicky, I . . ."

"No, Cas, please?" His raw-nerve sadness was unescapable. "You know, I've had that ring for a year. You have no idea how many times we've been out with that stupid thing in my pocket, but I couldn't ever do it. I knew you didn't want to change what we had, and I can't keep doing it that way. All I've been doing is delaying the inevitable."

"This is not what I want, though."

"Cassidy, you looked like you were going to throw up when I took that ring out of my pocket. I don't think you really know what you want, and that's not going to work. We need to be honest about it. I don't want to still be scheduling time with you, only waking up with you once a week when I get lucky enough not to have you get called out. That's not enough for me after two years. I need more." Silence flittered between us as Nicky absentmindedly ran the fingers of his free hand over the top of mine. "If I thought I could do it, I would, but I know I can't. We need to let it go, because keeping this going just means hurting more later, you know?"

"If I say yes, will that fix it?"

Nicky shook his head. "Stop."

"No, it's my turn now. If I sell my place and move into your place, set a date, plan a wedding, all the things you're asking for, can we fix it?"

He shook his head again, looking across the small room past me. "I can't handle going there right now. With everything you've been through tonight, this isn't the time to get into the what-ifs."

"It's the first chance I've had to talk about it, though. You've refused to even talk to me for a month. Why can't we reset? I can compromise."

"Can you put me first?"

"What?" I heard the words but wasn't sure how far Nicky was asking me to go.

"Can you quit your job and put me first?" The question came with sad laughter. "We both know the answer there, and it's just not something I can be okay with anymore. I am not a good loser, you know that. With you it is always going to be work that comes first, and after work there's always going to be Jenna. That is more time coming in third than I can be happy with, and I've been trying to pretend that I can deal with it, because I do love you, but I can't do this. Not any better than you could deal with giving those things up if I asked you to."

I didn't try to stop my tears. I wasn't worrying about being in control, only about stopping the end of the relationship I'd spent two years convincing myself I wanted. Each of us had spent time being stubborn, selfish at times even, but I'd thought we would get another chance. Maybe part of me thought I should have a say in whether or not we were over.

"I'm really glad you're going to be all right, Cas." Softly, he kissed the back of my hand before I pulled away. "I'll get ahold of Jamie for you, but I should go before one of us does something we regret."

I let my hurt respond. "Don't do me any favors. I can find my own ride," I said.

"Right on cue, Cassidy, right on cue," Nicky said with an almost amused shake of his head. "I'll at least let the nurses know you're awake."

* * *

True to his word, Nicky alerted the nurses, and an older Black woman in mauve scrubs came through the door with Lieutenant Miller right behind her. The nurse went right to checking machine readouts, and Nancy Miller dropped herself into the chair that Nicky had vacated. Her stress showed in the deepening lines across her forehead, and her shoulders slumped forward with the weight of the night.

"Have you seen Bryan? Is Alayna all right?"

"Bryan is still in surgery," she answered. "Alayna is going to be all right, thanks to you." She paused and then dropped the confirmation I wasn't sure I was ready to take in. "Our suspect, Will Dunham, was pronounced dead at the scene."

I was relieved that we'd managed to get the young woman out of the woods, but my partner wasn't safe yet. "I need to get down to where Bryan is." I tried again and finally got myself into a sitting position, pretending I felt sober as my body wobbled to starboard like a sinking ship.

"It's best for you to stay right where you are for the night," the nurse who still hadn't introduced herself said. "I've paged Dr. Green to check on you. He's the one who got you all cleaned up."

Steadying myself against a wave of dizziness, I sat up straighter against the bed. "I feel fine. Bryan is here, which means if I go to where he is, I'll still technically be in the hospital. I need to be down there with everyone else."

"Are you really going to push this, Cantwell?" There were dark half-moons under my lieutenant's brown eyes as she stared me down. Nancy Miller was done with the day. The case we'd all been living under was finally over, two of her officers had been injured, a suspect had been shot, and a young woman had been reunited with her mother. I knew the last thing she wanted was to deal with an insubordinate detective with a GSW, but we were talking about my partner. "A lot has happened tonight, including you also being shot. Yes, it's a minor wound, but a bullet still went through part of you. Your uniform and weapon have been collected as evidence, and we haven't been able to take your official statement because of all of what I just outlined. Would it be so hard to just do what you're told and stay here tonight?"

"You know what's more important to me right now," I said. I wasn't going to give in to abandoning my partner now.

She didn't get a chance to continue her argument before we were joined by Dr. Green, a fit man who I guessed was in his later fifties. He took the clipboard from the nurse and nodded while he read silently. "You were pretty lucky tonight, Detective Cantwell."

"Lucky enough to go home?"

The doctor laughed in a way that said he'd dealt with patients like me before. "It went straight through your thigh and somehow didn't hit any major arteries or bones, so we consider that lucky. It's going to take time to heal, though, and torn skin and torn muscle still hurts." He talked while filling out prescription notes. "I understand you want to be with your partner right now, which I know also means you're going to walk out the door when you're ready rather than come back up and spend the night with us."

I saw my chances of being released improving, but I was really wishing Nicky had been kind enough to bring some of my clothes I knew were still hanging out in his closet. A medical gown wasn't going to do. "Really, I'm going to be fine. No need to take up a bed."

"If you're going to insist on leaving, I'm going to insist that you come back for a follow-up with me in forty-eight hours. You also have to sign this."

"What's this?" I took the clipboard he handed me with its attached form. He followed up with a hospital-logo pen from his front pocket.

"This says you, as a non–medical professional, are deciding to leave the hospital against my advice as a trained medical professional." Under different circumstances, I thought, I would like Dr. Green. Sarcasm is an important personality trait. "I've checked on your partner's status.

You should know that he is in very qualified hands right now and will be with us for some time. You could easily skip signing that and wake up here tomorrow and enjoy a free breakfast with your partner."

"Thanks, Dr. Green, it's a good offer, but I'll see you in two days." I said it with a smile to appear more confident that I could indeed get myself out of here and back in two days.

"You're going to miss out on some pretty delectable Jell-O cubes, but I'll give you these." He put a set of green scrubs at the foot of the bed, along with a pair of purple socks covered in rubber grippy dots on both sides.

I was soon dressed and released with an additional order for crutches after I refused to let a nurse push me around in a wheelchair. With my leg strangely numb and throbbing at the same time, I limped to the waiting room of the ER, where Ana Ramirez was waiting with her in-laws, many people from our department, and Phoenix.

"Well, look at you being all tough-girl," Phoenix teased, once I finally reached an empty seat next to him. "I heard they were keeping you overnight. I was going to come see you."

"Doctors changed their minds, so I get to go home," I fibbed. Phoenix helped me into the chair with the cracked vinyl across from Ana, and she reached across the aisle to squeeze my hand.

"We don't know much yet," she said, one hand resting on her growing belly. "They said they were working on stabilizing him and then they were going to get him into surgery, but they haven't come out since."

"He's going to be fine—it's Bryan we're talking about. He's too stubborn for stuff like this to get him. And the guy who took care of me told me up there that Bry is in surgery, and he promised he's in good hands." I hoped to sound reassuring despite the fear attached to the images that still flashed behind my eyes—my unconscious partner in the dirt underground.

"Have you been questioned yet?" Phoenix asked.

I shook my head. "I'm barely remembering getting out of the tunnels, so they want to wait until I have less of the funny stuff in my system, and Lieutenant Miller said I could check on Bryan first. Is someone with Alayna?"

"Cole is with her and her family. Eric and the others are still up at the property. They'll be up there for days at this point, but she owes getting out to you, Cassidy."

"It was a team effort."

"You were the one who figured out the photo. You caught up with him. You were the one who eliminated the threat. I'm trying to give you some credit here, so take it." Phoenix offered a smile. "He ended up at another hospital, but I got word a bit ago that Sean Dunham made it through surgery. They said he's going to make a full recovery."

"Another win for the good guys." My memory bank opened up with another image of me pushing at Phoenix and ending up on the ground. I was sure there was more that I hadn't caught up to yet, moments still caught behind the fuzzy wall created by the anesthesia and medication. I tried to clear my head, wanting to force myself into clarity. "I think I might owe you an apology for up there. If I really took a swing, I'm sorry."

Phoenix tipped his chair back with a grin. "It was a weak swing, and you took yourself out, so we're all good. You also threw your phone at Cole, and I couldn't find that, by the way. Not sure who up there ended up with it."

I groaned at the new mention of my cell, which I'd assumed had been gathered with the rest of my gear. I never had dealt well with going into shock. "Either way, I'm sorry for trying to hit you, especially because I know it was you that got me out of there." I sat quietly. I hadn't been coherent enough, or maybe brave enough, to say it out loud to my lieutenant, but I couldn't shake the dread that I'd played right into his game. "I fell for it."

Phoenix understood my attempted confession immediately—the fear that a suspect had manipulated me into firing. He shook his head. "You don't want to talk to anyone about it until they take your official statement, including me, but you'll come out of this all right. You were on the right side tonight." I tried to agree, but my bottom lip betrayed my tough-girl shell. Phoenix reached under his seat and slid a blue duffel bag to my feet. "I've got Cole's Explorer, and you left that in the back seat. I figured you'd want it back. There might be something warmer in there."

I unzipped the bag and pulled out what I knew was inside—a pair of sneakers, regular socks, and a department-issued fleece. On top of the folded sweatshirt was the postcard that had been sent to my parents' house. The handwritten message, so much like Jenna's handwriting but not quite right, was taunting. Accusatory. *You should have been there!*

Phoenix watched intently as I examined what I thought I'd lost. "I found it in the fishbowl a while back. I saw your name and the message and figured it was probably related to the other stuff you told me about, and tonight seemed like a decent time to give it back."

For the first time I had the chance to study the image on the front, willing it to look familiar, but there wasn't anything unique about a wave of water and driftwood on a sandy shore. The postage sticker was stamped locally, four days before Jamie hand delivered it. Four days before

Alayna Keller was kidnapped. The back side still gave nothing away. I knew it wasn't Jenna who'd sent it, but the handwriting was disturbing. So close to being hers. Whoever wrote it was the same person who'd sent the swim photo and permission slip with the ladybug stickers. It was more taunts from someone who knew I should have been with Jenna when she died. Whether or not the taunts were from a killer was what I needed to figure out.

Delicately, I began picking at the corner of the postal barcode sticker that had been affixed at the bottom of the photo. I knew Phoenix was still watching as I scraped at the edges with my fingernails. After a bit of scraping, all I'd managed to do was separate the sticky adhesive side from the paper side, but it was enough to reveal a blue vertical line with another line at the bottom corner. A capital *B*? Maybe a capital *D*? I pushed a little farther with my thumb nail, and suddenly I was sure it was a capital *D*. The answer was right there. The next letter would be an *A*.

I slid the postcard under my uninjured thigh when a woman in surgical scrubs pulled an empty chair from the row to sit in front of Ana. We sat, collectively holding our breath, and listened while she explained the injury Bryan had sustained and what they had done, and what would still need to be done before he was released. Bryan's mother raised her hands to the heavens and cried in relief, and I knew I was safe to leave. I also knew where I needed to go. Hopefully, it wasn't too late.

"Do you think you could give me a ride to my car?" I asked Phoenix. I ignored the pain of pulling off the hospital socks and skipped replacing them, pushing bare feet into my Adidas from the bag. I pulled myself into the fleece and attempted to look ready to go.

"I am more than willing to give you a ride home, but you could barely put your shoes on just now. I don't see you being fit to drive yourself anywhere."

"Please?" I turned on my desperate face. "In the past few hours, I've watched my partner get shot, I've been shot, I've shot someone, and then I got officially dumped. I just want to pick up my car and be alone." I knew he meant well, but the postcard hadn't been sent to Phoenix, it had been sent to me, and I was more convinced than ever that I was being called out by a killer. Called to the place we'd never been able to find. Jenna Sutton's original crime scene.

Phoenix wasn't yet convinced. "Let me drop you off at home. I can help you get to your house, get you settled, and even get your car back to you tonight, free of charge."

"Or you could call me a ride to my car, since I seem to have misplaced my cell phone," I countered, unwilling to give in. "I just need to feel a few hours of normal right now."

"Fine." Phoenix surrendered. "If you can make it all the way to the parking lot without falling over, I'll take you to your car."

22

As if to prove my small part of the world wasn't the only part sitting off-kilter, an evening rain struggled to find its rhythm, switching from drizzle to downpour and back again, as I drove my Mini Cooper through the dark to my destination. I'd fought with Phoenix all the way to the parking garage about my pain levels and the meds I'd left the hospital with, but I'd won in the end.

"The offer still stands," he said when we made it to the underground parking lot at the FBI office I realized I would no longer be reporting to after tonight. No one had given me anything official—that was still to come—but policy and procedure said I'd be on leave for both my injured leg and my fired weapon. When I came off leave, I would be reporting back to my desk in the corner of our office with Bryan and the rest of our team. Whenever it was they let me come back.

"Thank you." I shook off his concern. "I really am all right, though. The meds are wearing off a bit, and I just want to sit by myself for a minute and then climb into bed."

"Let me grab this for you." Phoenix reached between us to the back seat and grabbed my duffel bag.

I zipped the bag closed and prepared myself to drop out of the front seat. The pain in my hip was heating up, and I worried if I delayed, I wouldn't be able to get myself in and out of my car, so I made my goodbye quick. The postcard had been sent just over one month ago, and I was sure now that it was meant as an invitation. An invitation to the place cops had looked for fifteen years ago but never found. I was afraid I was already too late.

* * *

The offbeat rain from earlier finally ran out, leaving behind a silent drizzle. I parked my Mini Cooper in the dark public lot at Dash Point Beach and grabbed the small flashlight from my glove box. I pulled the postcard off of the passenger seat and read the message again. *You should have been there.*

"I'm here now," I said to the empty parking lot when I opened my door and stepped into the wet night air. The mini light was compact and nearly as bright as my work flashlight, cutting through the dark as I limped my way across the parking lot to the path that would lead down to the beach.

* * *

"Am I a good person?" Jenna asked me. We were lying side by side on her basement bedroom floor, sharing a pair of headphones for the record player that once belonged to her dad. She'd put on her favorite from his classic rock collection—*Led Zeppelin II*—and turned off the lights. The only illumination was from the color-changing nightlight outside her door.

"Of course you're a good person," I said. "You're one of the best people I know."

"You're my best friend, though, so would you really tell me if you thought I was a bad person?"

I lowered my voice for dramatic effect and said, "Jenna Lee Sutton, I declare that you are a good person." We both giggled at my failed attempt at a southern accent.

"Am I a good-enough person to borrow your black sweater tomorrow?"

I laughed. "Yeah, you can borrow my sweater. I finally fixed the sleeve; it looks cool."

Jenna took my hand in hers and held both our hands to her chest. "Cassi, promise me that you'll always be my best friend?"

"Of course I'll always be your best friend. Why are you being such a weirdo?" I felt the shrug of her shoulders, then we were both still.

We stayed on the floor for hours that evening, moving only when we took turns changing out the record from her limited vinyl collection. There were no more questions of our friendship or her goodness, and the next day at school my best friend was her usual effervescent self. We met at our lockers after first period, and I traded my oversized black sweater with its new sleeve repair for her purple-and-green flannel. At lunch, we sat in our normal spot and planned out our escape. A plan that would give us total freedom to be where we wanted to be until Sunday afternoon. We went our separate ways after school with plans for me to pick her up after taking care of a few things at home. I never spoke to her again.

After she was gone, I wanted answers to that last night. I had no idea if her concern over being a good person was simply the angst of a sixteen-year-old trying to figure out who she was or a concern connected to a situation I was somehow unaware of. A situation that had led to her death. After her murder, that unknown created a fear in me that I'd missed my chance to save her that night, and the uncertainty still haunted me in my nightmares.

* * *

The beach on this October evening was almost empty, with only a middle-aged couple walking in the opposite direction several yards away. They paid no attention to me as they rushed to get off the beach before the rain and the tides came in. I slowly made my way down the collection of steps that led to the beach. With each unsure step, pain moved through my thigh like a wave. These steps, at least, were not as treacherous as the multilevel stairs that took visitors up to the most popular trailhead. I wasn't going to need those. The postcard had been clear: I would find what I was looking for at the beach.

I concentrated on each step in the sand to keep from wobbling, moving the ray of my light back and forth in front of me. I could see a new collection of large driftwood on the beach and started that way. Bryan's voice was loud in my head, nagging at me about training and protocols, but I pushed it out. In the same situation, my partner would make the same move, and I was as sure of that as I was of the increase in my own heart rate. There were moments you had to be prepared to handle on your own. I'd been able to stop Will Dunham, I reminded myself with a nervous laugh, and continued to talk to the darkness. "Why stop there?"

You should have been there. Here, if I was reading the postcard right. Dash Point Beach, a scenic water-access spot in the northern tip of Tacoma. It was a spot right out of my childhood. We'd been to the beach often as a family, and usually Jenna would come with us. We'd wander the trails and pick wild blackberries until our fingers turned purple. When we were young, we'd make up stories of wood nymphs and Sasquatch; when we got older, we'd talk school crushes and boy bands. It was nowhere near the party we were supposed to be at on the night she disappeared.

A large collection of new storm clouds rolled across the skyline like spreading ink, and I knew I was running out of time. A real storm was coming in, and the wet sand on a damaged leg was going to get annoyingly difficult to maneuver. Questioning my own sanity, I let my determination and guilt get me across the beach. Someone wanted me to come here, and I was already a month behind in the search for whatever they'd left me. Whatever it was could be anywhere by now—taken by someone else or washed away. A community bulletin board was on the opposite end of the beach, closer to the main trailhead. It was a long shot, but that was my destination. What better place to leave a message?

Keeping my focus on the driftwood against the ridge in the dark, I stopped at the sea debris to catch my breath. This was the beach from the postcard. From the right angle and with the right lighting, I imagined this might even be the same collection of driftwood from the photo. Minus the smaller bits and pieces collected by beachcombers that had made their way to different lives, the largest part of the structure was the same. The view across the water was lit up by the smaller islands in the Puget Sound, and my heart screamed from inside my chest when I realized what I was seeing.

It was beyond Maury Island, expanding farther into the sound and the Salish Sea. The southernmost tip of Vashon

Island was where two fishermen had found the body of Jenna Sutton in the water fifteen days after her disappearance. It was never believed Jenna had gone into the water from the shores of Vashon. The currents of the sound had carried her body to its final resting place along the shoreline. The small island of isolated residents, accessible only by ferry, was lit up against the dark water, and it all made sense.

You should have been there. I should have been *here.* This was where I'd needed to be that night in April. This was where I could have saved Jenna. The person behind the postcard wanted to show me where she died. My breaths were short and sharp, the pain stabbing at the center of my thigh with each step, but I kept going, my resolve to find the next message more powerful than my physical pain. The bulletin board maintained by the park rangers was usually full of trail updates, program schedules, and tide schedules. A pink flyer had been pinned to the top right corner, and my eyes fixed on it immediately.

One by one, I removed the pushpins from each corner and stared at the page in my hand. The pink had been my idea. The city was littered with so many signs and flyers. Missing people, missing pets, yard sales. I went to the copy place with my mom and insisted on the bright paper so it would stand out. The photo was her school picture—her brown hair in a high ponytail, her pink enamel *J* necklace that matched the *C* I wore in my own photo that year. The paper was newly faded, and someone had added one of her colorful ladybug stickers from the sheet now hidden in my tote at home. A wind gush folded the top corner over itself in my hand, and I caught the first glimpse of the handwriting on the back.

The message was unmistakable this time. The handwriting—still not quite Jenna's, but close—was in thick magic marker. Block letters, all caps, a small star under the single question mark. The words screamed out at me in Jenna's voice. *BEST FRIENDS FOREVER?*

A scream I didn't immediately recognize cut through the dark. For the second time in the same day, pain punched me backward, and I was falling.

Strong arms caught me about the waist before I could hit the ground.

"Cassi," Phoenix said. The familiarity hit me with an uncanny wave. Only Jenna ever called me Cassi. I finally gave in to the pain surging through my right side and let my legs fully slide out, and I felt him adjust to support my entire weight. I dug my fingers into my hair, and that's when I realized I was crying. The screams echoing out into the water were mine. "What the hell were you thinking?" he grumbled close to my ear.

"She was here. Jenna was here." My teeth began to clank together as my body registered its current load of adrenaline. "Why are you here? Why are you following me?"

"You weren't as sly as you thought you were about the postcard. I knew you were up to something and in no shape to be up to anything when we left the hospital, so I put a tracker in your bag when we left the hospital."

Relying on his strength, I made it as far as the collection of driftwood before my body threw up the white flag in surrender. I steadied myself against the driftwood, the missing-person poster still in my hand. My fingers let go slowly when Phoenix took it from me. A cold mist of sea water hit my cheeks, and I covered my mouth with both hands and cried. My muscles tensed with a shiver and continued to tremble. My adrenaline levels were hitting maximum on a day that had already put me through so much.

Phoenix grabbed hold of my waist again, and I knew he was speaking to me, giving me instructions, but the words came at me mangled and meaningless.

He eased us back to the parking lot in the dark, not asking me any further questions. When we got back to my car, he put me in the passenger seat of Cole's black Explorer. When I asked about my own car, he assured me it would be in my driveway by morning and clipped my seat belt around me. He'd folded the missing poster in half and put it in the inside pocket of his black Columbia jacket, then pulled out of the parking lot. I rattled off my address through chattering teeth when he asked, then sat back for the rest of the ride in silence.

* * *

My house was dark and empty when Phoenix pulled into my driveway. I made my way by myself to the couch, and Phoenix searched for the light switch, then sat across from me with his hands on his knees. "I am taking some blame here for this, because I shouldn't have let it get this far, but I think you should let me in a little bit on what you were doing down there tonight. I know the basics, but what is going on?"

I made a noise that was somewhere between laughing and sobbing. "I don't know," I said, and wiped my cheeks on my sleeve. "I told you someone was sending me stuff. I didn't know at first why. The first one was dropped off at my mom's house, and it was just an old picture of me and Jenna in high school. I didn't know what to think, really. Maybe it was just someone we knew from school who thought I'd want it. We'd just started working the Dana Mayhew case, so I tried to just put it away and deal with the nightmares it brought back."

"How did we go from sending school pictures to sending you to empty beaches?"

"The postcard." I shifted myself on the couch, laced my fingers together behind my head, and leaned all the way back, staring at the ceiling to avoid making eye contact. "The next things included messages. It made it a lot more personal, like I was being taunted."

"*Best friends*?" He repeated the question from the flyer. "You've gone far enough with this, Cas. We need to be realistic about what you might be dealing with, and you're going to have to bring in your side about the mail."

I couldn't answer. I didn't want to admit he was right on any of it. If I gave in and brought in these new details, they would be taken, bagged and cataloged, and added to a paper box in a storage room with Jenna's name on it. Lieutenant Miller would take my files and order me away from the investigation, and she'd make the same conclusion that Phoenix had come to: The person taunting me was possibly a killer. My chances of solving Jenna's murder would slip away just as someone was daring me to catch her killer.

I had to make two promises before I could convince Phoenix to leave me alone for the night. First, I had to promise to stay put. Considering I had no car and no phone, it was an easy promise to make, even without the bullet hole radiating pain below my right hip. I needed time to deal with what I couldn't sort through in my current state: a rescue, a shooting, a breakup. With all of it fighting for attention, the fact that I'd never fired my weapon before tonight was the only thought in the collection I was internally focused on. I couldn't dive deeper for now, unsure how to process saving a life and taking a life in the same moment and ending a relationship I'd thought was solid and fixable. I needed time to process the emotional tangles, and I could do that best alone, on my couch.

The second promise was that I would loop Lieutenant Miller in on the new evidence in Jenna's case. Once I made it known that I believed I was being taunted by Jenna's killer, I would be iced out of the investigation. Miller would collect everything I had, just as I was starting to make progress, and turn it over to someone else. Protocol after my shooting would put me on leave and the best way to keep sane through that process would be working Jenna's case, I explained to Phoenix, but he insisted the only way he was leaving was if I told Miller, so I agreed. We left the deadline open.

The missing-person flyer at the beach had been the piece I needed. I didn't have a name yet, but I knew where to start. After using my laptop to send a message on our sibling group chat to keep everyone away until morning, I swallowed down one of the white tablets Dr. Green sent me home with for the pain and pulled the lid off my bin. I put my old yearbook in my lap and opened the pages to the ones dedicated to the sophomore swim team. All of the usual suspects around our neighborhood and the high school had been looked at after Jenna went missing. I knew that because I had copies of the interviews. Less than a dozen of them warranted a serious look, and over time no one had made it to the level of *person of interest*, let alone *suspect*. I was sure now that the original detectives, including Miller, had missed something.

I studied each black-and-white photo, examining the faces. I was in the middle of our team picture with my arm slung around the shoulder of another swimmer. Jenna was the shortest girl on the team and was leaning back to back with a girl I didn't remember. I was still missing something. I went back to the cover page and scanned the faces, wanting someone to jump out at me. Despite the fog of the adrenaline and medication, I knew that somewhere in these pages of people we knew, I would find Jenna's killer.

That was the clue I hadn't caught before tonight. It wasn't random luck that they reached out to me, and it wasn't accidental that the first clues were sent to my childhood home. I turned the pink flyer over again and studied the message on the back. The memories of our last night together came back to me in tearful waves. *Tell me you'll always be my best friend,* Jenna asked me the night before she was murdered. I'd said yes that night, and the killer knew it. Jenna's killer knew her, and they knew me.

Freddy, on guard duty after having a stranger in the house, grumbled a few meows at the dark window, his striped tail flipping from side to side. He jumped from the window with a deep hiss the same moment I heard the side door in the kitchen jiggle. It hit me then how alone I was. With the pain meds kicking in, my body was heavy, and I didn't have my service weapon. Worse, I didn't even have my phone.

I pushed myself off the couch and grabbed the wine bottle that had been sitting empty on the side table since the night before. Barefoot, I edged my way to the kitchen with the bottle over my shoulder like a baseball bat and nearly dropped it as my younger sister came through the door full of hushed giggles. Sebastian was behind her, obviously nervous after our first meeting in my kitchen, wide eyes zeroed in on the wine bottle in my hand.

"Why are you coming in that door?" I couldn't delete the panic in my voice, but I lowered my makeshift weapon and put my other hand against the wall for support.

Meghan put her hands up with an innocent cock of her head. "I lost my keys yesterday, so I left this door unlocked so I wouldn't have to wake you up if I came home late."

"You can't do that, Megs. You can't leave the doors open." I let it go when she rolled her eyes on her way to her bedroom with a still-nervous Sebastian in tow. My head was swimming with the pain meds and making it all the way to my bed felt impossible, so I tried to get comfortable again on the couch. The tears started as soon as I lay down. My little sister lived in a fairy-tale world where every stranger was a friend, but Jenna had learned the hard way that not all friends can be trusted. I'd promised myself I would solve Jenna's murder, but with my new promise to Phoenix, I was running out of time to figure out which friend had betrayed her and who was now targeting me.

Acknowledgements

My first thank you goes to my husband, Rich, who pulled an old computer from the closet and later signed me up for a writing conference in Vegas. I would never have made it this far without all of his love and support. To the author, Mia Thompson, for her words of advice and encouragement. To my patient agent, Elizabeth Kracht – thanks for letting me be the first to send you ranty emails! Everyone at Kimberley Cameron & Associates. To Rebecca Nelson and the entire team at Crooked Lane Books. A giant thank you to all of the family and friends who have listened to me talk about this story of mine. Piper for asking for more. Sunny for suggesting the write nights at Beans. The original 3 in my old lunch crew. The wonderful women in the Sass and Chatter Literary Society who have read multiple drafts and given so much feedback. To Charlie for being my twin and checking in when I go quiet. Thanks to Laura and her Monday group, and the friends I've made there, especially Holly, Linda, Marji, and Sheri, who have spent time not on Mondays to tell me what they think. Love to

ACKNOWLEDGEMENTS

Alexandre for helping me realize what this life is all about, and Rylie and RJ for completing my circle. Thank you to my mom and dad, Kendall, Kat, and Walter, and my entire extended families for giving me the foundation I needed to get here. I'm sure I've forgotten someone but know that I love you all.